# A Garden Party
# for the Dead

*Also by Stephen Reardon*

The Equal Sky

The Middle Room

Madame Lamartine's Journey

Stephen Reardon

# A Garden Party
# for the Dead

© Stephen Reardon 2018

This book is sold subject to the condition that it shall not by way of trade or otherwise be lent, resold, hired out or otherwise circulated without the publisher's prior consent in any form of binding or cover other than that with which it is published and without similar condition being imposed on the subsequent purchaser.

Stephen Reardon has asserted his right under the Copyright, Design and Patents Act 1988 to be identified as the author of this work.

First published in 2018 by Stephen Reardon.
Printed and distributed by Lulu.com
ISBN 978-0-244-72803-8

*A Garden Party for the Dead* is a work of fiction. Other than recognised historical people, events and settings, all the characters and their actions are imagined. They are not intended to bear any resemblance to persons living or dead.

*Cover from an original illustration by Roger Birchall.*
*"Temporary War Graves".*
*Photography. Constantine Lourdas. Lourdas Photography.*

*A man knelt behind a line of headstones — evidently a gardener, for he was firming a young plant in the soft earth. She went towards him, her paper in her hand. He rose at her approach and without prelude or salutation asked: 'Who are you looking for?'*

*'Lieutenant Michael Turrell — my nephew,' said Helen slowly word for word, as she had many thousands of times in her life.*

*The man lifted his eyes and looked at her with infinite compassion before he turned from the fresh-sown grass toward the naked black crosses. 'Come with me,' he said, 'and I will show you where your son lies.'*

*When Helen left the cemetery she turned for a last look. In the distance she saw the man bending over his young plants; and she went away, supposing him to be the gardener.*

*Rudyard Kipling.* "The Gardener." Debits and Credits

*A Garden Party for the Dead* was first published in the centenary month of the end of the First World War on the Western Front. It is, in part, a small act of recognition by the author, of those men and women who continued to toil on the battlefields, sometimes at the cost of their own lives, for the dead who remained long after the living had returned home.

# Part One

*Service Deferred*

# *1*

EDWARD Dereham had been in isolation for several months when the assassination of Archduke Franz Ferdinand precipitated Europe into war. He had started spitting blood in January 1914 and, as his mother had been suffering with tuberculosis for some considerable time, the medical assumption was that Edward had contracted it from her. He had his doubts. Having lived with his mother through her drawn-out illness and having witnessed its advances and recessions, he felt his own symptoms were not the same. The doctor said that his reluctance to accept his condition was itself part of the course of the illness and packed him off to the sanatorium his mother had only recently vacated, for 'observation'. Although he was loath to leave her to the peremptory ministrations of the day-nurse, he convinced himself that he would be home before her next inevitable relapse needed the expense of a night-nurse he could ill-afford.

So as his 'observation' continued from weeks into months, his assumed medical condition kept him at arm's length from the turbulence affecting the rest of the world outside. He had already turned thirty-five which, together with his isolation, kept him from being bowled along by the euphoria driving so many young men to volunteer in those first weeks of the war. They included most of his own friends and acquaintances, a steadily dwindling number, in any case, as he chose quietly to distance himself from them even though he did not believe he was infectious. He came to regret this bitterly. But his instinct to comply with doctors – professional men like himself – together with his deep feeling of obligation (more than filial love, if he was honest) towards his sick, widowed mother, convinced him that not joining up was the right thing to have done. His real feelings he swept under the carpet, as he always did, calling them selfish. But in time they became too big to reject; he could not ignore the guilt and sense of personal failure he felt as so many marched away without him and never came back. He especially absolved Ursula, the woman with whom he had an understanding, from any obligation to him.

He remained at the sanatorium on the first occasion until the end of that year. 'Home in time for Christmas' had a rather different significance for him and he was relieved to be back to spend it with his mother and anxious to return to his solicitor's practice and pick up the reins again. The more-or-less-retired partner, James Bellingham, from whom he had taken it over some years before had kept things 'ticking over' in Edward's absence. This had meant little more than making sure the small number of regular paying clients were not entirely neglected, but he had not gone so far as to take on any new business. What with the expense of his sojourn at the sanatorium and his mother's continuing doctor's bills Edward could have wished that some of the wills which had suddenly been drawn up locally in Sunbury at the outbreak of war might have come his way. But the first lucrative flurry was over.

Back in the outside world the realities of the fighting in France were becoming brutally plain. The retreat from Mons was in the newspapers and on everybody's lips. Convalescing wounded, many with pitiful amputations, began to be seen publicly, adding to the pressures on Edward's loyalties, already being assailed daily by the national call to arms. Back in his solicitor's office he began to encounter a trickle of unaccustomed clients, forlornly seeking his advice about their lost or injured sons, as if that might bring them back or make them whole; mothers openly weeping and often, through their tears, voicing surprise that Edward was still at home, not having seen him in the neighbourhood and assuming he had joined up. Revealing he had in fact been in the sanatorium would hardly have been a respectable explanation invoking, as it would, different taboos and prejudices. Nor did he send any of them a bill.

Then one day, opening the morning's post – business not being sufficient to warrant a clerk – two white feathers fluttered out of an envelope. Staring at them on his blotter it was as if he had sent them himself. This was probably the moment that his nagging unease with himself crystalized into deep self-doubt. For the first time for a long time he took a decision he knew reflected his own true desire. He closed the office, put on his hat, and went to fetch his bicycle, having left it at home that morning. Without giving it much thought, his mind being very much elsewhere, he took the lower road along the river and so found himself at the recruiting office in nearby Kingston.

There was a small line of men in front of him, all by the look of them younger than Edward. The recruitment process seemed to move along quite swiftly. When it was his turn the sergeant at the desk made a swift, silent appraisal of Edward's hat, suit and tie and by some imperceptible signal conjured up an officer, a rather elderly territorial major, from behind a temporary screen.

He too looked Edward up and down: 'Do we know one another?' he asked. It sounded like a stock question designed to allocate men such as Edward to an appropriate social slot.

Edward replied that 'he didn't think so' and then to be helpful added that he was a solicitor in Lower Sunbury. The major grunted non-committally. 'Applications for temporary commissions can be made during basic training. Give your details to the sergeant and then go through for your medical. The doctor's here at the moment, so it shouldn't take long.'

Details amounted to his name, address, age and next of kin. For the first time since shutting up the office Edward spared a thought for his mother as he gave her name. Would she be his next of kin first or would he be hers? But there was no-one else. Then he went behind a separate set of screens for the medical examination.

The doctor was still dealing with the previous recruit who was stripped to the waist, telling him to breathe in and out as he listened to his rather scrawny chest and back. 'Get on the scales my lad. Hmm. A bit short – like the butcher's order. Here, pick your boots up. That's the ticket. Spot on the regulation,' and he called out, 'Baines – is it? Passed fit Sergeant. Next.' He turned to face Edward. 'Good Lord! Mr Dereham isn't it? What on earth brings you in here? Are you out of your mind?'

Edward realised with a start that the doctor was one of the consultants he had come across on the local panel. 'It's high time I joined up,' he said.

'Not in your condition. Can't allow it, I'm afraid. Besides, what age are you?'

Edward said he was thirty-six next birthday.

'Well you look older. That'll be down to your condition too.'

'But I've been discharged from the sanatorium, haven't I? And in any case no-one seems absolutely certain that it's TB I've got.'

'Discharged until the next time. I'm afraid you're the one who won't accept it, Dereham. I have very few doubts, myself.'

'Well, can't I pick my boots up to make the weight, too? In a manner of speaking, Doctor.'

The doctor made a wry grimace. 'Young Baines will soon be up to weight with a few helpings of army food, mark my words. But no amount of it is going to stop you spitting blood, and as like as not infecting those around you. That's what I have to think about. If you got sick – when you got sick – you'd end up occupying a precious bed and still have to be discharged at the end of it. No – the best thing you can do is go for spells at the sanatorium, keep your strength up, plenty of fresh air. I would have said go to Baden Baden, but that's out of the question clearly; you'll have to make do with Clare Hall.' He gave a snort of laughter. 'I should thank my lucky stars if I were you. I see a fair few young men who would give their eye teeth to be declared unfit. For some of them the euphoria of being swept in here by their comrades' patriotism disappears as soon as they have to take their shirts off.'

Edward was on the point of saying that he would rather take his chance of a quick death at the front where he could take a few of the Hun with him, than live at home with the slow sentence of consumption, but that would have meant acknowledging the truth of the doctor's medical opinion of him. Besides it would have been a piece of bravado he wouldn't have felt comfortable voicing.

'You're not married are you? No?'

It was more of a descriptive comment than a question. Edward could guess the implications behind it: less likelihood of infecting someone else close, the possibility that at his age his celibacy might put a question mark over his sexuality, which would be one less headache for the army since he was deemed unfit anyway. He felt like refuting that too, telling him about Ursula, who had not loved him as much as he had imagined he loved her; who had been content to be released from their bargain when first his mother's health and now his own put obstacles in its way. He had not blamed her. How could he? Whilst he wasn't accepting his condition was consumptive, he wasn't prepared to try and impose his conviction on her. It would have seemed like blackmailing her into marrying him. But as she had thankfully walked away he had naturally dismissed dreams of future relationships.

The doctor held out his hand. 'I'll be seeing you, Mr Dereham – not too soon I hope. Show me your handkerchief.'

Edward took it out of his pocket and offered it for inspection. It was clean he knew. No tell-tale spots of blood. They had been like that for some time now. The doctor grunted his satisfaction. 'That's good. Keep plenty – you know that. Use them around other people. And if you get any spotting, bag them and date them. You know that too.' He called out to the sergeant on the other side of the screens: 'Dereham, unfit, Sergeant. Are there any more?' It seemed there were not. 'Well, good-bye then. You'll be getting an exemption certificate in due course.'

Edward stood outside on the pavement, wondering what to do next. When he had bolted out of his office that morning he had given no thought to what would have happened if he had been accepted. Would he have had to go straight to the barracks here in Kingston or would he have gone to Hounslow on the Middlesex side of the Thames? That was his home county after all. He realised he hadn't even brought a toothbrush, or another clean handkerchief either. Would it have been like being sentenced at the sessions: down the stairs and straight into the van? When would he have told his mother? What would he tell her now? He found himself walking his bicycle back along the river up to Hampton Court, putting off the moment of dull anti-climax that awaited him when he turned the key in the office door. As he walked he could only think what rotten luck it had been to run across his own doctor at the medical. If only he had taken the road towards Hounslow and ended up at a different recruiting office. Perhaps he could do that now. Would they know if he did, that he had already been rejected?

The two white feathers were still lying on his desk. They fluttered up in the air as the draught caught them when he opened the door. They hung suspended for a moment before coming to rest in the empty tray labelled 'pending'. When his certificate of exemption arrived a few days later he carefully enclosed the white feathers in the envelope with it and put it back in the tray.

His mother's health soon took another turn for the worse and she was readmitted to the sanatorium, Clare Hall, out at South Mimms, which was just about as far removed from Lower Sunbury as it was possible to be in the county of Middlesex. It being much too far to bicycle, Edward took three trains to get to see her, a journey made even more difficult by the necessary wartime priorities. His visit was by contrast brief, as his mother was 'not to be tired out'.

When he was leaving the outside veranda where she like most of the patients spent most of their daylight hours whatever the weather, he was stopped by one of the doctors who knew him from his own recent time there. 'Mr Dereham, I really would not advise you visit us here unless you want to find yourself readmitted sooner than you intend. The less time you spend in the company of these patients the better and I'm sure you'll have your mother home soon enough. It is meant to be isolation remember.'

As he retraced the tortuous journey home he was relieved to have to take notice of the doctor's injunction. At the same time, of course, he felt guilty at being thus relieved and the sense of obligation towards his mother weighed all the more heavily.

The weeks slid by and the sanatorium doctor's prediction that he would have his mother home 'soon enough' took on a variety of Delphic interpretations. As for his own health, it remained stable. His cough was less troublesome, even though it was by now as much a nervous habit as a symptom of something else, and he could find no traces of blood in his sputum. Edward was thankful he did not have to find money for his own doctor's bills as well as his mother's sanatorium fees which, at five guineas a month, began to be increasingly noticeable, especially as there was very little new business coming the way of a sleepy Thames-side solicitor's practice, plus the fact that the regular clients on the books were never in a hurry to pay, if at all.

The summer of 1915 came and began to go. The progress of the war was difficult to fathom. Reports from the western front made the most of very little success as far as Edward could make out. Victories were claimed, yet no significant ground was made or if it was it soon seemed to be lost again. The Gallipoli campaign was an evident disaster. His copy of the Morning Post focused on heroic encounters or read like extracts from an abstract manual on tactics, while column after column was given over to casualty lists. There began to be rumblings that the flow of volunteer recruits was insufficient to supply the voracious appetite of the war machine.

Edward wondered if conscription were introduced, which was beginning to look more and more certain, whether it would mean a general lowering of requirements. Would the recruiting sergeants and the doctors be turning a blind eye to some medical conditions now? Would they review the cases of some of those who had previously been declared unfit? He struggled with his conscience not to wish his mother's death would be soon and release him to try his luck with volunteering again. But if he were successful what would become of her? The monthly five guineas for the sanatorium would run out soon enough and she would be relegated to the level of treatment not much better than that provided by indoor relief, the workhouse in other words. Then, with the lengthening of the shadows and the shortening of the days, autumn mists on the Thames brought on a touch of pleurisy, or so he convinced himself it was. There was still no blood, so he stayed well away from the doctor and dosed himself up with Dr. Collis Brown's.

After the turn of the year, conscription was indeed introduced and although Edward lived in hopeful anticipation of being called up, no summons came. After several weeks of fretful waiting he presented himself at the barracks in Hounslow – this time avoiding the recruitment office – only to be told that he would receive his call-up papers when his age-group ('if' his age-group, the officer put it, rather disparagingly) came to the top of the list. The young man's empty sleeve and a stick leaning in the corner behind him, Edward felt, did not justify him being dismissed out of hand like this – at least the officer was still in uniform. Surely, Edward insisted, he could nevertheless still volunteer? The officer asked him if he had volunteered before. Wrestling with his innate truthfulness Edward hesitated.

'You have, haven't you? What happened? Turned down on medical grounds? What is it with you people? At least you're not able to lie about your age. Take no for an answer, I should. Don't be in a hurry, it's not going to be over soon. Look at me! Stick bomb at Mons. Lucky still to have one arm left.'

Edward was taken aback at the officer's outburst. He would have expected something rather more encouraging from a serving soldier, wounded or not. It was his first real encounter with an attitude like this, not defeatist exactly, but implying a different kind of realism that seemed lacking in hope and spoke only of endurance. He was used to the anguished questioning of the bereaved mothers and, occasionally, fathers who sought some kind of comfort and redress from his professional advice, though he had none to offer, but otherwise he had little personal contact with men, like this officer, who spoke from true experience. Edward was an only child, so had no younger brothers fighting, coming home on leave with a first-hand account of it; no sisters with husbands at the war; no wider family either that were close, with cousins at the front; no relatives mutilated or gassed to give him any opinion different to those of the *Morning Post*. Feeling that he had been given a brief but salutary lesson, he took himself home, thinking all the way about how far he should allow it to weigh with his own desire to serve.

Crestfallen he bicycled back home to Lower Sunbury. As he removed his bicycle clips on the front step, this reminded him that he had not put to the officer any of the questions he had intended to ask, particularly how much notice one was given of call-up and where would he have to travel to? Presumably he could not take his bicycle. There was a telegram on the doormat, a sight that always created a moment of anxiety, although for him it was not that feeling of dreadful foreboding the same silent greeting would have brought to those neighbouring families with husbands and sons at the front. He took time to hang his hat, coat and scarf on the hallstand and put his gloves away in the drawer before carefully opening the yellow-brown envelope. The brief message was from the consultant at Clare Hall: *Telephoned earlier. Best you come soonest.* There was no further enlightenment, but Edward hardly needed any. He unhooked the telephone beside the hallstand and tapped for the operator. When she came on the line and asked him 'what number please caller?' he realised the sanatorium number was in his desk drawer at the office. 'It doesn't matter,' he said. 'I've changed my mind. Sorry.' And then after a pause, 'It wasn't urgent.'

'That's all right Mr Dereham. Have a pleasant evening.'

He re-hooked the ear-piece and went into the front sitting-room where he poured himself an unaccustomed whisky-and-soda, before putting a match to the newspaper fire lighters in the grate laid by the daily woman, Mrs Bale, and left for him to attend to. He knew someone of his middle standing in the village should by rights have a housekeeper living in, or at least a maid-of-all-work. But this was an expense he had dispensed with quite deliberately, in the former case because of the difficulty of getting someone to work in a house where it was known his mother, when there, was suffering from TB, and in the latter case because of the gossip that would assuredly attach to a local solicitor living alone in the house with a young girl from the village when, as now, his mother was away. A daily woman was quite sufficient for his modest needs.

While he waited for the fire to draw, the whisky-and-soda got to work on his inner-self, chilled from the bicycle journey from Hounslow. He thought about what he had just said to the telephone operator, that 'it wasn't urgent'. He knew what a telegram from the sanatorium betokened, especially after they had tried and failed to reach him by telephone, and he searched his emotions for one which might ignite a feeling of urgency. But he could not awaken anything other than guilty, cold logic which argued that he could not now get to Clare Hall before the next day whether his mother was alive or dead and that it would be hypocritical to telephone now and have to demonstrate feelings he did not truly possess.

When he called the sanatorium in the morning from the office to be informed his mother had passed away about the time he had been pouring himself another whisky-and-soda, his guilt was redoubled. His instant emotion then was one of relief that he would not now have to make the journey to the other side of Middlesex to sit by her bedside. The undertakers would fetch her home and a cheque for her final bill could be put in the post, perhaps even conveniently delayed, he reasoned.

It came as an enormous surprise to him, therefore, when she did come home and had been laid out in her coffin in the dining room, to find himself sitting beside her racked with sobs. These in turn led to a fit of prolonged coughing for the first time in several months and a suspicion of blood in his handkerchief.

There was just him at the funeral, there being no relations on her side of the family to contact. His late father had had a married sister, Rose, Edward knew, but he had never met her. After his father's death his mother had rarely spoken of her, and then only coldly, in passing. There was evidently no love lost between the sisters-in-law. Nevertheless, his solicitor's sense of correctness led him to reach down his father's file of papers where he discovered a letter in an envelope in his mother's hand addressed to Mrs. H. Grace. The letter began 'Dear Rose' and was informing her of the death of her brother, Edward's father. It was a brief impersonal missive, giving only details of the funeral arrangements but containing no sympathy, no expressions of her own sorrow. It had obviously not been sent – the envelope had not been sealed or stamped, but perhaps, thought Edward charitably, his mother had sent another, more comforting. He had been very young when his father died; his recollections of the funeral were very hazy and certainly did not include the presence of an aunt and uncle. Perhaps their absence from the funeral had been the cause of his mother's antipathy to Rose and her perpetuated estrangement.

His first instinct was to put the letter back in the file and forget all about it. After all there had been no contact with them as far as Edward knew. But again his solicitor's correctness prompted him to write a brief letter, on his official business paper informing his aunt of her sister-in-law's death and giving the funeral arrangements. Although he wrote as a relation it was the style of letter Edward was used to writing in connection with settlements of estates – not that he supposed his aunt and uncle, if they were still alive and at the address on the envelope his mother hadn't sent, would have any residual call on her estate. Edward was the sole beneficiary, but you never knew, perhaps there was an outstanding debt; he sincerely hoped not, but he felt it would be the right thing to do and would satisfactorily close the chapter on his parents' generation, leaving him the one family survivor and able to consign them all to the past. He received no reply to the letter before or after the funeral and chose to assume that, for whatever reason, it had been ignored or not received.

Towards the end of the summer of 1916 Edward did receive papers instructing him to present himself at Hounslow barracks prior to being called up. Despite now being at the upper end of the age limit for service the attrition on the western front meant there was a pressing need for a steady flow of new recruits. Knowing this Edward was hopeful that the health check would be sufficiently cursory for him to pass. The examining doctor was however rather more thorough than he was expecting. He listened carefully to Edward's chest and lungs and then did so again.

'Are you being treated for this?' he asked.
'For what?' said Edward cagily.
'Your lungs are in a poor state. Any history of tuberculosis.'
'I get a touch of pleurisy now and again.'
'Any in the family?'
'Pleurisy?'
'No. TB.'

'Not that I know of,' Edward said. And then to cover his conscience he added, 'I have no family I know of – so I can't be sure.'

'You need to get that checked out. Seriously. I'm going to give you a temporary deferral and refer you up the line for another opinion. Who's your general practitioner?'

Edward thought for a moment about giving the wrong doctor's name, but supposed it would be a breach of wartime regulations. He tried again. 'I'm sure I'm still recovering from that recent touch of pleurisy, Doctor. It's the weather. And I live close to the Thames. It's low lying, you know. Just pass me fit and I'll take my chances.'

At this the recruiting sergeant in the background cleared his throat and shuffled his boots, making the military presence felt. 'Can't say fairer than that Doc. Willing volunteer I'd say. We need 'em.'

But the doctor would not be swayed. 'If it were a question of flat feet and boss eyes, I would let it go, Sergeant, even pox at a pinch: he might shag the Huns to death. But if this man's consumptive, he'd be a liability to everyone around him…' the sergeant took an involuntary step back, '…Temporary deferral, back in two months. Wheel in the next one, Sergeant.'

Shortly after this, Edward was summoned to St. Mary's Hospital in Paddington to be seen by another consultant, a Dr Carradine. His cough had improved again by now and he hoped he might be able to pass muster on this occasion. He had not bargained with the efficiency of the military process and its determination to leave no stone unturned in finding new conscripts and uncovering malingerers. When he presented himself in the consultant's room, he soon found that his own doctor had already been approached and his medical notes sent through to Paddington where they languished accusingly in front of him on the consultant's table.

He pleaded with Dr Carradine that the diagnosis was mistaken; said that he had a recurring cough, true enough, but that it never came to anything; that he was always discharged from the sanatorium after 'observation' with nothing proven one way or the other.

'You're extraordinarily keen to get yourself killed – one way or another, I'd say,' said the consultant wearily, 'and that's not being defeatist on my part. I can say that to you because I cannot in all conscience pass you fit in the face of all this evidence – there are at least three opinions here, all in agreement. But,' he added hastily, 'I will of course examine you myself first.'

He took his time with the examination and even asked Edward to 'cough up some product' into a small pot, which he then put on a slide and examined under the microscope on his bench. 'Hmm,' he said thoughtfully. 'Let me listen to you again.' Once again he took his time.

Edward began to feel hopeful. 'I'm right, aren't I?'

The consultant told him to cough while he listened to his back. 'So away from me, if you please!' There followed a silence. Then he went back to his side of the desk and sat with his head bowed in thought, drumming his fingers faintly on the ink-blotter in front of him.

'I'll tell you honestly Mr. Dereham, I'm not sure…'

'So will you…?'

'…But I may not professionally pass a man fit for military service whom I suspect of having a serious infectious disease – whatever his motives might be for wanting so anxiously to join up.' He gave Edward a searching look. 'Something to prove? Or something or someone to escape?'

'I can assure you…' Edward began.

Dr Carradine raised his hand. 'Psychiatry not my department. I'll tell you what I'm going to do. I'll recommend deferral for six months and see you again then. If you present no change I will defer for another six months and if still no change I will pass you fit.'

'You mean, if I'm not dead in twelve months, you'll let me go.' Edward could not hide his disappointment. 'The war will be over by then as like as not.'

'As like as not. But that's my decision.'

## 2

IN February 1917, a few weeks before the date of his first re-examination at St. Mary's, Edward received an unexpected communication in a brown manila envelope marked 'OHMS' – On His Majesty's Service. For an instant he thought that it was call-up papers, that the powers-that-be had somehow relented or overruled the doctors. He tore it open and found to his surprise it contained a completed form and another envelope addressed to him. The form was headed HM Prison Brixton and simply stated that the enclosed letter had been approved for sending by the prison authorities. Edward rarely received any criminal work in his solicitor's practice although it was not entirely unknown. As he slit open the second envelope he tried to remember whether he had any existing client in prison but could call none to mind. The handwritten letter inside was addressed to him by name and read:

*As I gather you are in the legal trade from the letter I eventually received in here from you concerning your mother's death (for which my condolences) which was directed to my wife who has herself passed away some months ago and as you are in a sense family, I write to ask that you act for me in a confidential matter as my appointed lawyer. Anything that passes between us will remain privileged as between client and solicitor. I should perhaps say that none of the matter in question is outside the law, despite my current situation, the reasons for which you may wish to acquaint yourself with. Please arrange to visit me here at your earliest convenience and inform the authorities. I have the means to meet your fee.*

It was signed simply, *Herbert Grace.*

The abruptness of the letter and its lack of any information about the nature of the business involved in the proposed commission might have inclined Edward to reject it. But he recalled that his own letter to his aunt had been rather brusque in the circumstances. Still, it was evident from his uncle's letter that it was assumed without question that he would take on the business, whatever it might turn out to be. If the name Herbert Grace rang any bells he could not bring to mind in what context, other than the fact that his mother had written to a Mrs. H. Grace. He decided to write and accept the brief without first enquiring; he told himself it would be better to accept a client who was already in prison, without discovering what for, and therefore be able to act without preconceived prejudices. However, when he had posted the letter which he marked 'Client Confidential' to be on the safe side and enclosed it with one to the prison authorities informing them of his intention to act for Mr. Grace and asking to be told what the visiting arrangements were, his curiosity got the better of his professional logic.

On his way back from posting this and his other letters that day – of which there were precious few, business having declined even more since the folk of Sunbury had begun to suspect that the reason for his not being conscripted must be medical and probably therefore not unconnected to his 'poor mother's TB' – he called in at James Bellingham's house, his semi-retired partner. Edward found him in the front garden where a little to his surprise he was pruning the roses. 'Isn't it a little early for that?' he enquired.

'It's nearly spring and the sun's shining: I should really have done it last autumn. So what brings you to my blessed plot on a working day? I suppose that the sheer weight of importunate clients at your door has driven you to seek a moment's peace and quiet at mine, is that it? Will you have some tea? I am afraid my wife is out but the girl will make us some anyway.' He led the way indoors, calling out to the unseen maid, 'Polly, put the kettle on, we have Mr Dereham for tea.' He chuckled: 'Always enjoy asking Polly to do that, but I expect it gets on her nerves after all these years.' (Despite being referred to invariably as 'the girl', Polly was somewhere in her fifties by now).

When they were settled in the sitting room with tea and some sugared bread pudding that had been requested from the kitchen earlier by Bellingham, Edward came to the point.

'Does the name Herbert Grace ring any bells?'

Bellingham pursed his lips. 'Can't think of anyone locally. Not a client anyhow. No, the only Herbert Grace of whom I've heard, of course, was the fraudster. You must remember the case…three or four years ago. Big city swindle had been running for years, thousands went broke. He got a hefty sentence. Something like seven years – penal servitude mind: he'd double-crossed some very important people as well as numerous unforgiving nonconformist clergymen and their widows and orphans. There was even talk that royalty lost money with him, although that never came out in court…' He paused, lost in a little reverie. '…Yes, that's right. Herbert Grace. That was him. Could be dead now, for all I know. After all he was no spring chicken when he went to prison and penal servitude is no picnic. Thing was, the judge said the reason for the harshness of the sentence was that Grace made no attempt to pay any of the money back. In any case it was suspected that his visible moveable assets were only the tip of the iceberg and that he'd squirreled most of it abroad. Switzerland, I shouldn't wonder; that seems to be the up-and-coming place these days, they say. His non-movables were needless to say in his wife's name. Big estate somewhere. Part owner of a fashionable casino, they said, in France, near Le Touquet, along the channel coast somewhere. Very profitable. Easier to get to than Cannes, but quite out of reach of English jurisdiction. Might as well have been on the moon. Of course, as you well know, it's the devil's own job to recover the proceeds of crime if the villains won't cough up. There ought to be a law to make it easy: send the bailiffs in. Yes…good old Herbert Grace…that him?'

Edward had a sinking feeling that it might be him. But he didn't wish it so and after all Bellingham thought he was probably dead by now. So he decided not mention the letter he had received: client confidential, after-all-was-said-and-done. He was surprised, however, not to have even a vague recollection of this Herbert Grace's case, although it must have happened during his spell in the sanatorium which might account for it. He'd spent more of his time reading books there, trying to avoid the newspapers which were full of news of the war he could not join. Surely, he said to Bellingham, the case must have lasted for many weeks? On the contrary, Bellingham said, much of the evidence against Grace had not been contested, perhaps because royalty had been involved as unwitting promotors of his bogus companies and rather than put their highnesses on the witness stand and in the hopes of a lenient sentence the case was over in a relatively short time. 'Didn't want it running and running in the newspapers. Although there was a pretty harsh leader in the Times, I recall, which undoubtedly weighed with the judge. Grace was given no leave to appeal either.'

'You seem to have a good recollection of the case, James. How come?'

Bellingham said that was easy: a local worthy in Sunbury had lost money investing in Grace's swindles and had come to the firm for advice when it all came to light. 'Nothing we could do, of course, except put his name on the creditors' list. Fat lot of good that did, as I told him. Actually, I do seem to remember you were away Edward, and I was minding the shop. He wanted to give evidence in court – have his day and pound of flesh if nothing else. But he was relatively small fry and there were plenty of bigger fish in front of him in the queue. And, as I say, much of the evidence was uncontested. Grace must have felt very bad about that, I imagine, when m'lud handed him seven years penal. Maybe why he never came clean on the money afterwards.'

A reply from the prison came after about a week, informing Edward that he had been allotted a visit a few days later, but that as an appointed legal representative he would be able arrange to further visits with the gatehouse at the end of each one, or they could be arranged by him or his clerk by telephone. Edward smiled wryly when he read this, not because he did not run to a clerk, but in the absence of one of the recent automatic telephone exchanges yet in Sunbury he would have classed calling Brixton Prison as too tempting for the local operator not to eavesdrop.

On the appointed day he took the train to Waterloo, a harrowing experience in itself for him, as there he mingled on the concourse with dozens of men spilling off trains, recovering from wounds, and recently discharged from the main receiving hospital at Southampton. For them, many who were amputees, he could see the war was over, where for him it had yet, if ever, to commence. He wanted to talk to some of them, all of them, but angry shame overcame him, made him pull down his hat, turn up his overcoat collar and hurry in search of a bus stop.

The long walk from the main road where the bus had dropped him, along the length of the lowering wall of the gaol, past its main gate to the smaller, more discreet, visitors' entrance, soon snapped him out of this selfish preoccupation with his own lack of fulfilment. Instead his mind was concentrated on the misfortunes of this other section of the wounded population, albeit self-inflicted. Edward wondered what manner of life's victim he was about to encounter here.

After a careful search of his briefcase and the contents of his pockets a prison warder conducted him through several gates which had to be unlocked and relocked behind them, causing his spirits to sink further and further with each one they passed through: it felt as if he too was being punished for being there exercising his duty to represent an inmate. He was left in a bare room with a wooden table and two hard chairs while the warder departed to fetch the prisoner. At any rate he was relieved to discover that the interview would be accorded some privacy, although he wondered if the warder would remain in the room. He knew that he should be more aware of the rights of the lawyer and his client when conducting interviews inside prison but did not wish to demonstrate his ignorance of them by asking if they would be left alone. The dilemma was resolved, however, when the warder returned with his charge, announcing in brusque tones, 'One-three-four-seven, Prisoner Grace', and adding, 'I shall be next door if you need me, Sir. Just ring the bell: although I don't think he'll give you any trouble. Still, I can cuff him if you'd prefer.'

Edward, who had clumsily risen to his feet on their entering, stammered that would not be necessary. Neither he nor the prisoner spoke until the warder had left, locking them both in.

'Thank you for that, at least, Mr Dereham. I hadn't asked you here to offer you violence.' The stooped man proffered his hand first, indicating with his introduction that he felt very much in control of the occasion: 'I am, as you will have gathered, Herbert Grace, at your service, as I trust, by your presence here, you intend to be at mine. Forgive the state of my hand. They are both much calloused, I fear, owing to the nature of the tasks that they set you here. Shall we sit?'

Edward could not help glancing down at Grace's hands. His nails had all but disappeared and the stubs of his fingers had roughly healed over where they had once been. Grace observed his glance.

'Some of us still pick oakum, although I believe His Majesty's ships have only limited use for it now. However, the governor here has taken some pity on me lately and has taken me into his own office to clerk for him and catalogue his surprisingly extensive library. My quota of oakum has been reduced because of my good behaviour, and miraculously appears each night when I return to my cell already picked. It seems I have some Rumpelstiltskin here to thank for it.'

'What is it precisely – oakum?' Edward asked, feeling foolish at not knowing despite having heard of it, but not before having felt the need to find out.

'Old pieces of hard, tarry rope. You have to pick it apart to make caulking.'

'Just with your fingers? That's barbaric.'

'Well they give you a kind of hook. But mostly your fingers, yes. Still there are worse things some have to do. At least I got to sit down. But it is penal servitude after all.'

'But you don't have to do all of it any more you say? Somebody else is doing some for you. That cannot be fair on him, can it?'

'I quite agree, Mr Dereham, but I am hardly in a position to complain to the governor about lenient treatment. He would find that extraordinary. I am after all a gentleman when all is said and done. Such things still count for something, even in here. I have made a great deal of money, the kind of money most of the inmates here and the gaolers too cannot even comprehend – and yet as far as most of them are concerned I have harmed no-one in the process. Most of my victims, for want of a better word, were victims of their own greed. When I explain it to some of my fellow inmates – and I include the governor and his deputies in that – they are inclined to equate the losses my shareholders incurred with a bad day at the races. And in my own case ultimately, so do I.'

As Grace was delivering this short, personal panegyric, Edward took him in: a gaunt grey-faced man, probably once an imposing six feet tall, but now round shouldered, his appearance indicating that his incarceration, not surprisingly, was ruining his health. Bellingham had supposed he might already have died in prison and it very much looked to Edward as though it was only a matter of time. According to the back copies of the Morning Post which he had been unable to resist consulting before his visit, Grace was already in his sixties when sentenced three years earlier, but now it looked as though ten had passed since then. Looking at the man on the other side of the table Edward felt pity at his sickly appearance, especially when contrasted with the photographs of him in the Morning Post. At the same time he was irritated with his self-satisfied justification of his crimes and natural arrogance undiminished by his physical decline. While it was possible to regard many of those who had lost money at Grace's hands as driven to destruction by their own greed, many others, Edward had read, were small people who had been persuaded by others to invest savings and legacies representing the sum total of meagre wealth they could ill-afford to lose. These were the widows and orphans Bellingham had referred to, although Edward did think those pillars of the non-conformist church who had been keen to advise them and take a commission might have been less deserving.

Grace moved on from his general statement of absolution to the more specific: so far neither inviting Edward's approval nor yet offering any explanation for summoning him. He seemed to be establishing his right to be owed whatever service it was he intended to demand, without going through an expression of contrition. 'My company flotations were at the outset no more risky than most others that involve imagination, flair and a degree of courage on the part of the investors. Indeed, *The Rapid City and South Dakota Tramway Company* is a thriving concern as we speak although the shares on which the original flotation was promoted may have reflected a level of capitalisation not subsequently borne out. But, Mr Dereham, as a man of law you will know that inviting people to share in risk is not in itself reprehensible, even if the expected returns fail to materialise in the time specified or at the percentages estimated in good faith.'

Edward wondered what he was supposed to make of this codswallop. The reports in the Morning Post said that the gigantic sums involved in Grace's frauds had come about as a result of his transferring non-existent funds from one set of companies he owned onto the books of others he also owned to make them appear profitably capitalised when they were not. In this way banks and other lenders were duped into investing real money in the expectation of a profit which could never materialise other than by Grace repeating the process, constructing a tower of cards needing only a puff of wind to bring it tumbling down.

Grace had tried to persuade himself and the court that the potentially profitable investments such as *Rapid City and South Dakota* would have paid out in time to reimburse his other creditors. If not deliberate fraud it had been self-delusion of an incredible kind and had not stopped him from taking his own 'profit' along the way of more than half a million pounds. This presumably had bought amongst other things the large house with an estate and the part-share in the French casino Bellingham had alluded to – all in his wife's name, Edward reflected. He wondered whether his mother had had any inkling of this; whether it had been the reason for the estrangement from her sister and this man she had married, or had it been simply some mundane falling-out in the family.

'You will be wondering why I have arranged this meeting, Mr Dereham.'

Now we are coming to it, Edward thought. Perhaps Grace had detected from the lack of any response to what he had been saying that it was time to bring matters to a head, although from what he had heard so far Edward was more inclined to think that Grace had too much self-conviction to allow himself to believe he was not convincing others. It would have been this egoism that had enabled him to bestride his flawed business empire so easily, qualities he would have seen as flair, imagination and a degree of courage.

'Your mother's sister, your aunt Rose, my unlamented wife who had nothing but bitter recrimination to offer me, despite the fact that I made her a wealthy woman, with a fine house, servants and a very substantial income in her own right, has passed away while I have been here in Brixton. Undoubtedly she would have blamed her demise on that fact had she been in a position to do so.'

It did not seem appropriate for Edward to make any comment on this: faced with Grace's seasoned bitterness and his own lack of any connection with his aunt, any expression of his own sorrow or even murmured condolences would have been entirely superfluous; so he listened in silence.

'My wife left a will concerning the property in her name together with the investment income from a company I set up for her, quite legitimately in my view. A will which I had drawn up for her. I did not expect, of course, to be in quite the position I am now.'

The circumstances of his being in prison meant he had lost day-to-day control of the business arrangements he had obviously made to safeguard his wealth. It had consequently come as a nasty surprise to find that she had felt sufficiently wronged by him to have consulted a lawyer and had a codicil to the will drawn up – effectively a new one. It was short and sweet, said Grace, with considerable asperity. 'It provided that on her death her estate would be left elsewhere and not to the investment trust previously stipulated – one I had set up anonymously, of course, merely to replicate the arrangements for handling her money that were in place in her lifetime. Sheer vindictiveness on her part. I only wonder she did not have the effrontery to tell me to my face. Not that she would have been seen here, alive or dead. That's not to say I wished her dead, Dereham. I did not.'

No, thought Edward, that was probably because alive she had provided a legal front for his wealth. Even though Grace was oblivious of it, the irony of the fraudster himself defrauded was not lost on Edward. It struck him in that instant that he had been summoned by his uncle to contest this new will; that would be it. His mind began to race as he considered what his own ethical position ought to be when faced with such a commission. He was wholly unprepared for what came next.

'By your obvious look of surprise, Dereham, you are as yet unaware of the spiteful nature of my wife's revenge. She did in fact leave everything to your mother. Some piddling solicitor she found locally is the principle executor and needless to say I have no locus in the matter while I am in here. He must be seeking probate which as you know can be a very long-drawn out business, so I can only assume he intended to contact your mother when it came through. He may in any case not have been given her address – he certainly hasn't been in touch with me in here directly. For all I know he may not even be aware of my existence, although in view of the codicil you would think he would have made it his business to find out. I was merely allowed brief sight of a communication from some faceless government cypher informing me of my wife's death. I asked if I could see the will but as you may imagine, as the authorities here are not obliged to do that, I had to – let us say – come to a private arrangement. And now I have you.'

'But my mother is dead – as you know,' Edward stammered. He was astonished by Grace's revelation, not least because as far as he knew there had been no communication from any solicitor, piddling or otherwise, before or since his mother's own death, to inform her of the bequest. In his own professional experience this should have been standard practice. As for not having her address – well, the last known addresses of the beneficiaries should always be appended to the will, he knew that.

'Indeed, your letter made that clear. I saw no need to inform the governor of that fact. So Dereham, I guess that you are the sole inheritor of my wealth, unless of course your mother left everything to the women's suffrage movement or some such, which I doubt, you, I assume, being her solicitor executor.'

Edward – on whom the words 'piddling solicitor' were not lost – was hazy as to the rights, if any, of prisoners to take out actions in the High Court when it came to something like contesting a will while they were still serving their sentences. In any case it seemed implausible that Grace would be approaching him to do so on his behalf when he himself appeared to be the ultimate beneficiary. In fact he assumed his interest would probably rule him out. He said as much to Grace who retorted, 'I do not wish you to contest the codicil. I am only too well aware of the difficulties of our doing that from in here I can assure you.'

Edward was at a loss. He could not imagine what Grace might want him to do as a solicitor that would enable him to get his hands on his money once more.

'Part of the various bits of finance that went to make up the total, which she nominally controlled in her name, included, let us say, regular payments to a lady of my long-term acquaintance and her two children – I'm sure you get my drift. Amongst other things I have put a decent roof over their heads and have paid for the children's boarding schools. It suited everyone to have them educated away from home you understand.'

'But didn't your wife…?'

'My wife was unaware of the nature of these transactions. They were all dealt with by automatic payments made through a company bank account which was ultimately in her name but which I effectively oversaw. It was not an account she needed to access for her own income. As long as she had that and the house she took no interest in any other business matters which were in her name. She simply signed any documents I put in front of her. She had no curiosity about my business nor wished to. It was not until my affairs and the name of Grace were so ridiculously dragged through the criminal court that she took any action of her own, which was to punish me with that codicil.'

Edward stared unbelievingly at the man across the table. A month ago he had barely known of his existence, didn't know his name, yet now he was suddenly about to become the inheritor of his ill-gotten wealth or a significant part of it. And what about this lady – Grace's mistress he did not doubt – and her children – his too? They were all being supported out of this money that was coming to him. Something else occurred to him as well.

'If probate hasn't been granted yet…'

'Well, I don't know that one way or the other. As I say, no-one is very concerned in here about my part in it. That's why I have called for you…'

'...any bank accounts solely in your wife's name will have been frozen – I'm assuming you do not have power of attorney or a trusteeship...'

'As a convicted felon, rather difficult. I had omitted to do so before all this – rather remiss of me in the circumstances. But I saw no reason to and, you will appreciate, I intended to keep my name at some distance from my wife's affairs.'

'So the payments to your...to this lady and her family will also have been frozen. Unless your wife's solicitor has made some arrangement?'

It was the first time Edward had seen Grace's self-assuredness falter since the beginning of their meeting. The implications of one or both these propositions shook him visibly. That his wife and her 'piddling solicitor' might have delved into the payments to his lady without his knowledge or control, still worse that his wife might then have arbitrarily cancelled them out of vindictiveness wasn't anything he had remotely considered, being someone who had always taken for granted his ability to read every move. Just as bad though was Edward's pointing out that if the solicitor had not gone into the purposes of the payments from this account, the upshot would now be the same: no payments to the lady.

'You must establish the position, Dereham. Swiftly establish the position, and make sure that my poor Louise has not been left destitute.'

Edward was not entirely sure how he would make sure of that if the funds had been frozen, especially as he had no idea what kind of life the lady was accustomed to enjoy but Grace was now recovering his composure.

'I have access to funds of my own, as I believe I mentioned to you concerning your immediate fee, but you will have to make the arrangement, I cannot from in here unless I bribe one of the warders. But this is not a matter of sending a screw for a draft for a few guineas. No, not at all. No, you must ascertain Louise's position, draw up a deed of power of attorney in your name, have it witnessed and bring it to me for signature. At once mind, tomorrow, by the end of the week.'

Edward asked him when precisely his wife had died because it occurred to him that it now being February, the children's school fees could have already been paid for the year. Grace said it had been some time in the autumn, 'But I was not notified until January via the governor's office. This solicitor of Rose's wrote to the authorities – not to me.'

There came a loud knocking on the door of the room and the sound of the observation slide being thrust back. The disembodied voice of the warder informed them that time was up. 'If you wish to continue with the prisoner, Sir, you'll have to make another appointment at the gate on your way out. Come along please – this man's got work to do.'

Edward gathered up his papers. 'I'll have to see…Mrs, um Miss…Where shall I find her?'

'Mrs Louise Bolden,' said Grace. He gave Edward an address in Hove in Sussex which he wrote down: it was not a part of the world he was familiar with.

He picked up his hat and coat. 'And so, Mr Grace – he could not bring himself to call him 'uncle' – what do you expect me to do with your wife's legacy?' It was the question he really needed to ask, but hardly the one on which to end their interview so abruptly.

'Enjoy it Dereham, I should. Act in Louise's best interests and the children's, and mine too, if you would be so kind,' Grace said gruffly; for the first time evincing some awareness of his own dependency within the forbidding prison surroundings. 'What is it you most want to do with the life and liberty you have?'

'To fight,' thought Edward, jamming on his hat. 'But they won't let me.'

When he found himself at the gate he wasn't clear how he should proceed with Grace's business. Should he make another appointment then and there? Had his instruction been to draw up a deed of power of attorney and return with it for signature within the week, or had it been primarily to ascertain Mrs Bolden's financial position within the week? He decided to make an appointment for three weeks hence.

'Will you inform Mr Grace?' he asked the warder behind the desk.

'The prisoner? I shouldn't suppose so, no. Time enough for him to know on the day.'

Edward asked if he might write, then, to the prisoner and was grudgingly told that would be in order.

## 3

CAROLINE Crescent, Hove, included the terrace where Mrs Bolden resided, looking over pleasant gardens open at the southern end to the promenade. It was imposing without the grandeur of some of the neighbouring squares, sharing their presence, but not their ostentation. It was, thought Edward as he rang the bell, 'a good address', and one, he supposed, that had been chosen with some care by Herbert Grace to accommodate his mistress comfortably, without exposing her to undue speculation.

To his relief, the maid who opened the door was evidently expecting him. Immediately on returning home from Brixton, after some deliberation on the train he had decided to write informing Mrs Bolden of his intention to pay her a visit that week, stating briefly his reasons. He had not received a reply – there would hardly have been time in any case – so on his way to Victoria Station on a sudden impulse he had stopped at the post office to send a telegram confirming his arrival later that day.

The maid showed him into the spacious sitting room upstairs, with tall bow windows overlooking the gardens and a small grand piano set back from them. Mrs Bolden was standing by the fire, halfway down the room, which was lit. She was a dark-haired woman, quietly dressed, but in the modern style of a long blue skirt and separate blouse. Edward guessed she was little older than him, not much – late thirties or possibly early forties. He was drawn at once to her dark, almost violet eyes, not least because it was apparent she had recently been weeping. In one hand she was clutching a crumpled telegram which Edward assumed was the one he had sent from Victoria although he was at a loss to understand why it should have reduced her to tears. He struggled for an explanation; his very presence and purpose must have come as an unpleasant shock; perhaps he was the first direct link she had had since his incarceration, with her – what was he? – Her protector? Faced with her distress normal courtesies went out of the window.

'I'm so sorry,' he stammered. 'I shouldn't have turned up so abruptly, but I gave your…Mr Grace, my word I would waste no time. I sent the telegram today because I wasn't sure if you had received my letter. I'm so sorry Mrs Bolden, so sorry.' He blundered to a halt.

She made an effort to choke back sobs that were clearly about to engulf her again. 'Telegram?' she murmured. 'Ah yes, the telegram. But not this one.' She held out the creased buff-coloured slip for him to see. It read: *Regret to inform you 2nd Lt. Cornelius Bolden London Irish Rifles missing in action. Letter follows.*

'Your son?'

Mrs. Bolden nodded distractedly, her stifled sobs beginning to crumple her face like the telegram that was causing them. Edward felt he wanted to take her in his arms to comfort her, but his clumsy half movement towards her turned into little more than a helpless gesture, appearing to offer back the offending message as if it were too hot for him to continue holding. She took it from him without seeming to notice.

'Missing might mean he has been taken prisoner, mightn't it?' he offered. A few – very few – of those grieving parents and relatives who had come to his office seeking straws to clutch at, had subsequently been informed as much. Most had not. Subsequent communications generally presumed death. 'Or wounded somewhere…in hospital, I mean. They get mislaid that way sometimes, I've heard.'

She turned towards the window and gazed intently down towards the seafront, as if she might be searching for her son, seeing all the way across to France, or hoping for him simply to emerge from the edge of the waves and walk up the shingle.

'And why would he be mislaid like that?' Wouldn't he tell them his name? Why would they be sending a telegram saying he's missing?' Her voice had a soft, barely noticeable, Irish inflection, so unpronounced that Edward thought it might have been long-suppressed, only now set free by her pain. This thought made him conscious he had been mentally casting her in the role of the scarlet woman ever since he had become aware of her existence, only now to be rebuked by the gracious balance of her surroundings, her circumstances and her bearing which all spoke to the contrary.

'He might be…he mightn't be able to…might be confused.' What did he know? He could imagine. He had seen the young men at Waterloo Station, hadn't he? The state they were in now. What must some of them have been like when they came off the battlefields? Just *missing* was a terrible word to write to anyone, most of all a boy's mother; leaving her prey to every continuing nightmare; lacking death's completion.

'They say a letter will come,' he said. 'It may have more news when it does.'

'So he might be found alive somewhere? In hospital like you said?'

'Or a prisoner. Word comes through. They have ways…the Red Cross, I believe.' It sounded trite.

'What if he's…lying somewhere? Do they go looking for people who are missing?'

'Almost certainly.' But Edward didn't really know at all. How little those who were not there really knew: the conspiracies of silence and subterfuge; the soldiers themselves writing cheery letters keeping up the spirits of those they loved, especially those mothers like Mrs Bolden; the newspapers always making the best of a disastrous job. He was in danger of giving false hope, offering fictional platitudes which would in the long run be an affront to Mrs Bolden's dignity.

'They have special units who go looking for soldiers who are missing – even if it's been a little while.' The words came out. He so wanted that to be true, he believed it to be so in his heart. 'Someone will find your son, be sure, Mrs Bolden.'

She did not reply, seeming to dwell on the finality of what he had just said. Then she nodded decisively, as much to herself as to him, making firm this pledge, mentally spitting in her palm and shaking hands on it. Her crisis had passed, for the moment at any rate.

She made an effort at calmness, turning back from the bay window to face him, her features composed, her Irish lilt locked away again. 'You've news of Herbert, Mr...? I'm sorry I've forgotten your name in the midst of all this.'

He had rehearsed and rehearsed on the train down how much or how little he would impart to her, expecting that he would need to preserve a polite, professional distance from her and keep their relationship on a business footing. But the harrowing circumstances of this first meeting had instantly broken down any reserve he might have wanted to impose. He told her everything from the beginning; the summons to Brixton prison, the bizarre coincidence of the death of his mother and her sister Rose, the fact that he himself had become the unwitting beneficiary of a slice of Herbert Grace's wealth; how large a slice he could not yet say.

How much Mrs Bolden took in was impossible to tell. Her thoughts were wandering over some unimaginable battlefield in France; that he could see. He came to a stop.

'This must be so difficult,' he said, after a long silence broken only by the sound of embers dropping in the grate. He went over to the fireplace absently and replenished the fire with a few coals from the brass scuttle with the tongs. 'Would you like me to leave you in peace? I can return another time – tomorrow if you like.

Perhaps you have a friend who could sit with you. It's hardly fair to expect you to discuss all this stuff with a complete stranger when you must be feeling so…' He trailed off lamely.

'Yes that might be best.' She lifted her gaze where it had followed his attention to the fire and looked at him with her violet eyes as if to fix his face in her mind for when she would see him again. 'No I don't want anybody. I'd rather be alone I think. And May is here if I need someone. She lives in while her man is in France.'

'So shall I come again tomorrow, then? Or another day?'

'Tomorrow would be grand.' She even smiled a little.

'Shall we say eleven?'

'Yes, and stay for lunch, why not?'

She accompanied him to the front door. As he turned to say goodbye on the steps she said, 'Thank you for being here when this came.' She was still clutching the telegram. 'You are a good, kind man, Mr Dereham, so you are. I can tell.'

Edward raised his hat and turned down the crescent trying to look as though he had somewhere to be.

He returned to Caroline Crescent at eleven the following morning, having spent the night in a shabby hotel in one of the adjoining squares where his lack of luggage had not been questioned. The bathroom along the corridor from his room had not been at all inviting, so not having a razor in any case, he had found a barber's nearby after breakfast from which he emerged hoping that his close shave would make up for the lack of a clean collar.

Mrs Bolden received him in the sitting room again. Her face revealed the signs of a sleepless night and she too was wearing the same clothes as she had on the previous day. However, when he enquired how she was feeling she assured him she was in a much better state of mind. He didn't accept the platitude for one minute of course, but he took it as a signal that she wished him to press on with the business.

'Mrs Bolden,' he began.

'Louise, please,' she interrupted. 'I feel that we are almost related in a manner of speaking. Although I know we are not,' she added hastily and gave him that half smile he had seen briefly the day before. 'And may I call you something other than Mr Dereham? It's obvious that our paths will be crossing from time to time and as it seems Grace and I are to be beholden to you, I would rather you were not a stranger.'

For a moment Edward assumed she was talking about Herbert Grace. 'Yes, call me Edward please. After all he is my uncle by marriage, so now that he is a widower he would of course be free to…to bring you into the family, so to speak.' He stammered to a halt and blushed to the roots of his hair, realising what she must have supposed he had been about to say. This time she laughed properly and put a reassuring hand on his arm.

'Bless you no, Edward. Grace is my daughter – our daughter I suppose I can say to you. We called her Grace because, well because it was a way of giving her his name as he couldn't marry me and give his name to me.'

'And is – was – your son not his then?'

'No. No he is not,' she corrected him and Edward again blushed awkwardly, ashamed he had referred to her missing son as if he were dead.

She said she already had Cornelius, when his father, her husband Joseph Bolden had walked out of their lives. Whether he had deliberately deserted them was unclear. He had been a young employee in one of the legitimate city businesses Herbert Grace had acquired and had come to the attention of the board of directors as a rising star. When it had been looking for someone to investigate opportunities across the Atlantic Joseph Bolden was dispatched to the United States. He landed in New York, headed out West by the new railroad and was never heard of again. No word at all, Dereham asked her, wondering if he might have made it as far as Rapid City, South Dakota? He did not ask her how her relationship with Herbert Grace had come about, judging it would be indelicate despite her frankness so far. Edward assumed that it would have grown after the disappearance of Bolden, that Grace had offered her comfort and succour in her distress. But, he thought, they could just as easily have been having a liaison of some kind before that. To admit to that would cast her in a rather different light, although it would not have altered his opinion of his uncle.

Legally, however, there was part of the business that he felt he needed to broach. 'How long is it since you or anyone heard anything of your husband? I take it your daughter Grace was, er, was born after he disappeared, and she must be, how old now?'

'She is nearly twelve years old. Cornelius was already five when she was born.'

Edward did a quick calculation. 'So your husband Joseph has been gone for seven years, if not more?'

'That's right. It must be eight or nine.'

So, he thought, Louise would be free to marry again – to marry Herbert Grace, if that made sense. But then she would probably be pursued for the rest of his wealth if he died and she inherited it. Edward pictured the newspaper headlines and shuddered inwardly, fervently wishing he could stop thinking for a moment as her legal adviser, all the time conjuring up issues he would rather not raise with her. But he knew she was alone and vulnerable. He had no obligations to her, not even ties of blood. His brief, which came from a convicted felon still serving a long prison sentence, amounted to no more than an entreaty for him to act in her interest as power of attorney, by dispensing his ill-gotten money which in all probability would be forfeit to the authorities as soon as its whereabouts became apparent. No, the reality was that Louise Bolden's entire world would now depend solely on the emotional generosity of one Edward Dereham. He could see with startling clarity that he had no choice but to care for her as he would a song-bird he had found on the back step, left there for dead by next door's cat. Yet startling as it might be, it was nevertheless a self-revelation that made him glow with anticipation.

They had lunch in the small dining room at the rear of the house behind the sitting room and overlooking a small garden. From its size and the shape of the table Edward deduced that, despite its elegance, it was not used for lavish entertaining which spoke volumes for Herbert Grace's discretion. But nor would he have described the house in Caroline Crescent as a love nest. It was very much a home and where, he guessed, his uncle would come and go very much as the man of the house and, if not as a husband, certainly as the father of the children. Edward almost expected to see a portrait of him on the wall, the absent paterfamilias presiding over his circular inlaid rosewood table.

They discussed her daughter's schooling (fortunately he had been right and the next year's fees had been paid). He found it odd to call her by that name as until then he had associated it solely with his uncle, her father, a man he had formed no good opinion of and therefore with whom he had no wish to tarnish his daughter's image. He mentioned his confusion to Louise, but not of course the reason for it.

'Well, I do have a pet name for her,' she said. 'I call her "Gee" – her initial. To be honest with you, Edward,' she confided with him, 'I had the same trouble with her name as you do. It was really Herbert's idea and I went along with it. She's very happy with it though – Grace Darling is one of her heroines.'

'And does she know that he is her natural father, and that you aren't…you know?'

'Aren't married, you mean?' She fell silent. Then she said, 'They haven't really arisen yet, all the explanations. I think she's worked some things out for herself about Herbert and me, but not that he is her father. We always called Joseph "daddy" because he was to Cornelius, and Gee has always been Grace Bolden at school. Herbert spends most of his time here when the children are at school. We don't do things together in the holidays much.' She stopped, sobs welling up inside her. Edward took her hand awkwardly across the table, but she took it away gently, on the pretext of taking a sip of water from her glass. 'I have to stop talking as though nothing has changed in the last three years. Herbert is in prison and forbids me to go there – and I'm not so sure I would have the courage in any case…Now my son is gone, God knows where. And shouldn't he be still at school? God knows he should. And I never saw him go, God knows. And now I'm punished. All the men in my life missing: as good as dead to me and me not been to confession since I cannot remember when. And now I'm punished for my sins.'

She half collapsed forward onto the table, her shoulders shaking with great gulping sobs which she had given up trying to suppress. Edward put his hands over hers and this time she did not try to remove them. He wondered helplessly what he should say or do: something told him that words of reason would be of little comfort. He felt for her, succumbing to the repressed flood of grief from all its causes over a long time, as he had felt when he had sat by his mother's coffin in their house; as someone who had craved the physical contact for so long absent from him, as it must have been too for Louise. He left his hands where they were over hers, wishing he could stand behind her and fold his arms tightly around her. But he could not. Convention and manners held him in check.

After a while she drew herself up and dabbed at her eyes with a tiny handkerchief. Edward hastily pulled out his own, which was fortunately still clean from the day before, and gave it to her. She chose to blow her nose loudly in a way that said, that's over and I've pulled myself together. 'There now. Let's go back to the other room and we'll get May to bring us some tea – or coffee if you would prefer.'

When he judged the moment might be right, he broached the subject that had been nagging away at him ever since he had done the age calculations. 'Cornelius, your son…he must be barely eighteen.' He did not repeat the mistake of using the past tense.

'He's just had his eighteenth birthday. He wrote and said he had had a good time with his comrades and thanked me for a parcel I had sent to help him celebrate. I don't think he was at the front just then. But they're not allowed to say where they are, I know.'

'But the telegram yesterday said he is a second lieutenant.'

'Yes. It did, didn't it? I haven't given that much thought. He didn't go back to school after the Christmas holidays last year when he was just coming up to his seventeenth birthday and went and volunteered for the London Irish Rifles. I should have tried to stop him, but he was already in France before I knew what he had done. We'd had a bit of an old set to about Herbert a while earlier. I hadn't said anything about the trial or anything. Cornelius must have seen his picture somewhere in a newspaper and realised who he was. Well, you can imagine. And I thought it best to let sleeping dogs lie when he joined under age. He'd have gone this year anyway. God forgive me!'

Edward feared she would break down again, but she did not. He felt an oddly curious emotion, not quite envy and not quite resentment. It had been so easy for her son to join up even though he was technically ineligible. Not only had he hoodwinked them about his age, it was obvious that his public school education — he'd probably been in the cadets, hadn't he? — had walked him straight into a junior commission. What had the recruiting officer said to Edward — applications for temporary commissions can be made during basic training? Now 2nd Lt. Bolden was missing in action. Did Edward Dereham wish it was him instead?

If it had occurred to Louise that Edward himself should have been in uniform she did not mention it. He wished he could say something about his circumstances, his health, his persistently being declared unfit in the face of his own instincts to the contrary. But the fact that Cornelius Bolden was missing in action acted as a huge reproachful barrier, making all his explanations sound to him like feeble excuses.

She, however, regarded him as her knight in shining armour and perhaps needed no explanations about any other uniform. For two months now the regular payments to her bank account had been missing, as Edward had supposed they might be while probate was being sought, of which Louise knew nothing, of course. The manager at her bank had not been notified of any reason why the regular payments had ceased, and Louise had been reluctant to get him to pursue it, knowing that it would inevitably lead to unpleasant disclosures and explanations regarding the origin of the money. Fortunately she had sufficient cushion in the account to allow her to pay her bills for a while yet but she had been miserably contemplating having to write to Herbert in prison if a third month's payment was missed. This was a step she shrank from taking, in the main because he forbade it, presumably to protect her identity and their relationship. Edward thought this a remarkably flimsy protection for Louise in the event that something should go wrong with her finances, as indeed it had. But he had already seen that Herbert Grace still liked to think that he was master of his affairs, even though he was picking oakum in Brixton. His natural arrogance would have made him blind to the weakness of his arrangement for Louise as it had been to that of his own business edifice.

Edward assured her that her payments would continue, although privately he was not sure quite how he would manage that, especially when he saw from her bank statements how much they amounted to.

It was still preoccupying his thoughts when he alighted from the train at Sunbury station later that evening.

# 4

As it turned out, resolving Louise Bolden's finances was not Edward's only preoccupation in the days following his visit to Hove. Two letters arrived in quick succession: one from the War Office department dealing with conscription telling him that his period of temporary deferral was at an end and that he should report back to hospital for a further examination within two weeks, and that failure to do so would result in...*etcetera, etcetera.* The other was indeed from Dr Carradine, the consultant at St Mary's, saying the same thing without the threatening tone and giving him an appointment early in the following week.

On the day of the appointment Dr Carradine called him in to his room and immediately asked if he had been spitting blood since the last appointment to which Edward replied truthfully that he had not. He removed his waistcoat and shirt at Carradine's request, who then tapped him, applied his stethoscope to his back and front, and then as before asked Edward to cough and spit onto a small glass slide, which he then examined under the microscope.

While he was staring into the eyepiece he said, 'Tell me, have you ever had an x-ray taken of your chest?' There's no mention of one in the medical notes I have been sent.'

Edward said he had not. 'There is no machine at our local hospital, as far as I know. In any case my doctors have always been convinced of their diagnosis – because of my mother having it, I suppose.'

'Hmm. What about South Mimms? Didn't they give you one there?'

Edward said he had never been offered one. He assumed that by the time one needed to go to South Mimms, the diagnosis had already been accepted. 'If it hadn't been for the war, I would probably accepted it myself more readily, but it's been…you know…'

'Keeping you out of the army? I have to say I admire your determination to fight for King and country. I often think I should be with Almroth Wright at one of the hospitals he's running around Boulogne – God knows, half my young physicians are over there, but someone has to keep St Mary's running and I suppose it has to be the older ones like me. Come on, put your shirt back on and we'll go and take your picture, see what your lungs look like – not that it's all that definitive for lungs. Not like broken bones and such. They've got machines in Boulogne now, by the way. So finding bits of metal inside the casualties involves less guesswork, less digging blindly. But shadows on lungs now. Could be anything. Just proves a point that something's there or it isn't.'

After the x-ray Edward sat in the waiting room while the pictures were being developed or whatever had to be done with them – he didn't know, but he assumed it must involve dark rooms and chemicals. After a surprisingly short time, however, the consultant called him back into his room. 'It's as I thought,' he said, holding the plate up to the window for the best light, 'inconclusive. There's a shadow there all right. But as you haven't had an x-ray before now, I've nothing to compare it with.'

Edward wondered what the point of it was, then, but was too polite to say so. He didn't feel this was getting them anywhere.

'The thing is,' said Dr Carradine pursing his lips as if he was talking to himself and Edward wasn't there. 'The thing is, given the length of time you're supposed to have been developing this

TB, I would have expected to see a bigger area than this.' He pointed to the small, shadowy patch on the picture with his pencil. 'This looks to me more like a small fibrosis of some kind, or some old damage that has healed up and scarred.'

'And would that account for me spitting blood when I cough, like opening an old wound?' Edward asked. 'Not that I have lately,' he added hastily.

It was possible, the consultant conceded. 'But on its own this is, as I say, inconclusive. The safest course is to hope that there is no recurrence after time, no increase in the frequency and amount of your spitting blood.'

Edward felt his spirits sag. For a moment he had hoped he might have been about to change his mind and declare him officially free from infection, but instead it was clear he was going to have to wait longer. The bitter disappointment showed on his face.

'Another six months, Dereham. That's all. Good God man, I'm probably giving you your life back in more ways than you think.' He stood up and proffered his hand as a sign that their time was up. As Edward was leaving, the consultant said, 'If it weren't for the regulations, I might just be persuaded to give you the benefit of the doubt in less time. If you're so keen to do something for the war you ought to find a job that doesn't involve the armed services and their damn regulations.' Instantly he must have regretted seeming to contradict his own medical opinion, because he added, 'Not that you shouldn't wait. Have to consider the people around you too, if you are infectious.'

On the train back to Sunbury he shared his carriage with two convalescent soldiers in their hospital blues. He tried to think of something to say to them which wouldn't sound patronising, and he began to feel uncomfortable in his suit, with his bowler up in the rack next to their forage caps glowering down at his hunched, guilty figure. Burying his head in the Evening News' reports of more action around Ypres and against the Turks further off in Mesopotamia, he mulled over the consultant's parting shot. Was there in fact something he could do that might get him out of civilian clothes, something valuable for the war? He thought about the hospitals along the channel coast the consultant had mentioned. Was there work there he could do which didn't involve being in the military? But he quickly saw that he would have to say why he wasn't already in uniform, have to present his exemption paper. They would hardly let him work in a hospital if they knew his own medical situation. Still, he thought, he would pursue the notion: why not? There might be a backdoor of some kind, some organisation which might not be too particular about the reason for his exemption. He tried to recall whether his exemption or his temporary deferral specifically mentioned tuberculosis. Did it just say 'medical exemption'? Perhaps he could make something up if that was the case; something that wasn't an infectious disease. After all, he reasoned, he had always been convinced he didn't have TB – and he didn't believe his consultant thought so either.

The two soldiers left the train at Richmond, where their military hospital evidently was, both on crutches manoeuvring themselves adroitly down from the carriage step. They were, unusually, wearing Red Cross armbands – to emphasise their status presumably, Edward supposed. Red Cross, he thought? Worth a try.

When he arrived home having had to push his bicycle all the way from the station to his house in Lower Sunbury because of a flat tyre and no pump, it was already dark. He was therefore rather alarmed to see a man's figure propped on the shelf in the porch where his dead mother's over-wintered geraniums still stood in their pots.

Edward called out to him from the gate, asking what his business was. The man stepped out of the porch into the light afforded by the street gas lamp. He was hatless and wearing a heavy, dark blue coat. 'Name of Dereham? I've a message for you.'

Edward advanced towards the burly figure, still rather alarmed. 'Message from whom?'

'Name of Grace. Says you know him.'

A neighbour walked by with his dog on the other side of the street. He wished Edward a good evening. 'Nothing wrong, Mr Dereham?'

'No, no, nothing wrong, no. Late client.' He laughed, he hoped reassuringly, turned round to his visitor and crowded him back up the path to the front door. 'You'd better step in for a moment.'

When he had lit his own gas in the entrance hall, Edward could see the man's serge coat was uniform issue; he had an irrational thought he was from the gas company, or perhaps even a bus conductor, except they were women these days, things being how they were. Then when he saw the numbered collar and crown insignia on his tunic half concealed underneath the coat he realised with a start that this messenger was actually a prison warder. The entire situation should have been clear but Edward tried to believe he must be doing his uncle a kindness out of the goodness of his heart, acting as a messenger; but his own better feelings were soon dispelled.

The creased envelope the warder handed over bore the appearance of already having been opened and resealed. 'Grace says you'll give me half a sov' for my expenses making the trip.' Edward doubted this: it would certainly be a generous tip on top of the handsome bribe he would already have received. But he made no demur; even he could see that to have done so would have incurred some kind of trouble for his client. He opened the missive – it was too brief to be called a letter. His uncle clearly assumed it would be read by its postman, however much he had been paid to deliver it, and, Edward thought, its contents might have been incriminating in some way if he had been caught doing it; who could say? It was unsigned and just said: *Come and see me. I need news of our business. I gave you a week and I have heard nothing.*

*You know how important this is to me. Reply by return. Sed nihil revelandum.* Edward took the point, but was slightly disappointed the entire thing had not been in Latin as he could have managed it. But then if the whole thing had looked like code, his gaoler probably wouldn't have brought it.

'Wait here while I write a reply,' he said curtly, hoping he sounded sufficiently resolute, as it occurred to him he must be compounding some heinous offence under the criminal justice provisions. He went through to his study, sat at the desk and thought hard. There was absolutely no point in allowing himself to be bullied by Herbert Grace from inside prison, even though he was strictly speaking his solicitor. In any case he had made no progress with his counterpart in the business of probate, being more concerned with the question of his medical examination and its consequences. So, taking care not to use his headed writing paper he wrote: *Your instructions are being carried out. Satisfactory arrangements are being put in place for the third parties. You will receive a visit in two or three weeks.* He just stopped himself automatically signing it and then began to have more misgivings. Would it be better to tell the gaoler to sling his hook and that as a respectable solicitor he couldn't possibly receive client communications in this underhand and certainly unlawful way? But after weighing up the possible reprisals that might entail against Herbert Grace he just added: *Do not communicate this way again as there will be no further reply.*

Returning to the entrance hall he found his messenger idly examining the miscellaneous collection of umbrellas and walking sticks stored in an oriental porcelain urn by the door. One, he had just discovered, was a rather handsome silver-mounted sword stick. It had been there for longer than Edward could remember, an object he had been forbidden to touch as a child and which as an adult he no longer had any desire to. The gaoler had half pulled the hidden blade from its Malacca scabbard as Edward re-emerged from the study and said sharply, 'Kindly put that back, if you please.'

With the blade still half drawn his less and less welcome visitor gave Edward a dirty look, deliberately waiting before pushing the steel back with a slow hiss. 'Frightened of burglars, are we? Quiet spot like this, there's no knowing, is there?'

Edward made an effort not to feel intimidated in his own home. In fact he was conscious of an unaccustomed sensation stirring inside him and realised it was anger. Without comment he handed his envelope over, together with the demanded half sovereign he had retrieved from the cash box in his study drawer. At this the other man assumed a tone of mock indignation. 'That was half a sov' to bring it. It'll be another to take a reply. I'm taking quite a chance.'

The anger quietly brewing inside Edward increased. He felt exhilarated by it: it pushed aside that natural deference he instinctively employed with people to whom he felt under an unwelcome obligation which he wanted to be over and done with. 'You are indeed,' he said. 'Quite a chance. So I wouldn't push your luck if I were you. Coming into my home and threatening me.'

'Threatening you?'

'With that blade.'

'I didn't threaten you. I didn't even know it was there.'

'You found it without any difficulty, didn't you?'

'Now you look...!'

'No you look.' Edward was warming to his offensive; his thought process lining up his actions and their various possible consequences and ticking them off with careful precision. 'You came here unasked: I assume for a hefty bribe and now you're trying to extort more money from me. It's immaterial to me whether you return the message – I've told Grace not to communicate like this again. You can take yourself off and be thankful I don't have you taken in charge for corruption in public office and what else besides.' He opened the front door. The man barged past him without a word. But he nevertheless stuffed the letter into his pocket as he went.

Edward had been feeling rather sorry for his uncle, being beholden to such an unpleasant and obviously corrupt individual as this, but the fact that he had opted to take the letter despite Edward's provocation rather made him think that Grace and his gaoler deserved one another. It was hardly likely, was it, that a man like Herbert Grace would make use of someone he wasn't able to control? It was just what he had tried to do to Edward during his visit and was undoubtedly what this evening's illicit letter was supposed to achieve. He remembered what Grace had told him about being relieved of much of his oakum picking, which in his innocence he had taken at face value.

As his anger now began suddenly to subside he felt distinctly shaky; he went into the sitting room and poured himself a stiff whisky. The house was quiet and still; not even the black marble clock on the mantelpiece was ticking; it had not been wound for some time – probably not since his mother's death. He stirred himself to put this right and then went through to the kitchen to see about supper. There wasn't much in the larder, some cheese and a jar of pickled onions his mother had preserved about eighteen months previously. He must remember to ask Mrs Bale to fetch something in. Come to that he must pay her. It was some time since their paths had crossed in the house. He unscrewed the onions and sniffed them dubiously. High time, he thought, to be in uniform, to be in France, to be gone.

Even so, his professional obligations, such as they were, to Herbert Grace, and the personal obligations he had assumed more readily to Louise Bolden, did preoccupy him. After his frugal supper he began to give thought to his next course of action. Grace wanted him to take power of attorney, but the more Edward thought about that, the less inclined he felt to find himself responsible for administering his uncle's remaining hidden assets. Probably better to see what he could do about speeding up the probate process regarding his Aunt Rose's inadvertent legacy. He had already obtained probate of his mother's estate, so there should be no obstacle to his receiving Rose's bequest himself directly, although there might be an issue over death duties to be resolved. But that should be dealt with by his brother lawyer, whoever he would turn out to be. He had not, he realised, found out yet the name and address of the 'piddling solicitor', Rose's executor. Grace had said he had not been in touch with him in prison, but that he had been notified of his wife's death presumably by the prison authorities. Edward resolved to telephone the governor's office the next day, even though there was every possibility that the local operator would be unable to resist eavesdropping on a call to Brixton Prison. Still, he did not want to make a special journey for such a small thing. He would have to be firm with her.

After hanging on for what seemed an interminable time while someone in the prison governor's office hunted through the documents relating to prisoner one-three-four-seven H. Grace, Edward was eventually told that a department in the Home Office generally notified the prison of the death of prisoners' wives or children 'if it came to their attention'. He was grudgingly given a name and the telephone number of the Home Office where he then spent another interminable amount of time being passed from pillar to post before one official who was inclined to be rather more helpful came up with the business address of one Lloyd Garwood, of the firm of Garwood and Potter with offices in Surbiton. When Edward was thanking him profusely for his time and trouble, the helpful official said Rose Grace's name had rung a bell because he had been asked to obtain a copy of her will by someone in the Governor's office at Brixton. He couldn't remember who. It had been returned later and was still stuck on a file. He wasn't sure what he should do with it but it should probably go back to the Registrar's office. Edward assumed that whoever had asked for it at Brixton was the same Rumpelstiltskin who also arranged for his uncle's picked oakum quota to be lightened.

It was encouraging that the solicitors were based in Surbiton, because he could at a pinch bicycle there from Lower Sunbury if necessary. Perhaps their location explained why Rose had chosen to consult them out of the blue; it might be that Grace had a country estate in that vicinity, which would be well on the way to Hove, too.

Edward penned a brief letter to Lloyd Garwood on his own official stationery, saying that he was the sole beneficiary and the executor of the estate of his late mother, whom he understood to have been a beneficiary of her sister, the late Rose Grace. He saw no need to mention his dealings with Herbert Grace.

Without looking to see if his own practice required any attention that morning, he took the letter straight to the post-box. When he had done this he reproved himself slightly for letting himself be seduced by the thought that his own interests here were likely to be far more lucrative than those of the few clients needing his attention.

His conscience was pricked some more when, instead of returning immediately to his office to remedy this neglect, he carried on up the road the mile or so to Sunbury Cross and went into the public library. Settling himself down with the stiff-covered portfolios of recent copies of the Times and the Morning Post, he browsed through them for anything he could find about the work of the Red Cross. Anything which might get him into the thick of things; anything that might even get him into some kind of uniform.

# 5

LLOYD Garwood's reply came within two days, which Edward found remarkable, being himself well-used to solicitors' procrastinations, although he liked to think he was not himself overly prone to it. What this unusual speed said to him was that matters regarding Rose Grace's probate must have already come to a head. The letter said as much; probate had been granted, and as Edward's mother had been the sole beneficiary of Rose's will, everything would now come to him, subject to the usual proofs. Garwood, too, having noted Edward's relative proximity to Surbiton wondered whether it would be convenient for him to drive over and bring them himself rather than posting them, assuming he had access to a motor in these difficult times, 'or a taxi from Kingston might not be out of the question'.

Edward wrestled with his decision. He was of course immensely curious as to the size and scope of his accidental inheritance. He was also keen, as a lawyer, to find out if the odd circumstances of Rose's will and the fact that she had been used as a front for her husband's ill-gotten wealth, was something that Mr Garwood, 'the piddling solicitor', had been aware of. Personally he wasn't entirely sure whether the High Court of Chancery might be entitled to be made aware of these facts or whether as solicitors and executors either of them were under any obligation to inform it. But he assumed that while Rose would have been comfortably off and would undoubtedly have been the sole owner of whatever property she was living in, Herbert Grace would have been careful to keep the lion's share of his assets to himself, safely invested abroad to avoid investigation. Hadn't there been talk of shares in a casino in northern France, for instance? Edward wondered where Grace's cash might be – in France too? If so what might the war have done to that? He had a vague idea that the price of gold had risen enormously since 1914. Once again he rebuked himself for letting his thoughts wander in that direction. He had never been close to serious money in his life and he was alarmed at the ease with which its infectious quality could run through his system.

When he awoke the following morning he was still torn between getting his bicycle out and riding over to Messrs Garwood and Potter in Surbiton, and setting about pursuing his own burgeoning scheme for getting into the war. After an even more frugal breakfast than his previous night's supper – the toasted remains of the stale loaf and some jam from which he had first to remove a layer of mould – he put on his hat and coat and wheeled his bicycle out of the porch. But although he set off in the direction of the iron bridge at Hampton Court, he wobbled slowly along, his control of the bicycle reflecting his indecisiveness. However, his uncertain route took him past James Bellingham's house, and with a firmer sense of purpose he dismounted, left his bicycle at the garden gate and knocked at the door. Polly, the maid, answered it, and said rather severely that Mr Bellingham was at his breakfast and Mrs Bellingham was 'not yet down.' Edward couldn't tell whether her severity was aimed at both of them for being so tardy, or at him for presuming to interrupt them so early. She left Edward in the hall and went through to the breakfast room to announce him, but James Bellingham had already heard his voice and bluffly summoned him in.

'Morning Edward, join me in some eggs? I've only just started. Can't have you sitting there while I finish – feel like a monkey at the zoo, and I guess it's something that can't wait at this hour. Good God! Is that the time already? The perils of retirement, eh?'

Edward could see Polly's scrambled eggs in the chafing dish on the sideboard were done softly, just as he liked them. The slight gnawing in his stomach reminding him of the meagreness of his own recent repast at once overcame his embarrassment at interrupting Bellingham's own breakfast unannounced. He helped himself to a plateful and some bacon besides; only when he was well into it did it cross his mind he had probably eaten Mrs Bellingham's.

Bellingham waved aside his belated apology. 'Nonsense, nonsense. Sarah'll probably only have toast anyway. So – to what do I owe this early call of yours, Edward?'

'Do we know anyone connected with the Red Cross, James? I don't mean collecting locally for soldiers' comforts. I mean anyone well connected with it – its administration and so forth. Or someone who might know someone.' He trailed off, looking for something helpful from his occasional partner.

'Aren't they run from Geneva?'

'Yes, but there must be people in this country. I thought you might know somebody – you know, through your lodge.'

'Ah, the lodge. You've always turned away my overtures in that direction, haven't you? Anyway the masons are a bit more Knights of St John than the Red Cross. Tell me what it's about, Edward, I may be able to think of someone. I assume this has something to do with your inexplicable wish to overturn the verdict of the Army Medical Board. You don't want to take any notice of those damn white feathers by the way. I've not heard a single criticism of you from any of the people who matter round here.'

Bellingham was the only person to whom Edward had confided his frustrations at being turned down for service by the doctors, and of course, he was well aware of Edward's condition, having stood in for him at the practice during his visits to the sanatorium. But he never sought to distance himself physically or emotionally from Edward, never questioned the honesty of his stated determination to get into the army somehow, even though, for his own part, he was inclined to accept the doctors' opinions.

Edward cleared his throat. 'I've been reading some of the letters to the papers and the reports of the work the Red Cross are doing in France on recording the location of the battlefield graves. I think they've even had groups searching for soldiers who have been posted as missing, although from one report I read, I don't think the army are letting them do that anymore.'

'And you thought you might be able to sign up for that?'

Edward gave a short laugh. 'Well I could hardly be accused of endangering the health of the dead, could I?'

'I assume it's not work people do on their own, though, Edward. I know you're convinced the doctors have got it wrong. But you'd still have to persuade the powers-that-be.'

Edward leaned forward excitedly across the breakfast table. 'That's it though. They've sent me to see this specialist up at St. Mary's in Paddington and he is inclined to agree with me.'

'So he'll sign you fit, will he?'

'Well probably, yes. At the end of my current deferral though. But he suggested I might look for something non-military to sign up for in the meantime,' Edward fibbed. 'So I thought of the Red Cross. I could just write in, of course, but an introduction always helps. So I just wondered.'

'I'll ask around, Edward. There's a lodge meeting tomorrow as it happens. But you know, the Red Cross wouldn't exactly get you into uniform, would it? I thought that mattered to you.'

'Perhaps that wouldn't matter so much, actually,' Edward mumbled uncertainly. He wanted to tell Bellingham how forcibly he had been struck by a report he had read in the Morning Post about efforts Red Cross Units were making to find those posted missing. But the thought of what a fraud he had felt at the sight of Louise Bolden clinging to her hope that 'missing' did not mean dead made him silent.

'You've changed your tune, there, young Dereham. Still I'll ask about. Leave it with me. Now, tell me, what was all that about

Herbert Grace, the last time we spoke? Was it the city fraudster after all? You didn't seem to know.'

Edward hesitated for a moment. But after all, he thought, James Bellingham was his own executor and if anything should happen to him, whether on the battlefield or in Lower Sunbury, he would want Louise Bolden's affairs to be left in capable hands. So he told Bellingham everything – almost everything; he left out the bit about Rose Grace's codicil. He made it sound as though Herbert Grace had consulted him about Louise Bolden's financial arrangements, simply because of their distant family connection. Time enough, thought Edward, as he remounted his bicycle and set off to cross the river at Hampton Court, to confess that he had inadvertently been made heir to a large, illicit estate. How large still remained to be seen.

Garwood and Potter (Solicitors and Commissioners for Oaths) were located above a draper's shop in Victoria Road, the main street in Surbiton. As he mounted the stairs to the first floor Edward reflected ruefully that he should probably have informed Garwood of his intention to call; he hardly wished to have to repeat his bicycle journey. Still, as he took in the shabby state of the outer office and the absence of a clerk, he felt less presumptive and more in control. He rang the small hand bell on the unoccupied desk but there was no response. He knocked on the frosted glass door of the inner office and tried the handle. It was locked. There was a scrap of paper on the floor which must have fallen from the desk. On it a handwritten note informed him that Mr Potter was in court and that Mr Garwood might be found in The Victoria Hotel if the matter was urgent.

Edward looked at his watch. It was getting on for midday; by the time he had finished his explanations to James Bellingham and the inevitable questions they posed, it had been getting on for eleven o'clock. His bicycle ride had rekindled his appetite despite the good breakfast he had eaten at Bellingham's, so he decided he might as well seek out Garwood and some luncheon at the pub.

Although there were several possible candidates in the saloon of The Victoria who could be Garwood, only one had a bowler hat, which was beside him on the bar. Edward, who was himself wearing a cap today having bicycled, approached its owner fairly confidently. 'Mr Garwood, is it?' he ventured.

'Indeed, indeed, Mr er?'

Edward introduced himself. Garwood shook his hand warmly and offered him a drink. 'I'm having a glass of madeira myself, it being before noon, if you would care to join me.' Edward declined this suggestion, saying that he rarely drank alcohol and not in any case during the day. He immediately felt dishonest about this, in view of the large whiskies he had downed lately, admittedly in the evening while under some stress. It also sounded sanctimonious. 'I'll have a ginger beer, though, all the same. And I wouldn't mind something to eat too.' Somehow he had assumed that the Madeira must be a precursor to lunch, but the way Garwood seized on the novel possibility of eating something indicated that one Madeira was simply the precursor to several more.

'Capital idea. They do a very good Barnsley chop here, I'm told. We can commandeer the little snug bar at the side. We shouldn't be disturbed there.'

The barmaid said they hadn't had the Barnsley chops since the beginning of the war, to Edward's relief, knowing the size they could be. They both settled for liver and onions. Edward had a ginger beer while Garwood followed his Madeira with a bottle of stout. While they ate they talked in general about their respective practices and the effect the war was having on business. Edward was careful to keep his personal situation to himself. From the way Garwood referred to Edward he evidently assumed he must be too old to have been called up, particularly as he had yet to see any of Edward's proofs including his birth certificate. Garwood was thankful, he said, that he had no sons at the front; he only had daughters, although one of them was training to be a nurse. When they had finished eating, Garwood filled a curly Peterson pipe and signalled through to the main bar that he would 'take a glass of port'.

'So, Dereham,' he said when he had got the pipe to draw satisfactorily, 'I expect you are aware you are in for a tidy penny, a very tidy penny indeed. Stroke of luck your mother… er' He just managed to hold back the solecism he was about to unleash. 'Er, your mother being written into her sister's will at the last minute, like that. No knowing where the estate would have gone if she hadn't. Not that she had any intention of dying so soon, when she came to see me. That was very unexpected. At least I assume it was.'

Once again Edward was aware of the infected tide of wealth coursing through his system. He fought it, refusing to let himself ask 'how much'.

'Why do you say there was no knowing where the estate would have gone?' He had a slight sinking feeling that some question of judicial confiscation of Herbert Grace's loot was about to loom, although if that were a fact it would surely have happened regardless of the terms of the will.

'Well otherwise she would have been intestate as far as I can fathom. Her will originally left everything to some kind of foreign trust administered by a firm of lawyers on the continent. Antwerp I think it was. Wrong side of the western front anyway by the sound of it. No idea what we're supposed to do when someone's estate is left behind enemy lines. Put it in a holding account I suppose until the hostilities are all over. What would you think, Dereham? Ever come across that?'

Edward said it was probably a matter for the Bank of England in wartime, but he wasn't sure.

'Hmm. Well, anyway, it didn't come to it because Mrs Grace left it all to her sister instead. Your late mother.'

'Did you ask her why the will was so dramatically different? Did she explain why it had been drawn up in favour of this overseas trust or whatever it was?' A suspicion was beginning to form in Edward's head that Garwood hadn't the faintest idea who Rose Grace was.

'She told me that her husband had wanted it that way – your uncle by marriage that would be, of course. But now that he had died...'

'Died?'

'So she said. But surely you would know that.' Garwood looked at him a little strangely. Edward felt he would be asking for his proofs next, which indeed he should have done at the outset had not several large glasses intervened in the formalities. 'I barely knew my aunt Rose,' he explained truthfully. 'In fact I cannot really remember meeting her when I was a child, although I suppose I must have done. And I certainly have no recollection of him...from that time,' he added, thinking that perhaps it would be better not to offer Garwood any information he was not legally bound to supply him with. The phrase 'piddling solicitor' again insinuated itself into his head, in spite of his feeling professionally a little disloyal about it. But he was fascinated by the fact that Garwood had so little curiosity about what would surely have seemed to any lawyer an extraordinary change of intention for what was obviously a very large bequest.

'So you didn't handle any of her husband's business then? Who did probate on his own will – not you?'

'No, no. Not me. No idea who. Must have been some while earlier that he died. Didn't see the point. He wasn't a beneficiary of her first will so I didn't pursue it. D'you think I should've done?'

Edward didn't respond. He was almost tempted to reveal the true facts about Herbert Grace, just to see the look on Garwood's face, but he restrained himself. His first instinct to volunteer only what was necessary was the right one with this man, he was sure. Garwood clearly took no reply as a sign of approval of his actions – or lack of. But the exchange must have prompted him to pay some better attention to his executor obligations. Wiping his mouth on his handkerchief he said in a slightly more brusque tone that perhaps they should now repair to his office 'and go through the formalities' before discussing the detail of will. Back in his inner office, however he at once produced a decanter of sherry, with an apology for the fact that it was now after noon, but that he was 'a Cambridge man', which meant nothing to Edward, who declined it anyway.

Once Edward's proofs had been superficially scrutinised and unsurprisingly accepted Garwood set about the reading of Rose Grace's last will and testament. As he had said, everything was originally left to what sounded as if it could possibly have been a trust administered by a Belgian bank. Edward hadn't heard of it either, but he didn't say so: in view of the codicil that followed it hardly mattered. Strictly speaking although it was a codicil to her will, in fact it acted as a new one, completely denying the terms of what had gone before, leaving cash in the bank and removable goods to Edward's mother and her heirs as well as transferring the deeds of property to her name. Everything would have otherwise have been put into safe deposits and investment accounts somewhere in Europe, waiting for Herbert Grace quietly to claim it, which now of course the codicil together with his straitened circumstances prevented him from doing.

'As I told you,' said Garwood, with a great deal of vicarious satisfaction, 'having done the probate, it all amounts to a tidy sum, a very tidy sum indeed.' Edward waited, not wishing to give him the satisfaction of witnessing a display of vulgar impatience. Garwood began to itemise the totals held on deposit and in cash accounts in several banks, Edward silently totting them up in his head. As the sum continued to mount up he began to feel sick to his stomach. Whatever Herbert Grace may have done in creating illusions with other people's investments, there was nothing at all insubstantial about what he had created for himself.

And this, thought Edward, was presumably just a fraction of his wealth, his insurance against the unforeseen which he had conveyed to his wife to keep it safe for a rainy day. Had he, in spite of his enormous self-belief, some inkling of his inevitable downfall?

'There is also a substantial portfolio of stocks and shares. That's a bit outside my field I'm afraid. I generally put a rule-of-thumb value on those for probate – I mean it's all notional that kind of thing. I can't see the point of paying for a professional valuation which is going to come up with the same figure as I would. It wasn't queried, it never is provided you're not too greedy. Came as quite an eye-opener to me, I can tell you. You see the original will put no value on any of the trust holdings or the shares. Quite an eye-opener. Oh yes.'

Edward asked if he could see the list. He smiled to himself when he saw *The Rapid City and South Dakota Tramway Company* amongst a number of respectable and well-established names. Evidently Herbert Grace did believe in the future integrity of some of his own felonious ventures. From the notional value Garwood had placed on them it was easy to see that he had no knowledge of the part this faraway transportation company had played in the downfall of a monstrous crook.

'And what do you intend to do with the house and estate?' Garwood asked. 'I could arrange to have it put on the market. That's more my forte, although I imagine you do a fair amount of conveyancing yourself. Not that the property market is particularly strong, what with the uncertainties the war brings.'

'Where is it?' Edward asked. 'I assume it's in this vicinity.' There had to be some reason why Rose Grace had chosen Garwood to administer her will; proximity seemed the most plausible. However, he was surprised when Garwood said it was down beyond Hindhead on the borders of Surrey and Sussex. 'How did my aunt come to you to act for her?' he queried. 'I'd have thought she could find a firm locally.'

'I must admit I find that a little odd, too. There was no other connection I'm aware of. She just walked in here unannounced one day. She told me she had been visiting a friend who had recommended us.'

'So, what? She asked you to obtain a copy of her original will – from the bank? Who were the original solicitors?' Edward felt he should arm himself with whatever scraps of information might come in handy in view of the dubious provenance of his aunt's estate.

'No, she didn't. She had the original with her. Apparently it was kept at home. It's all above board. The change of executors was all properly witnessed as you can see.' Rather defensively Garwood pushed the will across the table so that Edward could see the signatures. The other executor was the partner, Potter. He started to make a note of the legal firm who had dealt with the first version of the will, but Garwood interrupted. 'No point really. I can tell you the firm has ceased to function, the main, or maybe he was the only partner, died. And he…'

'…was the principal executor, I suppose, was he?'

Garwood nodded.

'Who was the other one? No let me guess – her husband. Her husband who, she said, has since died.'

Again Garwood nodded. It was all very convenient, thought Edward. He was ready to believe that his devious uncle had deliberately searched out a solicitor who was already on his last legs to draw up that will, like executing the slaves who had built the secret passage and knew where the entrance to the king's tomb was. That would chime with the original document being unusually in his own keeping. If all had gone to plan Herbert Grace would have been the sole executor of what amounted to his own will. He was on the point of asking Garwood whether he had asked to see Grace's death certificate, but stopped himself: it was a stone he did not need to turn over. Instead he asked who had looked after her funeral arrangements.

'We did of course. That was her wish. She was buried at Brookwood. I did attend. Naturally, there being no other next-of-kin contactable.'

Edward suddenly recalled his astonishment at having been informed first by his uncle of the bequest to his mother. 'That's another thing,' he said, 'why didn't you write to my mother telling her of her sister's death? You should have made it your business to get her address when you drew this up.'

'But we did. Look here it is.' Garwood turned to a page at the back of the will. 'Anyway I wrote to her at this address. I assumed you must have seen it, otherwise how would you be here now?'

Now, thought Edward, he really doesn't know Grace is alive, if not entirely well, in Brixton. And what in the world had his mother done with Garwood's letter?

'So tell me,' he said, 'what's it like, this place near Hindhead?'

'Quite big. I've only been there once – to value the contents and so on. We are still paying the housekeeper but we let the parlour maid go. There's a head gardener still, but the two under-gardeners are both in the army. I know this because when your aunt came in about the will she told me how sorry she was not to be able to hold her garden parties now that the war had taken her staff.'

'And since her husband had died?' Edward wanted to add 'in prison' but it seemed an unnecessary complication now.

'And that too, presumably.' Garwood still gave no inkling that he knew anything of Grace's history. He opened his desk drawer and took out a tin box. 'Here you had better have these keys. I'm not sure what they fit – the housekeeper Mrs...ah...Mrs Aitken I think it is...she has the main set of course.'

## 6

JAMES Bellingham called round to the office a few days after Edward's visit to Surbiton. As he walked in Edward guiltily assumed he had somehow found out about his dubious inheritance and had come to add his own admonishment to Edward's chastisement of himself; he had done little else since returning home with the documents detailing the size of the fortune he had come into, to say nothing of several banker's drafts made out in his favour for what seemed an enormous amount of cash.

Clearing his throat nervously, he waited for the ethical homily he felt sure he was about to receive. So he was completely flummoxed when Bellingham said, 'It's not the Red Cross anymore. It's a thing called the Graves Registration Unit – or it may be a "Directorate" by now. The Red Cross have handed over the job over to the army.'

Edward hastily readjusted his thinking, thankfully clearing his mind of the debilitating thoughts of Herbert Grace's money, but admitting in their place another sinking feeling. 'Well bang goes my scheme for getting into uniform by the back door. If the army is running things, I mean.'

'Well hold on. They are and they aren't. According to my chum...'

'At the Lodge?'

'As it happens, at the golf club. Another social forum you have chosen to avoid despite the business it can bring in. But more to the point, he's quite a senior civil servant – in the Treasury. They have fingers in all sorts of official pies. He says the army is insisting on running it but that they are having to take on all kinds of staff, civilians as well as retired officers, invalided out and so on.'

'Did your Treasury friend say who I should talk to?'

'Not exactly but he gave me their address. Part of the War Office in St James's Square.'

Edward looked doubtful. 'It always comes back to the army, doesn't it? They'll want to know why I'm not called up and then my being medically unfit will have to come out. I'll be back to square one.'

'What about this consultant you're seeing at St Mary's. Could he help?'

Edward thought about it. It might be worth a try. He hadn't coughed since his last appointment there and it had been the consultant's suggestion to try and get in by the back door. He decided to write as soon as Bellingham had gone, asking for another appointment, but without spelling out why, other than he urgently needed to talk about things they had previously discussed.

Rather to his surprise this letter was answered almost by return of post. He was offered an appointment the following week, 'as it is clearly a matter of some urgency.' When Edward thought about this it dawned on him that the consultant must have assumed he had had a relapse. When he replied to confirm, he was still careful to say nothing concerning his real reasons in case they should lead to the consultation being postponed or withdrawn altogether.

Another 'matter of urgency' demanding his attention that morning was an interview his bank manager was requesting 'at his earliest convenience' to discuss his mounting overdraft. Although such summonses were not unfamiliar to Edward, he had been spared them while he had had to pay his mother's medical bills. Even so they never failed to fill him with dread. Curiously this one was no exception: his newly acquired fortune was still sitting like a stone in the pit of his stomach and, far from seeing it in the circumstances as an enormous piece of good luck, he was trying to persuade himself he needed to be rid of it. It was only the prospect of having to deal with the awful provenance of the money and estate when it became public, as he convinced himself it would as soon as he tried to disembarrass himself of it, which had prevented him putting the banker's drafts on the fire. The lawyer in him argued that the existence of such a large amount of wealth, made up as it was of property, investments and cash, could not simply be made to disappear up the chimney with no questions being asked. Shedding the responsibilities of ownership, however they may have been foisted on him, would entail careful disentanglement. Moreover there were others to be considered. People on the estate – *his* estate for goodness' sake. Surely he owed them some consideration even though he didn't even employ a live-in maid and barely communicated with his daily?

Also there was Louise Bolden to be considered. Despite allowing herself to be cast as 'the other woman' complicit in betraying Rose Grace, Edward could not get it out of his head that Louise had been chained by Herbert Grace to a rock of misfortune, like some Andromeda waiting hopelessly for a hero, but resigned to an inevitable monster of the deep, one that had already devoured her son. He knew he needed her to be the surrogate for all those deserving but anonymous widows and orphans; she was the one victim of his uncle's crimes Edward could really touch.

It did not help Edward's dread of Mr Mitchell, the bank manager, that he was immensely tall, so tall that he stooped, pulled over by his own gravity perhaps, making him mildly asthmatic, and giving his voice a soft, menacing rasp. Nor did it help that Mr Mitchell almost regarded him as a professional equal, making him temper his normal magisterial superiority with phoney sorrow for the financial difficulties of a fellow burgess. He made

Edward smart at the disappointment he was causing the bank rather than blink in the face of its wrath.

Mr Mitchell's handshake was perfunctory, and he did not offer Edward a glass of sherry. He would, he said, get straight to the point as he was sure they were both busy men. Edward sat quietly, interjecting an occasional 'tut-tut' and 'I had no idea', as the shameful neglect of his finances was laid bare. The bank manager came to his peroration, wondering 'when Mr Dereham intends to clear the outstanding balance, which is considerably above the overdraft limit he and the bank agreed during his mother's difficult final months?' deliberately voicing his conversation with Edward in the third person as if he were simply there as a member of the jury at the trial of his own irresponsible behaviour. Mr Mitchell waited, resting his elbows on the desk, fingertips delicately touching in front of him in an attitude of still-life silently reinforcing his question.

Edward did indeed feel justly chastened. He had allowed matters to run on much too long without thought, and not to have sought this meeting of his own volition with Mr Mitchell was nothing if not discourteous. A professional practitioner himself, he knew only too well the irritation caused by slow payers who regarded settling their debts as a defeat.

Genuinely apologetic he said, 'I think I should be able to clear most of it.'

'When, may I ask? What is the bank to understand by "most of it"?'

'Well, all of it, I suppose – now.'

Mr Mitchell began to thaw slightly. 'How precisely? Do you have cheques to pay in? You should have said, you know. It would have saved us some of this unpleasantness. Can I assume that your clients are at last settling their accounts? If that is indeed the case, it is good news. But is there more to come, I ask? Will we simply be staunching the flow temporarily? I fear I cannot continue indulging you with an overdraft of this size without any prospect of it coming to an end, as I have already made clear.

We may have to think carefully about mortgaging the house, now that it has passed to you, although with the war dragging on, values are not what they were.'

For a moment Edward thought the bank manager was referring to Rose Grace's house, which, of course, he knew nothing of. But the moment was enough to jog him out of his old world into his new one. Not in an especially triumphant tone he said, 'I do have these to pay in,' as he delved into his brief case and produced the manila envelope containing his banker's drafts.

Mr Mitchell took the small sheaf of papers from him and having taken in the nature of the first banker's draft on the top, laid the pile down, carefully perusing each document before turning it face down and gently smoothing it to create a second pile alongside. When he had digested them he sat back in his chair, wheezing. Then pulling a small inhaler from his pocket he inserted it into the corner of his mouth and pumped the rubber bulb vigorously half a dozen times. His wheezing became shallower, but he did not attempt to speak. He took a silver propelling pencil from the inside pocket of his jacket and began to turn the drafts back over again, this time noting their various sums on his pad. When he had finished he drew a line and totalled them up. Bent over he looked fixedly at the result for a while. Then he picked up the drafts again one by one: it almost looked as though he wanted to hold them up to the light. The only sounds breaking the silence of the office were the ponderous ticking of the pendulum case clock over the fireplace behind him and his rhythmic wheezing.

After a while he sat back in his chair again. 'I have to ask you – are these genuine, Mr Dereham?'

'I'm afraid they are.'

'Yes, well that's as may be, of course. But it is most unusual for a country branch like this to see a dozen or more drafts drawn on as many different banks. I mean to say, there are some merchant banking houses here which frankly I have only ever read about in the financial pages. Never dealt with any of their instruments and I wouldn't know a forged one to be honest. But surely this is clients' money you are holding on their behalf, Mr Dereham? Good business, I grant you. Very good business. Let me see, now – on deposit this would make, how much? I'd need to work it out, but even short-term, worth a handsome commission for bringing us the business. How long would you be leaving it invested with us? Weeks? Months?'

'It isn't clients' money. It's mine, I'm afraid.'

'All yours? Where did you get it from? It's a huge sum – look!' Almost accusingly Mr Mitchell pushed his pad across the desk. Edward began to get irate. It was as if he'd unjustly been asked to turn his pockets out by the head of house at school. He began to regret having brought the drafts to his own branch of the bank. He should be able to rely on Mr Mitchell's total professional discretion, he knew, but he had a sinking feeling he could be about to become the talk of the golf club, especially when Mr Mitchell said, 'Do you realise these deposits will make you far and away my largest customer?'

'I don't think you need to know where the money has come from. All the drafts will be honoured in four days I believe and I will give you further instructions on what is to be done with it. In the meantime, would you be good enough to put it in my personal deposit account? Be sure not the business account.' Edward spoke curtly. All at once it was if the money had asked him to defend it. He tried to reinstate the sense of oppression it had laid on him at first, its infective corruption, but could not: Mr Mitchell had succeeded in dispersing Edward's guilt simply by unconsciously implying it might exist.

The bank manager looked taken aback at the change of tone which had been introduced. He tried a more emollient approach. 'Look here, Dereham, my dear chap, I'll need to tell head office something about this amount of money. I mean to say. To be perfectly frank they'll want to know if it was honestly come by. Y'know, a sum of this kind at the Sunbury branch. I mean to say.

It's more than all my market gardeners put together, and they're my biggest customers. Normally expect to see a fortune like this being deposited in Lombard Street: followed by a decent lunch, I shouldn't be surprised. Ha-ha.' But his attempted laugh only set him wheezing again and once more he had to reach for his inhaler.

'You can tell head office it was an unexpected legacy, if you like,' said Edward. 'That's the truth of it, anyway.'

'Not your poor mother surely? No we've dealt with all that, haven't we?'

Edward and the money had confided enough, however, and he was not prepared to be any more forthcoming. He certainly did not wish to give Mr Mitchell enough information to have him hunting through the lists of published wills column in the *Times*. It was a sobering thought: Rose Grace's estate was large enough to have appeared there. The question was, would anyone have made the connection with Herbert if they had seen it? He had been intending to hand over the deeds to her house for safe-keeping at the bank, but now thought better of it. As a solicitor he was perfectly capable of looking after them himself in his safe at the office and the less the bank knew of his inheritances the better. Kicking himself for not having done it straight away, he resolved to open a private account with a different bank in the city, preferably one with safe deposit box facilities. His reluctant acceptance of his aunt's legacy seemed to be complete: its sickness seemed to have created a dependency in him.

The following week he attended his appointment at St Mary's. Unusually the consultant kept him waiting. When Edward was eventually called through, Dr Carradine was very apologetic. He had been totally taken up with problems at the Boulogne military hospitals.

'There are quite a few St Mary's people there,' he explained. 'It's almost an outpost of ours. That's why they bring me their problems if the army authorities can't help. They're desperately short of x-ray machines and related lab equipment – film processing and so on. Would you remove your waistcoat and shirt please?'

As Carradine began his examination, Edward said he was sorry to hear about Boulogne. He had assumed from the conversation they had had at the earlier appointment that the hospitals were well-provided with the latest equipment.

'They were…breathe in and out through your mouth, please…The problem is the hospitals are simply burgeoning. The whole of the channel coast from Etaples and Le Touquet along to Wimereux on the other side of Boulogne is mile after mile of hospitals. Some are just tents and wooden huts now all the suitable buildings and big houses have been commandeered. And breathe out. And now the Huns have started bombing them from the air. We've lost three x-ray machines that way. Turn round and face me please. Keep breathing in and out, if you would be so kind, while I listen. Better safe than sorry. The trouble is the machines take time to build and they aren't a priority. Can you believe it? Turn around again, please. And cough. Again.'

Edward did as he was told. 'So what is to be done?' he asked.

Carradine said that the best solution was there on the doorstep. 'The machines are French after all. Marie Curie has been working wonders. But the French need them just as much as we do. Cough and spit in the dish please. I have the contacts in Paris. I could pull strings, but at the end of the day I don't have the funds. I'm afraid the Medical Corps will have to talk to their French counterparts. It'll take ages, I expect. And every day we need to look at shrapnel wounds. Any blood since we last met? You can put your shirt back on.'

Edward said no, there had been no blood. As he was adjusting his tie he said, 'I've been giving a good deal of thought to what you said about getting a job in France that mightn't involve the military.'

'And?'

'I was wondering about the Red Cross.'

'Really? Doing what?'

'Well, there's something called the Graves Registration Directorate. It's been run by the Red Cross but I think the army might have taken it over now.'

Carradine frowned. 'I've heard about it. There's been correspondence in the *Times* off and on. But I don't see how that would help your perverse cause if the army is running it. You'll still need to pass the medical and I need another few months clear of blood before I would consider…'

Edward interrupted him. 'The thing is, I understand that this Graves Registration organisation is a bit of a mix of army personnel and civilians. I could get in as a civilian, couldn't I – without a medical? What do you think?'

Carradine looked at him thoughtfully. 'You're determined to get yourself killed and get me struck off.'

'But you did say…'

'Let me have a good look at what you've given me on this dish. You can wait outside, if you wouldn't mind. I can't have your imploring eyes boring into me while I try and concentrate. You're as bad as my dog.'

Edward went and sat in the corridor. There were several others doing the same, including some young men in uniform with hospital invalid insignia. One of them, a second lieutenant in the Grenadier Guards according to his badges, suddenly started retching into a handkerchief. Edward half rose to his feet looking for somebody to call but the young man motioned with his free hand for him to sit back down.

When he could speak he grimaced apologetically. 'Sorry about that – it's not catching. Gassed. Not too bad thankfully. You?'

'I've had some chest problems,' said Edward awkwardly. 'But I'm hoping the doctor is about to give me a clean bill of health.' He wanted to say his condition was not catching either, but as he struggled to find the right words he was saved by Dr Carradine calling him back in.

'I'm prepared to give you a "to whom it may concern" letter in general terms. It won't get you into the army – mainly because it won't be on the right form for them. In any event I'd have to refer your case back from whence it came. Everything has to be on the right file, you see. Neat and tidy, according to the book. I don't have to do that yet because you're still covered by the six month deferral I signed. I shall say that in my opinion you have some historic lesion which is prone to rupture through coughing. But I'm not going to go so far as to say that you are fit for any kind of duties. That's down to you. If you can persuade the Red Cross or this Directorate to take you on that's your affair. But mark you, Dereham, if you start spitting blood at all regularly, I'm trusting you to get yourself out of whatever you are engaged in and back here sharpish.'

Edward thanked him profusely. At last he felt he was getting somewhere. As he was putting his coat on he had a sudden blinding inspiration. It penetrated and illuminated him in a way nothing had ever done before. It was as if he had come through the crisis the fever brought on by his wealth had caused. Suddenly he was no longer dependent on it: he was over that. He was in control. He reached for his cheque book.

'You said you didn't have the money for the x-ray machines in France. How much would you need?'

Giving money away, especially a large sum running into several hundred pounds, was no easy matter. Once Edward had managed to overcome Carradine's disbelief and scepticism at his offer, the problem of whom a cheque should be made out to and how the money was then to be directed and properly accounted for assumed an apparently hideous proportion. It seemed almost to dwarf the matter he sought to resolve, replacing vital x-ray machines.

Carradine did not therefore immediately erupt with gratitude – not that Edward was looking for any; the fact that he had found a way of redeeming the sin of Herbert Grace's fortune was more than sufficient. Not until a month had passed and the harassed consultant had established that directing Dereham's anonymous (Edward insisted on that) donation was not going to turn out to be simply adding another insoluble problem to the one he already had of finding non-existent machines, was he able to write thanking Edward with anything like profusion.

During that month Edward wrote on his own business letter paper to the head of the Graves Registration Directorate, the splendidly named Brigadier Fabian Ware. In fact it was a name vaguely familiar to Edward from his recent searches in the Times and Morning Post. His first instinct was to steer clear of approaching someone with military rank, fearing that he would simply be swept back under the army's administrative carpet. But Bellingham had been alive to this difficulty too.

'My man at the Treasury...'

'You mean your man at the golf club, surely.'

'Just listen. This isn't for my benefit you know. My man at the Treasury knows Ware personally, from meetings and so forth. He says he is happy for you to pray his name in aid if you decide to write. Anyhow, this man Ware isn't a soldier, it's an honorary rank of some kind. Apparently he really knows how to get things done. Used to be editor of one of the dailies I gather. Bloody nuisance was how my golfing chum put it. That'd suit you, too, wouldn't it? Honorary military rank? So no harm in trying, eh?'

The address was Winchester House, St James's Square in London, sounded pretty grand to Edward so although he felt deflated as the days passed without an acknowledgement, he wasn't entirely surprised.

Edward also set his mind to venturing once again into the stony heart of Brixton Prison. He wasn't sure whether it was the edifice itself that filled him with foreboding or the prospect of facing his manipulating client across the bare wooden table.

'You've taken your time,' Grace growled, as soon as they had dispensed with the warder's presence (Edward was glad it was not the man who had paid him the unwelcome visit). 'Typical solicitor, I suppose, although I had hoped you would be better at keeping your promises than most I've dealt with. What's the matter? Haven't you been paid enough?'

Edward failed immediately to see what his uncle was driving at and made the mistake of saying that he had not put in a bill as there was no mechanism for doing so, given the circumstances of prison.

'So a significant part of my worldly goods and estate count for nothing do they?'

Edward was cut to the quick. He had managed to make himself subservient to Grace by a too clever repost. Added to which his client was in the right anyway: he had taken much more time than he had promised and had made no effort to contact him other than a curt anonymous note via the threatening warder. In any case he had no way of knowing that had been delivered. All told he had behaved in a way he deplored in many of his professional brethren.

He took the only sensible way out by trying to change the subject. 'You will be encouraged to learn that I have visited Louise in Hove…'

'So it's *Louise* is it? You evidently don't always waste your clients' time then. You needn't think you can rest your boots on that fender. Caroline Crescent is still safely under my lock and key.'

Edward assumed this was simply a vulgar innuendo, so he did not ask Grace to explain, although he made a mental note to check on the leasehold arrangements for Louise's house and if it was rented. It was extremely remiss of him not to have done so when going through the accounts with her. So once again the felon had managed to wrong-foot him over his lack of professionalism. Edward suspected his grumpy aggressiveness indicated that Grace was beginning to see him too as just some piddling solicitor, especially when he demanded to know what was happening about the power of attorney.

'It shouldn't be necessary,' Edward said loftily. 'I have made financial provision for Mrs Bolden out of the proceeds of the money from your wife's legacy to my mother.'

Herbert Grace's face grew dark. 'Don't dress it up Dereham. You're setting her up with your money, aren't you? You suppose that because I'm in here you can ride rough-shod over my legal instructions and feather your own nest into the bargain.'

Edward was angry and appalled. Angry because once again his professional behaviour was being properly called into question, and appalled because he could not dismiss out of hand Grace's interpretation of his intentions towards Louise Bolden. His angry outburst had scored a direct hit, catching him unawares. Edward did not want him to be right, but perhaps he was.

Then suddenly his uncle relented, seeming to accept he might have gone too far. 'That was uncalled for, Dereham. Uncalled for, I realise. It's generous of you, what you are doing. And I suppose, a safer course of action for her while I am in this damned hole. Leave no accounting trail you don't want to have followed is a useful maxim in life, eh?'

Edward made no comment but he couldn't disagree, when it came to distancing his own name from his uncle's millions. But the tension between them had eased and he moved on.

'Her son is missing in France. I was there when the telegram came.'

'Cornelius? I didn't even know he was in France. Surely he cannot be old enough?'

Edward told him what he knew. 'It seems they took him early. Didn't question his age. He was already a second lieutenant.'

'Was? So you assume he's dead then?'

'Was, that is, when he went missing. He might still turn up – prisoner of war, or in hospital somewhere. There's dozens of them you know, all along the French coast from Boulogne. They can't keep track of everyone.'

'Why aren't you out there? Are you too old?'

Edward looked at him in silence for a moment and an urge to confide in this convicted felon came over him, as if his own questions and uncertainties could be shared out in here and remain locked up with him when Edward departed. He told him everything, his recurring ill-health, his refusal to accept the doctors' diagnosis. His burning need to belong to what was happening in France.

When he had come to a stop, Grace said, 'It sounds to me that you don't so much want to fight for King and country as to get away from something here. There's plenty in this place have taken that option, and I can understand why they would. But with you it must be something in your head. It cannot be to escape your debts, now can it?' and he started to chuckle until his laughter turned to a racking cough. It was the first time his magisterial mask had slipped in front of Edward, but he did not join in or offer his own explanations. This was the second person to question what really lay behind his need to join up: Carradine had supposed it was a death wish.

'And my daughter, Gracie? Are you looking out for her with my money too?'

Edward said that her school fees were all taken care of now, but that he hadn't met her yet.

'She must be growing up fast. Best she doesn't know about me. Louise and I always let her think Bolden was her father too, you know. I was just an honorary uncle when she was there. A bit like you, really, I suppose. Does she wonder what has become of me, d'you think?'

For the first time Edward saw a hint of something more human in the man, a contrast to the autocratic fantasist persuading himself of his right to order other people's lives and their money. But he did not respond to the question. He didn't wish to prompt any sudden instructions about Grace, the daughter, he might not be able to fulfil. All the same, he made up his mind to draw up a power of attorney. He would send his uncle a form to sign.

# 7

As he made his way laboriously up the driveway in the fearful old fiacre and its equally decrepit driver he had hired from the station, Edward found himself wishing for the first time in his life that he could have been arriving somewhere in a motor car of his own. The horse in the shafts wheezed to a halt without bidding some yards from the front entrance and deposited a quantity of dung in the canvas container slung behind it.

'D'you want me to wait?' the cabman demanded.

Edward gave it some thought. 'How much to wait?'

The cabman sniffed disparagingly and said, 'It would be cheaper than coming back if he wasn't going to be long.' He had noted the absence of any luggage. Edward had an innate mistrust of cab drivers whether of motor taxis or of horses, largely borne out by being professionally involved in their licensing disputes in front of the magistrates. Now he tried to convince himself that he had enough money, probably actually there in his wallet, to buy the entire contraption, horse and all. But despite his spontaneous donation of hundreds of pounds towards six of Marie Curie's new mobile field x-ray machines, he still could not banish an instinctive penny-pinching attitude to cab fares, and probably numerous other items of lowly expenditure he could list if he put his mind to it. As he wrestled with this conundrum in front of the house, Hillcote Grange, which was, by all accounts his, and began to take in its gardens and the orchard, the pasture beyond that, he wondered if Herbert Grace had accumulated his fortune by being careful with the small things and lavish with the large.

Reluctantly therefore, he told the cabman to hang on, rang the bell and waited.

He had not pre-announced his intention to visit, partly not wanting to be pigeonholed as the new owner until he had ascertained the lie of the land, and partly to make it in the nature of a surprise inspection so that he could judge how reliable and trustworthy this housekeeper would turn out to be. Since he had no intention of taking up residence himself – a prospect that depressed him just thinking about it – a dependable chatelaine would be essential. The idea of selling the house and estate did not fill him with any enthusiasm. That way there was every chance that the circumstances of his coming into Herbert Grace's fraudulent wealth would become public and the scandal would devolve to him. Edward had also convinced himself that he would continue with his modest solicitor's practice in Lower Sunbury, until such time as, by hook or by crook, he would leave for France.

After a short interval the door was opened by a woman probably in her fifties. She was rather well dressed, Edward noticed, and severe-looking, although this may have been owing to this unexpected summons.

'Mrs Aitken?'

'I am. Yes.'

'Good afternoon. I'm Edward Dereham, the new owner.'

Mrs Aitken's severe look deepened. 'She left it to her sister. She told me she was going to. Have you bought it from her then?'

Edward made a mental note to have no further dealings with Garwood and Potter. They had clearly made no attempt to keep Mrs Aitken in the picture. All they seemed to have done was arrange Rose's funeral and sack a maid. He glanced towards the cab driver who was making no effort to move his horse and vehicle out of earshot. 'May I come in? I don't wish to conduct my business on the doorstep.'

Rather grudgingly Mrs Aitken stood aside to let him into the large square entrance hall. He took it in curiously. It was open to the full height of the front of the house with a vaulted timber roof and marble-paved floor. At the far end there was a heavy, dark wooden double staircase ascending to galleries running back along the length of the hall on either side. Several doors gave off these galleries to the left and right. From the outside it had not been easy to determine the age of the house. It was a mish-mash of alteration, stretching over one or probably two centuries. The marbled hall didn't chime particularly with the timbered ceiling which suggested that originally the house might have been thatched. Edward's first impression was that it had once been more modest and changing owners had attempted to add fashionable grandeur as time passed. He did not warm to it.

When he began to explain to the housekeeper how he had come to be the unsuspecting inheritor of Rose Grace's estate, Mrs Aitken started to unbend. The fact that it had come completely out of the blue to Dereham on Rose's side of the family was somewhat of a relief to her, although she put in hastily how sorry she was that he had had to lose his mother in the process.

As she led him around his new ancestral property she unwound even more. It was evident she needed to get something of her chest. 'That solicitor – he never set foot here but once, when the undertakers came for her – Mrs Grace. She wasn't laid to rest for another fortnight. I had no instructions or whether I should go to the funeral. I didn't even know if I had to prepare a funeral meal, if there would be mourners.'

No effort had been made to clear the house of its contents. Mrs Aitken said she had had no further instructions from Garwood and Potter other than to continue to manage the house and let the maid go. 'She's getting more money, anyway, working at Dennis's in Guildford, now they're making munitions for the war as well as fire engines.' The head gardener, she added, was doing his best on his own, but was fighting a losing battle. There had been no-one to pick the apples last year; he had got the local school children in to gather some and had given the farmer next door the run of the orchard with his pigs for the fallen fruit, 'but they were making a terrible mess of the ground, so Mr Kirby said he wouldn't do that again in a hurry.'

Edward guessed he ought to seek out the gardener, while he was there, but his heart was not really in it. He could just imagine how a tour of the grounds would go, undoubtedly in ill-fitting borrowed gum boots, Mr Kirby grumbling about the lack of staff, his own increasing inability to cope what with his lumbago, whilst harking back to the prizes he used to take at the county show and those idyllic garden parties Mrs Grace used to have before the war.

More to the point, it was only a matter of time before one or other of the retainers raised the question of Mr Herbert Grace. It was inconceivable they did not know of his downfall and imprisonment. Mrs Aitken asked him if he would like to see the bedrooms and the upper part of the house. When she showed him into Mrs Grace's room she became rather defensive when Edward asked where a door on the far side led to. It was the clothes closet. 'I've taken a few things. Mrs Grace always gave me some of her dresses when she had no further use for them. We were much of a size. I hope that's all right, Mr Dereham?'

He nodded. After all, there was no-one else to lay any claim to his aunt's clothes. A thought occurred to him. 'What about jewellery? I assume she had some.' He had not brought the probate details with him, but was now beginning to suspect the executor had not made a particularly thorough inventory. Garwood had spoken about his 'rule of thumb', but an estate like this must have been entirely beyond his experience. The codicil to Rose Grace's will would have given very little indication of the sheer size of the business he was being asked to take on when she had turned up at his office out of the blue.

Mrs Aitken said the jewellery was 'in there,' pointing to a small safe in one of the wardrobes in the closet.

'Do you have a key?'

The housekeeper said that the solicitor had taken it with him.

'Did he – Mr Garwood – did he look in there then?'

Mrs Aitken said he had. 'He said it looked like mostly costume jewellery. I told him I didn't think it was, knowing Mrs Grace. But I suppose he knew best, being a solicitor and used to this sort of thing. It hardly ever came out of the safe anyway so it was difficult to tell. To be honest, Mr Dereham, it's not my place, but I didn't think much to the solicitor. He didn't want to spend long here because he had a train to catch. I didn't think he was altogether sober.'

Edward searched through the keys Garwood had given him and found one that fitted. He lifted out the several jewellery cases inside and opened them one-by-one. As he examined the necklaces, brooches, rings and the precious-looking contents he was none the wiser himself. Garwood had dismissed them as paste and presumably put a probate valuation on them as such. He made no comment to Mrs Aitken other than to say that 'the solicitor was probably right.' A weariness was coming over him. Whilst he had begun to find a way of coming to terms with Herbert Grace's money, the sudden permanent reality of this house and grounds felt as if he had shed one millstone from round his neck only to hang another one there – even bigger. Perhaps he should think about selling it after all. At that precise moment he would have cheerfully given it away to the cabman at the door if he could have been certain his anonymity would be preserved.

'Will you stay here Mrs Aitken?' he asked as they went back downstairs.

'That depends. Are you going to live here, then?'

'Probably not, no.'

'You'll sell? Or rent it out?'

Letting it was a possibility he had not thought about until then. 'I don't know. Maybe.'

'Well I suppose you'll have to decide. I'll stay until you do at any rate, if that's what you want, but it's a big place to have all to myself, even though I've my own two rooms. I used to wonder why Mr Grace kept such a big place what with having no family. They used to entertain, it's true, although most of the time he wasn't here. I wouldn't be surprised if he hadn't had…' She broke off, clearly sensing she was going too far.

This was the first reference she had made to Henry Grace. Even though he had been steering well clear of the subject Edward wondered why. 'So weren't you surprised the place was left to my mother? It would have seemed logical that it would all come back to Mr Grace.'

'Well how could it, when he died in prison?'

According to Lloyd Garwood, Rose had put about this myth of her husband's death. He had made no mention of his being in prison though, unlike Mrs Aitken. For a moment Edward fantasised that in some other world, perhaps it was true that Herbert Grace had indeed died in prison; and that it was an unquiet ghost had summoned Dereham to Brixton to settle his affairs. The low opinion he had already formed of Garwood made him almost suspect that he had happily accepted the fiction, in case of legal repercussions, questions of forfeiture of Grace's ill-gotten gains, and a great deal of tiresome toil with little in it for him. He, himself, chose nonetheless not to listen to a small voice telling him to examine his own conscience, unwilling to bracket himself with the tipsy brother-solicitor.

'Did Mrs Grace tell you he had died in prison? I suppose she did. It wasn't reported in the newspapers as far as I can recall.' He wanted to ask her what she had thought of Grace going to prison, how much she knew of the crimes he had committed, wanted to say she had been misled by her late mistress, that he was still very much alive. But that small voice inside urged him against unravelling this story which Rose Grace, in her angry loneliness, had chosen to tell herself. No fraud had been committed by it; no-one had been disinherited by it, no chapel widows or their children had been impoverished by it. Only Henry Grace had had to suffer that sudden shock of betrayal he had cynically visited on others. That same small voice also told Edward he didn't need to hear Mrs Aitken's inferences on his inheriting all this for which Grace had gone down.

Mrs Aitken agreed she hadn't seen anything in her newspaper about Grace's death in prison, but she didn't appear to find that remarkable. 'And I won't be sorry to be moving on if I have to. The place gives me the creeps – knowing where the money came from – just like it did Mrs Grace when they found him guilty. Poor soul, it was nothing to do with her, was it?' This was said with a tone of finality and Edward was thankful to let it rest there.

The housekeeper had led the way to the back of the house where her own parlour was. She offered Edward a cup of tea, apologising again for the fact that the Holland covers were still on in Mrs Grace's day room. A stocky figure was in the act of letting himself in by the back door to the garden.

'Boots, Mr Kirby,' Mrs Aitken called out sharply. 'We have company, the new owner Mr Dereham. Poor Mrs Grace's nephew,' she added.

'I guessed when I saw that there carriage out front. I was going to ask the driver to bring it round the back so I could have the manure, but the cheeky beggar wanted a shilling. Afternoon Sir. Will you be wishing to look over the gardens, then?'

Edward said he would find him after he had had a cup of tea, and was given directions to his hut. 'I mustn't be long though, I've already kept the cabman here over an hour.'

Mr Kirby's domain bore only the vestiges of its undoubted former glory, but despite his sorrow and frustration at the decline of the gardens since the war, he did a very good job of bringing them back to life in Edward's imagination. The rose garden must have been magnificent when there had been enough men to prune them back. The bushes were in flower now, true enough in chequered beds of red, white, gold and pink, but the signs of two or three years' of neglect were apparent even to Dereham's untutored eye.

'Shame,' he said. 'Will you get it back the way it was, d'you think?'

'Depends if we get any boys back when it's all done. Our two were lost at Wipers a month back. Same day. That's what comes of putting them all in the same battalions. Whole villages go sometimes, I've heard. My roses – begging your pardon, Sir, - *your* roses, I should say, are the least of it.'

It came as a revelation to Edward that he had proprietorial rights over the flowers and fruit in the gardens when he would have had difficulty making just one bloom by his own efforts. Even his mother's geraniums had looked after themselves, although he had remembered to bring them into the front porch for the winter when she had asked him. Still, the nurture of the roses, and the care and replenishing of the herbaceous border along the length of what Mr Kirby said was a seventeenth century garden wall, and the peaches that had been espaliered on it, were every bit as much his responsibility as the jewellery in Mrs Grace's cases, every bit as much his to maintain or dispose of.

Mr Kirby inadvertently confirmed this discovery of his. 'Mrs Grace used to win prizes at the county show with her roses. She took gold year after year.'

'But they were yours really – not hers.'

The gardener gave him an old-fashioned look. 'I was just the gardener, wasn't I? You might as well say that the corn in the field is all the work of the ploughboy, or the harvesters. But it's the owner what makes it happen, the owner what takes the risk, who says let it be so. Look what's happened here now I've been left to my own devices. All gone to rack and ruin.'

Edward wanted to say that it was unfair for Mrs Grace to have taken the prizes which surely belonged to the skill and knowledge of Mr Kirby, whatever his station. But he could see that his experience, based on a few pots in the front porch, a small, round bed of marigolds that reseeded themselves every year with no intervention by anyone other than the Almighty, and an unkempt lawn running down to the river Thames, was nothing on which to base his new-found relationship with these gardens at Hillcote Grange. No, here a man could create and achieve, learn and direct, without the necessity of bending his own back or getting the soil under his own nails. These grounds called for a team, for more than one head, and as Mr Kirby said, without them it all goes to rack and ruin.

'Mrs Grace – my aunt – used to host spectacular garden parties, I believe?'

'Oh yes indeed, Sir. That's when the greenhouses really came into their own.'

'Floral decoration?'

'They was mainly cut from the garden, the arrangements. They were a sight too. Mrs Grace had a way, and showed the girls how. No, we used to get the cucumbers and tomatoes ready. And we had our own lemons for lemonade. And she showed cook – my wife that is – how to make the lavender cake everyone was so partial to. We have a vine too – let me show you the vine.'

Mr Kirby almost led Edward by the hand to the square, brick-paved yard where the greenhouses were built backing onto the east, west and south-facing walls, each one joined to the next, but separated by insulating doors. Heating pipes ran through them all, but connected in such a way, Mr Kirby explained, that the temperatures in each green house could be controlled individually. The greenhouses felt distinctly warm in the late June sunshine, even without the heating pipes, now disused and cold. The wooden staging was mostly empty, although Mr Kirby had some annuals in pots ready to be planted out and quite a few were already past their best. Mr Kirby tutted to himself and pinched out here and there as they made their way through to the vine.

'I try to organise myself, but it breaks my heart to cut down on everything. So I end up doing too much not very well. Here's the vine.'

Edward thought it looked in pretty good shape, not that he was any judge although he was familiar with the vine at Hampton Court. He said as much to the gardener.

'No – well. It all needs pruning back. Much too many bunches coming and they'll weaken one another. Needs what we call a green harvest about this time. I'll try and have a go. Need to lose about a third I'd say, maybe more. They're eating grapes see. Not as if we were making home-made wine, although Mrs Grace had a go one year. Turned out a bit musty as I remember.'

Edward could see the dozens of bunches of tiny green grapes, no bigger than mustard seeds some of them. To his untutored eye it looked like the promise of a fine harvest. For a moment he actually found himself contemplating telling Mrs Aitken he was staying on – so that he could roll up his sleeves and set about helping with Mr Kirby's green harvest. The thought reminded him of the cabman and his fiacre still waiting out at the front of the house. 'I must be going,' he said, shaking the gardener's rough hand. 'Thank you for showing me all this. Try not to despair. I'll see what can be done.'

Mr Kirby didn't look convinced by this. He pulled a wry face. 'Perhaps you'll be holding a garden party before long then, will you?' he chuckled gruffly, 'To remember Mrs Grace – but perhaps not that villain of a husband of hers, beggin' your pardon.

Thus was the nebulous spell broken; the magic that the garden's past had begun to weave was rudely undone.

## 8

THE cabman had demanded half a sovereign for his waiting time. Edward thought this outrageous and said five shillings would do, but the man was not to be bargained with seeing as his fare was not a local and as good as marooned at the Grange if he chose to abandon him. Besides, he argued, Edward had luggage now, where before he had none. This was because Edward had decided to take the jewellery cases with him after all. Mrs Aitken had looked out a valise for them that must have belonged to his uncle because it had the initials H.D.G. stamped on it. Edward wondered what the middle initial might stand for, his uncle having only ever signed himself 'Herbert'. And as he speculated about it he too found himself thinking of Grace in the past as if the fiction of the dead man had become reality. Rather than admit total defeat at the hands of the cabman he demanded that he should first drive his vehicle round the back of the house and deposit the horse manure wherever the gardener wanted it, 'and no shilling for it either.' While the cabman was grudgingly doing this, Edward took his leave of Mrs Aitken at the door, saying he would be in touch about the arrangements soon. He felt only too conscious of sounding much as Lloyd Garwood must have done on his one and only visit, but a plan was already forming in his mind for Hillcote Grange.

    The following day over breakfast he found himself having a conversation in his head with Louise Bolden and felt a sudden surge of adrenalin in his stomach which he put down to pangs of guilty conscience as he had not been in touch with her since

March and it was now nearly the end of June. He thought about sending her a telegram to arrange to visit but thought better of it in view of what had happened previously with a telegram. So he wrote her a brief letter, asking her to call him if she had access to a telephone. He could not remember having seen one at Caroline Crescent, but there again, his mind had been elsewhere. Anyway, he thought, a short delay would give more time for the ideas which were beginning to form to gain some proper structure.

The regular quarterly payments made for her maintenance had been briefly frozen after Rose's demise, as he had feared they might. But not for any censorious reason; only because they were innocuously described in one of the general purpose accounts as 'Bolden Miscellaneous Subscription Account'. As they were paid out quarterly only two had been missed while probate was being obtained and as both accounts were at the same bank, Louise Bolden had seemingly been allowed to continue to draw money in the expectation that it would shortly be granted. In any case, as Edward assumed, she was not a profligate spender and judging by the generous amount going to her each quarter there would have been a cushion, enough to last some while. What he had not discovered from the documents in his possession was any record of rent being paid on Caroline Crescent. He could only assume that Herbert Grace had purchased the lease, which of course was entirely in keeping with his desire to own. The lease was no doubt in the name of an anonymous trust and the deeds deposited with a bank somewhere in occupied Belgium. Edward made a mental note to ask Louise Bolden what she knew of it, if anything.

After breakfast he walked round to his office, posting his note to Louise on the way. He checked his own meagre delivery and examined the state of his equally exiguous in-tray. There was no new business coming in and still nothing from the Graves Registration Directorate. Otherwise the post brought him only one small cheque, so long overdue that Edward had long-since stopped requesting payment and forgotten all about it. He was slightly amused now that he felt no satisfaction that the fee had been paid as he would have done a month or so earlier; similarly he felt relieved that there was no new business in the pipeline where before it would have been a cause of nagging worry. But nevertheless he did ask himself whether this was what he really had had in mind when convincing himself he would keep the practice going despite his new-found fortune. Perhaps that was just a ploy to reinforce his anonymity, to shade him from the glare of notoriety he still feared his uncle's wealth could focus on him. How to relieve himself of the moral burden of criminal riches was an argument he found he was continually having with himself now, and if he was honest he wasn't desperate to conclude it one way or the other. 'Give the money back' was easy enough to say but almost impossible to accomplish in a way that the little people most deserving of recompense would benefit. Giving it away to a pressing cause, as he had eventually managed to do with the mobile x-ray machines seemed to fix his anxiety, but as time passed it was returning like a craving to be satisfied again.

He sat drumming his fingers slowly on the desk, staring into some far distance in his head. Then he suddenly straightened his shoulders and picked up the telephone. The operator came on the line and asked him what number he required. He asked for directory.

'That's me today, Mr Dereham. I'm on my own for an hour or two.'

'Well, I need the War Office in London please, Operator.' Edward laid stress on her proper title; he was not best pleased to have his identity so readily acknowledged. He took it as a sign that his calls were probably of interest to the ladies at the exchange, recalling with a start he had just asked Louise Bolden to telephone.

'I'll get them on the line, Caller. Please hang up.'

He waited and was just about to call the exchange again when the telephone rang. 'Putting you through, Mr Dereham,' the operator said, for all the world as if she were his personal secretary.

The switchboard operator at the War Office wasn't inclined to be quite so obliging, interrogating Edward more than he would have wished, given that the local exchange was listening, about why he wanted to talk to 'someone senior concerned with requisitioning property for military use.' So by the time he was put through to a principal civil servant he had already rehearsed the small fib he had decided on for the benefit of the ladies at the Sunbury telephone exchange.

'I am a solicitor acting as an executor of an estate. It includes a largish country residence which is of no use to the main beneficiary at present. It might, we thought, be suitable for some military purpose.'

The principal started to request chapter and verse, but when Edward pointed out that as he was not calling from an automatic exchange it might be more secure to write now that he knew to whom he should address correspondence, the official took the point, slightly crestfallen at having been justly rebuked.

When he replaced the telephone Edward felt a wave of relief. It was as if he had done penance for the sin of his wealth. The thirst for absolution had been slaked – at least until the next time.

Louise Bolden called him as soon as she received his letter. She did indeed possess a telephone at Caroline Crescent: Mr Grace had had it put in as soon as the automatic exchange had come to Hove. Of course he had, thought Edward.

'It might be useful if I made a note of the number, just in case,' he said, knowing full well that they should not be saying too much over his line. 'We aren't on the automatic exchange yet here in Sunbury – if you catch my drift.' He said he had business to discuss with her and that he would come and see her the following week if that was acceptable.

'Of course. Will you stay? Shall I have May make up the guest room?'

Edward imagined the ears pricking up at the exchange and wished Louise had not just revealed she was not from the Sunbury locality. He willed her not to mention Hove, or worse still, Brighton. 'It's all right, I shall go to the hotel,' he said, something telling him it was in any case not appropriate for him to accept the hospitality of a woman of his own age living on her own. She may have picked up his hesitancy because she didn't try to press him. Curiously though, he experienced more butterflies fluttering violently in his stomach as he replaced the receiver. It occurred to him that if there had been no-one eavesdropping on their conversation he could have been ready to take up her invitation.

The next day however, he received a letter from the civil servant at the War Office suggesting they meet at Hillcote Grange together with a Royal Army Medical Corps officer who happened to be based not far from Hindhead. Edward replied by return, agreeing, even though it would mean postponing his visit to Hove. Accordingly he wrote to Louise saying that some pressing business had come up. But even as he sealed the letter he felt serious disappointment, far more than was justified, if he was honest. Then as an afterthought, for which he rebuked himself, he wrote a short note to Mrs Aitken at Hillcote. At least this time there was no need for her to be taken unawares by a visit.

When Edward emerged from the station at Hindhead on the appointed day, the ancient fiacre and its curmudgeonly driver were nowhere in sight. His initial relief at not having to renew their acquaintance soon evaporated as he wondered how on earth he was going to get to Hillcote Grange. As he stood perplexed he felt a light touch on his sleeve and turning he saw a fellow passenger who had followed him off the train.

'Mr Dereham is it?'

Edward said he was.

'Thought you must be as we're the only ones getting off here. I'm Partridge. War Office. We spoke. You wrote to me.'

Edward shook his hand. 'There doesn't appear to be a cab, I'm afraid. I'm a bit stumped.'

'Not to worry. Major Rees is meeting me here with transport – in fact there he is now.'

A large berlin motor drove into the forecourt. An officer was sitting in the back and a uniformed soldier wearing a Red Cross armband was at the wheel in front of the partition. Partridge introduced Edward and they both squeezed in alongside the Major.

'I'm afraid I only have a hazy idea of where Hillcote Grange is,' said Edward. 'I have only been there once before and was taken by the station cab.'

Major Rees was reassuring. 'My driver has already checked the route. The house is marked on the ordnance survey.' Then, presumably alluding to the driver he added, 'He's not a conchie, in case you were wondering why he's not in France. He's done a good stint but he's been shell-shocked. Driving me seems to help. I deal with a lot of cases like his now. I shan't be sending him back to the front. But he'll probably come back to Wimereux with me when my blighty tour of duty is over.

Edward wanted to say he knew of the hospitals in Wimereux; wanted to say that he had heard they had their x-ray machines again after the enemy bombing; wanted to sound as though he had some sympathetic knowledge of Rees's war and his driver's. But he felt very uncomfortable at the way the Major had mentioned the driver wasn't a conscientious objector, as if he was really inviting Edward to explain his own civilian status without actually asking a blunt question. He wanted to say he was medically unfit. But Major Rees, being a doctor, might want awkward explanations, mightn't he? Wedged between him and Partridge in the motor car he did not relish trying to persuade them he was not actually infectious, though he firmly believed it himself.

Partridge fortunately chose this moment to bring the subject back to Hillcote Grange. 'So, Dereham, who is it you're executor for?'

Edward told him that in fact the house had been left to him by his late mother for whose estate he was acting.

'So it was your mother's house?'

'Yes. But she didn't ever live here.'

Partridge looked slightly nonplussed. 'I assume you have all the papers with you – deeds to the property and so forth?' He obviously wanted to reassure himself he wasn't in the hands of an imposter. 'It's in good repair is it – if your mother didn't live there?'

'I'm not offering the army a ruin, no. You'll see for yourself.'

The conversation turned to the war and the prospects for the next big push. Soon the motor car turned in through the gates to the Grange, and in a short while deposited them at the front entrance. This time Mrs Aitken, forewarned, was standing outside to meet them. Edward introduced the housekeeper.

'And do you come with the house?' the major asked. It was said in a jocular way, but Mrs Aitken who must have assumed these were prospective tenants responded firmly, addressing herself more to Edward, 'I shall be giving notice. So you may wish to advertise. I'm going to live with my sister over at Albury.'

'So no, then,' said Edward, 'Mrs Aitken evidently doesn't come with the house.' He felt rather put out at having this business broached here before they had even set foot inside. But when all was said and done, Mrs Aitken owed him no favours and certainly now that his aunt was no more, the house contained for her only its unpleasant association with his uncle.

After Partridge and the major had been given a tour they took themselves off conspiratorially into the small library off the main hall, leaving Edward alone with Mrs Aitken.

'What about Mr...er...Mr Kirby?' He found it difficult to refer to staff just by their surnames, especially when they were only his servants in a manner of speaking. People like the major, or

Dr Carradine at St Mary's, even Lloyd Garwood referred to him as Dereham: it was done as a signal of class brotherhood, although the first to call the other by the surname alone was generally staking precedence: unless they were just sucking up as in Garwood's case. But referring to staff by their surnames had an entirely different tone, enunciated differently to put people, even women, in their place and keep them there. It had never come easily to Edward, even at school. Perhaps his apparent deference to people like the gardener, and the housekeeper herself, was a reason why she in return felt little towards him. He had given the cabman a flea in his ear though, hadn't he? But then he thought, that had been due to his growing irritation, not a natural acceptance of the lower orders' place.

Mrs Aitken had no such inhibition. 'What about Kirby? Do they want to see the gardens? I can fetch him round.'

'Well they might want to. But I was thinking more about his position here. Will he want to leave now, too?'

'I shouldn't suppose so – no. He wants to see the gardens come back again, he says. When this dreadful war is over. He thinks life will go back to what it was when she had her garden parties here. Says he should be here for when the boys come back. But there's two we know who won't be and it's not over yet is it? In any case I can't see them coming back to gardening, can you Mr Dereham?'

The two visitors emerged from their purdah. The major raised his eyebrows in the housekeeper's direction and she immediately made herself scarce. Edward felt usurped, as if the army had already assumed an occupying role in the house. Perhaps it was just doctors, he consoled himself; they had a superiority all of their own anyway.

Partridge did at least ask if they might go back into the library to talk. 'Any chance of some tea?' he asked. Edward nodded and started to go in search of Mrs Aitken.

'Shall I get the bell?' the major said, ringing it anyway. Was there disapproval in his voice or was it his imagination? And it occurred to Edward then that he had still not given the major an explanation for his own lack of uniform. After a delay not quite bordering on unacceptable, Mrs Aitken put in an appearance and Edward perceived that the major's air of disapproval was being occasioned as much by her as by himself. It was probably due to her frosty response to the major's patriarchal joviality earlier at the front door – although Edward had not acquitted himself of his own lack of resolution in dealing with her.

He cleared his throat to issue what he hoped would be an authoritative request for tea, but the housekeeper forestalled him. 'I've laid out the refreshments as you asked Mr Dereham. In the small sitting room – I hope that's all right, seeing as the Holland covers are off in there.'

Edward could have hugged her. 'Would you like to show us through Mrs Aitken? Thank you.' He was damned if he was going to call her just 'Aitken' and in any case she was far too well dressed in his aunt's clothes.

Considering the privations of wartime, wonders had been worked with the tea. Over sandwiches, raised pork pie and a Victoria sponge, washed down with whisky and soda as an alternative to Darjeeling, Partridge expressed the army's considerable interest in Hillcote Grange. 'We are in need of convalescent homes and Major Rees thinks this will do very well. Very well. Now as to reimbursements. Under the requisitioning procedures of course, these are laid down. Not overly generous I must admit, but we are at war when all is said and done. You will get a full inventory and any loss or damage will be made good when the hostilities are at an end. Not long now we expect, eh?'

Edward had been giving some thought to the future arrangements, anticipating that his offer of the house would not be turned down. 'Just make good any loss or damage. As to reimbursement, I am willing to forego that.'

'Very patriotic of you, I'm sure,' said the Major.

'But with the proviso that the gardens and the orchard are recovered and regularly maintained under the supervision of the head gardener here, Mr Kirby.' Edward placed some emphasis on 'mister'.

Partridge was inclined to express some doubt. 'I'm not at all sure we could expect convalescing officers to undertake gardening duties, could we Major Rees?'

'What about men like your driver – shell shock I believe you called it?' said Edward. 'Mightn't gardening be good for men like that, officers or not?'

Major Rees pursed his lips. Edward judged he didn't like being second-guessed, but his professional egoism wouldn't allow him to reject Edward's suggestion. It had shrewdly hit the right spot with this doctor, a self-proclaimed specialist in this field. 'Indeed, I do recommend this kind of activity in appropriate cases. I assume there wouldn't be any objection to putting up a few huts for other ranks – over there perhaps.' He pointed through the library window to what had been the paddock on the other side of the orchard. 'You don't have any horses there now, do you?'

Edward said there were not. But he wondered to himself if his aunt had kept one or two, a pony perhaps at any rate.

Their business over, Partridge said brusquely he would write to Edward with a decision about his terms for Hillcote Grange. His tone made it clear that the War Office had taken control; as if Edward's gift-horse was a slightly knock-kneed offering whose teeth would have to be counted. Edward didn't mind: once again his uncle's burden had been lightened.

The berlin was at the front to take them back to the station. Partridge got in first. 'You coming back with us, Dereham?'

Edward wasn't sure he wanted to take the train all the way back to London with the civil servant. The conversation would be bound to turn to personal matters he would honestly rather avoid now, especially about his aunt and Hillcote, or his own civilian status. He turned to the housekeeper who was holding the front door. 'I shall stay if that's convenient, Mrs Aitken. We have some things to discuss, don't we?'

'Of course, Mr Dereham. I'll keep Mrs Kirby back.'

Edward called across to the waiting berlin and told them he was staying on. 'I'll get a train in the morning.' He thought a moment and added, 'Would you very obligingly order me the station cab, if he's there – nine o'clock?'

Much to his surprise Major Rees leaned out of the window and said he would send his driver for him, if he would like. Edward said he didn't want to put him to any bother, but the major replied, 'No bother. Least I can do in the circumstances. Very good thought of yours – the gardening.'

Edward watched until the car had turned out of the gates and then went back in with Mrs Aitken. 'Keep Mrs Kirby back, you said. The cook?'

'Yes, I got her in for the tea.'

'And very good it was too. So, is she still employed here, then?' He tried to recollect if Lloyd Garwood had said anything about a cook, although he vaguely remembered Mr Kirby saying something about his wife and lavender cake on his earlier visit. He hadn't taken it in.

Mrs Aitken looked flustered. 'I was told to let the maid go, but nothing was said about cook.'

'So, I'm still paying her?'

The housekeeper confirmed this was the case.

'And does she cook for you?'

Mrs Aitken said in a manner of speaking, she did. 'I go to the cottage for my supper sometimes.'

Edward smiled to himself. 'That's all right then. But I'd better have a look at the accounts hadn't I? After supper, of course!' He wanted to say to her that he would be happy to take his supper in the cottage too, but Mrs Aitken – perhaps anticipating the solecism he was about to commit – forestalled him.

'Mrs Grace used to take her dinner in the small sitting room when she was alone, which was mostly, later on. Where you had tea. Would that suit – seeing as the covers are off?'

Edward said it would, knowing he had been kept in his place and probably saved Mrs Kirby embarrassment and the trouble of tidying the cottage from top to bottom as well as preparing his meal. 'Nothing too grand tell Mrs Kirby. Not after that wonderful tea.' They agreed seven-thirty and Edward said he would stroll in the gardens until then as it was a fine evening.

'I opened up the principal guest bedroom too, in case you wanted to stay,' Mrs Aitken said, adding, 'but you've brought no things have you?'

'Oh, that's all right. I can manage for one night without a night shirt and I think there's just about another day in this collar. But perhaps you could find me some wash things – and a razor?'

'Leave it to me, Mr Dereham. This was a grand house in the entertaining way at one time. He used to bring royalty here on occasion. We have gentlemen's things of several sizes.'

Edward was relieved to hear that she wasn't offering anything that might have been Herbert Grace's, even though at one time, before his incarceration had bent and wasted him, he and Dereham would have been much of a build. He went through to the back area and let himself out to the cobbled yard. There was a small stable block with two sets of double doors. He peered into the first which was unlocked. It housed a small pony trap and several bicycles – he recognised one as being a Rover Safety like his own, but of an earlier vintage, perhaps the first edition which had won the gold medal at the famous Stanley Show in the eighties. He noticed all the machines were gentlemen's, so presumably his aunt had not used a bicycle. He struggled with the idea that Herbert Grace had ever bestrode one, although he mused that it would have been in his character to want to own the gold medal winner – he may even have had shares in the Rover company. Edward made a note to check his late aunt's portfolio, out of interest: and there it was again, the money, insinuating itself into his head when his guard was down, like an over-familiar acquaintance presuming to let himself in by the back door on getting no reply from the front and then calling up the stairs. This image reminded him sharply of the contrast between this experience, however brief it was to be, at Hillcote Grange and his spartan existence in Lower Sunbury, answering his own door and scraping mould from the top of the jam. There was no help for it: he must get to France, with or without a uniform. That way he could hide from his fortune; and who could say he would not be transformed when he returned, like those boys who would not want to be gardeners again?

The second set of doors was locked. Edward examined his bunch of keys and tried one or two that looked as though they might fit. One did, and he pulled the doors open. Inside was a large object covered overall with a heavy calico dustsheet. Stepping inside he bent down and struggled to lift one corner at the front. It was quite tightly secured all round with cord fastenings, but he could just make out the lower half of a motor car wheel. He straightened up, his curiosity enormously aroused, but uncertain whether to interfere with the fastenings. Rather like his aunt's jewellery, he had to keep reminding himself that the house and everything in it was his; that he wasn't acting as a solicitor for someone else. But even the house at Lower Sunbury had been his mother's first.

A polite cough behind him made Edward turn. Mr Kirby was standing outside in the yard. To his discomfort the gardener removed his hat and held it in front of him.

'It's a motor car, is it?' Edward said lamely.

'Yes Sir, that it is.'

'I didn't know there was one.'

'It was meant for Mr Grace. Want to have a look?'

Kirby came in to what was now revealed to be the garage and performed some sleight of hand with the cord so that the dust sheet hung freely.

'Would you take the other side, Mr Dereham, Sir, and help me fold it back. It makes it easier to get it back on, that way.'

They folded the cover back little by little so that it finally slipped to the floor at the back of the car in a neat concertina.

'That's the ticket, Sir, all ready to put back over.'

Edward didn't know much about motor cars, never having aspired to one himself. He hadn't even known the make of the army's berlin that had picked him up from the station. He was fairly sure, however, that he hadn't seen one like this before. It looked expensive and still had a lingering smell of newness about it, no doubt sealed in by the calico, which puzzled him.

'I'm not familiar with this model. Can you tell me what it is?'

'I believe it's a Sunbeam 12/16, Sir. So the man who delivered it from London told me. It hasn't been out on the road since then, of course. Mr Grace…he went away just before that. And then of course…well, he passed on.'

'So he never actually drove it? Did he drive, or did he have someone?'

'No he always drove himself, did Mr Grace. He had a Vauxhall before this, but to tell the truth I don't know what happened to it. He took it out one day and never came back here with it. I think he must have gone back to London in it. I never saw it again. And of course…they came for him in London, the police did. He never came back here. I asked Mrs Grace, when this arrived, I asked if she wanted the man to take it straight back to where it come from. But she said 'no', he might need it when he got back. And then of course he passed away.'

'So does it still go? If it hasn't been on the road since it was delivered?'

'Bless you, yes! When I say it hasn't been on the road, I have started it up from time to time and let it roll out into the yard. The man what delivered it said to do that, otherwise it would have to go up on blocks. I thought he should take it back, but Mrs Grace wouldn't hear of it.'

A thought struck Edward. 'Did the solicitor that came – Mr Garwood – did he see it?' He couldn't recall having seen a motor car mentioned on the probate inventory.

'I couldn't rightly say. I didn't show him. I don't know whether Mrs Aitken did. Probably not. She wouldn't have got the cover on and off on her own. I generally get my wife to help me, when it needs a start-up. She never mentioned Mrs Aitken asking her, when that solicitor chap was here, begging your pardon, Mr Dereham Sir. I knows you're one too, but we none of us cared for t'other chap.'

Edward asked about the trap next door and whether there had once been a pony to go with it. The gardener looked slightly uncomfortable. 'You'd best ask her about that – Mrs Aitken.'

Edward thought it best not to pursue the matter with him. 'Then I shall. By the way. I may have some good news for you about the garden. I may have got you some help.'

Mr Kirby looked at him shrewdly. 'Is it the army? I saw that officer with you earlier.'

Edward said nothing was cut and dried, but he was hopeful. 'I'd be grateful if you would keep it under your hat for the time being.' He didn't have much expectation that the gardener would do that however.

Back in the house Mrs Aitken informed him that she had laid out some things for him in the guest bedroom. Nothing formal as he was dining alone, although if he preferred he would find a dinner jacket in one of the wardrobes. Edward was taken by surprise at the suggestion: he had never changed for dinner at home even when his mother was alive, only doing so on the rare, very rare occasions when they might have entertained. The housekeeper had laid out a choice of two or three fresh shirts on the bed, all brand new and unworn he could see. She had judged his size to a nicety. Out of curiosity he examined the dinner suits. There were also three of slightly differing sizes in the wardrobe. He had to assume they had not been made to measure if they were simply intended for forgetful or unexpected guests – like him, he thought half-smiling. He tried one of the jackets; it fitted him pretty well. Holding the trousers and waistcoat against himself in the mirror, he could see that those too would do very well. Before he knew what he was really intending to do, Edward had picked out an evening shirt, still wrapped in the maker's tissue paper, from the small choice in the wardrobe drawers, as well as a black tie and studs.

So it was that, bathed and transformed into an elegant dinner guest in his own house, he descended to Mrs Grace's small sitting room, looking for all the world as if he expected to find others, similarly attired, enjoying pre-dinner drinks. While of course there was no other company, Mrs Aitken had set out various bottles, glasses and a syphon on a small side table. A larger, round table by the French windows looking onto the garden had been laid for one. Edward examined the drinks and although his hand hovered slightly over the whisky, thought better of it and poured himself a glass of sherry.

Mrs Aitken came in. She gave him an appraising look. 'Well, it's been a while I must say.' Her glance took in the glass of sherry. 'Will you ring when you're ready for the soup?'

Edward felt he should offer some explanation for his dressing for dinner, not wanting the housekeeper to think he had felt reproved by her for wanting to dress down and eat in the kitchen. But by the time he had thought about it, she had left the room. And in any case he couldn't be sure it wasn't the truth. He did feel reproached, simply by her presence in Hillcote, with her knowledge of how the house had been, how it had worked for his aunt Rose in the days of innocence before she had so suddenly and cruelly discovered what kind of man she was married to and where the money had come from to pay for it all. It was as if the house too had been cruelly let down and wanted him know it, through the medium of Mrs Aitken's disapproval. Perhaps, Edward thought, when she leaves, the final vestiges of the house's happier time would go with her.

Catching sight of his appearance in the gilded mirror above the mantelpiece he felt deceitful, because he had tried to play the part of some earlier guest who was ignorant of the guilty secret Herbert Grace had visited on this house. It was time they all moved on. Aunt Rose had moved on and in a sense had taken her husband with her, Mrs Aitken was moving on, and although

Hillcote Grange could not physically move on, it would be reborn, becoming a place of healing and restoration set in the gardens of its redeemed innocence, in the caring hands of Mr Kirby. Even he would be moving on, no longer the gardens' servant but raised up to be their master.

## 9

SUMMER 1917 was well advanced when he received a reply from the Graves Registration Directorate. In France the British allies had attacked at Arras and managed to take Vimy Ridge, but from what Edward could make out reading between the lines of the newspaper reports, all along the Western Front the conflict was bloody and inconclusive; casualties and deaths mounted relentlessly. The third battle of Ypres had begun in July, but the torrential summer rain in Flanders and the unexpected need to transfer troops to shore up the front in Italy meant that the looked-for advances to the south and east of the Ypres salient were becoming literally bogged down in Passchendaele.

The letter invited him to an interview in, of all places, St James's Park. Edward knew that the Directorate were in St James's Square; it was there he had written to Fabian Ware, so he assumed that an error must have been made and got overlooked. Added to the long delay that had elapsed since his first approach, he felt that this too did not augur well. However, when he arrived at the Park, planning to walk across and up into St James's Square, he found to his amazement that the lake had been drained and its rather slimy bed was now dotted with temporary wooden huts connected by duckboards. Number 26 St James's Park, which he had taken to be a misprint proved to be one of these.

To his relief he was expected, but his heart sank when he was directed to a desk occupied by a man in military uniform, clearly an army officer of some kind, or so Edward assumed. He resigned himself to the inevitable questions about his health.

'Mr Dereham is it? My name's Baker. I'm seconded here from Kew.'

This didn't mean anything to Edward. His immediate thought was that there must be an army depot or some such at Kew. He knew there was a barracks at Hounslow which wasn't too far from Kew. Feeling he should respond he asked Baker if this was indeed the case.

Baker looked blank and then laughed. 'No, no, not at all! Penny's just dropped. I'm here from Kew Gardens. This uniform's confusing. Been given a General Service rank some of us. I'm a captain, for my sins. Makes it easier for the army to put us in the right compartment when we go to the front. I'm just a bit too old to fight apparently. I expect you are too. Am I right?' He opened a file in front of him which Edward could see had his name on it. 'By the way,' Baker went on, obviously not expecting a reply to his rhetorical question, 'really must apologise for us not getting back to you sooner. Oversight, I'm afraid. We've been a bit at sixes and sevens lately, what with the changes that have gone on. You know – Red Cross and so on. And the move here to the park. Your letter got stuck in Ware's office while he was up to his ears with the Prince of Wales and the Prime Minister – I expect you know. So are you a gardener?'

Edward was on the brink of declaring he had little or no interest in gardening, but something told him that might not be a wise response: Baker's question had not simply been an ice-breaking pleasantry; if he was from Kew Gardens and had been made a temporary General Service officer, knowledge of gardening or at least a keen interest in it, could be critical.

'As a matter of fact, I'm in the process of planning some recovery work with my gardener for the gardens at Hillcote Grange. Do you know it? It's not far from Hindhead. It was my late Aunt's place and now it's my responsibility.'

Captain Baker looked interested but admitted that he had not heard of the house. Edward decided to press his luck. The fact that he was in the presence of someone in uniform who was more interested in horticulture than in his health made him a little reckless. He knew he must not totally misrepresent himself, but surely the very fact that he now owned gardens that had been splendid once by all accounts, and employed a full-time gardener with a cottage in the grounds, entitled him to claim more than a casual interest in gardening in polite circles. He was the decision-taker for a gardening endeavour that still demanded his attention even though the best part of its labour force was lying dead in France.

'The rose garden was magnificent before the war came. But of course, most of the men have gone away to the front. Sad to say, I know at least two won't be returning.'

Captain Baker commiserated, saying that they had similar difficulties at Kew. 'However, we have managed to recruit some ladies to fill in. They do very well, very well indeed. I shouldn't be surprised if they didn't stay on when it's all over.'

Edward told him how he was lending Hillcote to the army as an officers' convalescent home. 'They will look after the gardens – under my head gardener, Mr Kirby. He even hopes to get the greenhouses fired up again, assuming there will be a fuel allocation. The doctors think it's splendid rehabilitation, especially for the nervous cases - shell shock I think they're calling it.' Then thinking it wise not to prolong the gardening conversation any further than was necessary, he stopped talking.

Captain Baker had opened the manila file with Dereham's name on it and was reading Edward's letter. 'You don't mention your gardening interests here, I see.'

Edward was perplexed. 'No, I didn't. I didn't suppose it would be of interest. Is it…of interest, then?'

'Very much so. You will have seen from the newspaper reports that we are intending to create cemeteries for those who have fallen in France – and on the other fronts too, although that may prove more difficult perhaps.'

Edward began hazily to understand, although he realised he might not be as up-to-date on the role of the Graves Registration Directorate as he should be, considering he was seeking a post with it. 'So, what then? Might I be planning cemeteries, is that it? In charge of gardeners?' He wanted to pull himself back from the brink of dishonesty, but at the same time he did not want to retreat from it entirely, if there was a real possibility of employment at the front. He had come this far already.

'Not the planning perhaps,' Baker said. 'But, yes…directing work. Would that be a problem?'

Edward took the bull by the horns. 'I'm willing to try anything. But truth be told, I'm a country solicitor by profession. I wouldn't want to overstate my gardening expertise. You know how it is with these big houses,' he added.

Captain Baker looked disappointed. 'Yes. That's what you said in your letter. I just thought from what you were saying, you might have something more to offer from a horticultural point of view than most of the chaps we are getting pushed our way. Not that we are likely to turn you away. We're not getting very many volunteers for the kind of work we're doing. What sort of solicitor are you? Crime or conveyancing?'

'More conveyancing than crime,' said Edward, glad to be back on firmer ground.

'Land acquisition, that sort of thing?'

'Yes, that sort of thing.' There had been a few acres of building land some little while ago he recalled. He had acted for a local small-time developer in Hampton. The account still had not been settled.

'We do need people to negotiate with the local authorities in France. Some of their mayors can be a bit difficult about giving up land even though it's been agreed with the government. How's your French?'

Edward may have felt he could bluff it out on the horticulture, but professing fluency in French was another matter. 'Not good,' he confessed. 'Schoolboy. I don't think it would stretch to carrying out land deals.'

Captain Baker's air of disappointment deepened and he relapsed into silence. Edward could see his opportunity slipping away. 'There must be something I can do,' he said.

'Yes, I'm sure there is. Question is…what? We need drivers for the mobile teams. More to the point we need the vehicles for them to drive in the first place. Getting transport out of the army is well-nigh impossible. We're not a priority especially when there's a big push coming up.'

Edward clutched at this straw. 'I have a motor car. You'd be welcome to that. It's a Sunbeam 12/16. Not very old.

Baker began to look less gloomy and Edward felt his earlier recklessness returning. He heard himself say, 'In fact I could probably lay my hands on another one if it comes to that. Would we be able to ship them across to France though?'

The prospect of acquiring two vehicles was clearly beginning to excite Baker; so much so he forgot to ask if Edward could drive. Edward had already decided this was a bridge he would cross when he came to it.

'I'm sure we could get the army to requisition them. They'd be only too pleased if it meant we were pressing them less about finding transport. Then they could ship them across for us along with our other supplies and stores. Would you mind giving them over to the army like that?'

'Not if it means I can go with them,' said Edward.

'Goes without saying,' Baker replied. 'Goes without saying.' Then as a slight afterthought he added, 'You might have to go into uniform, like me. Is that a problem for you? I mean to say…' He appeared suddenly confused at having alluded to Dereham's civilian status even obliquely; clearly embarrassed he blushed visibly.

For Edward it was as if a sudden shaft of sunlight had broken through the clouds in his head, illuminating him from the inside; Baker's age and his reference to Edward's earlier was almost certainly meant to stand for those other possibilities that might get in the way of military service and were best not subjected to scrutiny by the authorities. Being just too old was a happy antidote to enquiries into conscientious objection or sexual proclivities.

Edward wondered which of these might really concern the man from Kew Gardens to whom it had not occurred to ask if he might have failed the medical. 'Not at all. Not at all,' he said, and the interview was at an end. As he stood up and made for the door to the hut, he waited to be summoned back, to be asked about his fitness, but the call never came.

It was now several weeks since he had written to Louise Bolden, putting off his visit to Hove. What with the appointment with the Graves Registration Directorate and dealing with the correspondence with the War Office arising from the future arrangements for Hillcote Grange he had neglected to contact her to rearrange their meeting. He wrote to her rather than use the telephone and found himself adding a postscript asking if he might after all take up her earlier offer of a bed for the night. Although he told himself that his reason for not telephoning her was to avoid tittle-tattle at the exchange, he suspected that it was Louise's status as his uncle's mistress which was colouring his dealings with her. She had been his secret pleasure and Edward had to confess to himself that he gained excitement from being the guardian of that knowledge. He tried not to think of her as 'a kept woman' and everything that might entail; his feelings about Louise were a more complex mixture. As he had prepared himself for their first encounter and on that journey to Hove, he had regarded himself as her lawyer acting to protect her finances, as if she had been made a widow by the imprisonment of Herbert Grace, in the same way, as he would discover, his wife, Rose, had chosen to become one. And while he still thought like her solicitor, his emotions had been rapidly transfused with something more softly protective by his arrival at the same time as the telegram announcing her son was missing. Right from the beginning of that first meeting her normal social protections had dissolved and so, too, had his own flesh melted. Edward was only too aware how easily he might have taken her in his arms as she wept. Whenever she came to mind he tried not to allow her status and her vulnerability to become confused. But nevertheless he had added the postscript.

No sooner had May shown him in than it was apparent that Louise herself regarded him as something more than a lawyer she had met only once before. She came forward and took his outstretched hand in both hers greeting him at once as 'Edward.'

'There's still no news of him,' she said as soon as she had enquired about his journey down.

For a brief, very brief, instant Edward thought she was talking about Herbert Grace, but the gatekeeper who should watch over thought and tongue was being vigilant. 'That shouldn't lead you to give up hope,' he said. 'I shall write to the War Office for you and see if there is anything more to be learned.'

'You're a kind man. But it's been months now. Anyway a letter came.'

'A letter? Yes the telegram said one would, didn't it?'

'I have it upstairs. I can show you. It was from his superior officer – a Captain Carey it is. He said Cornelius was in some attack and failed to arrive at the objective. He said the attack was successful. *Successful.* I suppose that's meant to be a comfort to me.'

'Did he say where this was?'

'Not exactly. I should like to know.'

They looked at one another; they were both talking as though he was dead. Edward went to say something.

'Don't. Don't. It's better I think of him as gone now, than I find out for sure in a week, or a month or a year and I have to grieve my heart out all over again. Now what have you got to tell me, Edward? Shall we go into luncheon and talk?'

As they were having the soup which was pea – May apologised for the lack of ham in it, blaming shortages – Edward asked Louise if she had heard anything from Herbert Grace, but she said she had not. 'I wrote a letter to him after you'd come. I told him you had been and were taking care of things. And I told him about Cornelius.

Edward's heart jolted. His uncle hadn't mentioned a letter from Louise on his last visit to Brixton. So had his accusations about the arrangements he had made for her been a game of some kind? A personal letter would have been read by the prison authorities, so they might easily have worked out Louise's identity and her relationship with their inmate. Before he knew it he found himself thinking furiously if they would be able to trace the current whereabouts of Grace's fortune, assuming they were looking for it. A letter from her after all this time was an act of compassion and forgiveness, a need to share her grief about her missing son with a man she still felt had a right to know. But Edward's instant reaction had been to wonder if the money was safe – his money. He tried to feel ashamed but what he really felt was guilt. Guilt because once again the money was finding him out, using him to preserve itself. 'What exactly did you say, Louise?' he asked.

'I didn't send it. I...I don't know...I thought it might get back to Gee and the school. Or Cornelius's regiment, or something.'

Edward breathed again. 'If you would like to write a letter to him, it might be better to let me send it as his solicitor. That way it wouldn't be so public. But I should tell you that I have been to see him again, so he knows about Cornelius and Grace's schooling. He's very concerned to protect you all from...from any unpleasantness because of him.'

May came in to clear the soup dishes and bring in the next frugal course. When she had left the room again Edward asked if the maid knew about Herbert's imprisonment.

Louise said she did. 'She doesn't gossip, if that's what you were thinking. She's too fond of me and the children to have us the talk of the crescent.'

'So what about the neighbours? Friends and acquaintances here in Hove?'

Louise smiled slightly. 'I do know the rules, you know, Edward. As far as the world is concerned I am Louise Bolden, a widow – or as good as. My husband went missing in America more than twelve years ago leaving me with a young son to bring up. It's mostly true after all, which makes it all the easier to live the lie.'

'And what about your…about Herbert?'

'We never entertained. I don't suppose anyone knew who he was. The people in the Crescent are far too discreet. Nobody ever asked his name. After all this is Hove, not Kensington. It's almost Brighton!'

'They'd get a shock if they did know who he was,' said Edward.

'Well yes, of course they would. And I expect I would have to move, if people found that out, wouldn't I?'

'I suppose you might have to. But I wasn't talking about his being in prison. I mean they'd have a shock if they knew he owns most of their houses.'

Louise stared at him in amazement.

'He has a company that owns most of this side of Caroline Crescent down to the Lawns – including this one of course – as well as the mews cottages and stables at the back that go with them.' Edward had done the searches after his visit to Brixton, anxious to know what his uncle might have meant by 'having Caroline Crescent safely under lock and key'. The entire terrace was owned by the trust in Antwerp and let on six-monthly renewable leases, including Louise's own house. Herbert Grace had been shrewd enough to provide Louise with her own status as a tenant rather than put his own name on the deeds, but not so generous as to give her the ownership outright. Edward's searches had also revealed that the six-monthly lease renewal was already due.

'Who pays for the lease on this house, Louise?' Neither she nor any of her neighbours, come to that, could possibly be sending money directly to an address in Antwerp.

Louise looked puzzled. 'Well, I always thought the house belonged to Herbert. I've never been asked for any payment myself. But I suppose if it belongs to this company of his that amounts to the same thing surely?'

Edward said it probably did. But she was now clearly not convinced. 'Am I not safe here in my own house? Are they stopping him having this company, now he's in prison? Have they just found out about it?'

'No, they don't know about his company. He's been careful to keep his name away from it partly, I should think, to protect you.' But he knew this had not been the principal reason for his uncle setting up the trust. Of course, when he had first set up the financial web with the Antwerp trust at its centre, the purpose had been to keep his real money remote from the tottering edifice of his fraudulent companies. The question which intrigued Edward, however, was where the payments to it were going now that it was behind the German lines? So after luncheon he asked to look at Louise's bank accounts again. From the drawer of the writing desk in the morning room she produced a sheaf of written statements, of which the most recent had been produced on a typewriter. However, the columns of payments in and out mostly showed cheques drawn to cash at the bank's Hove branch by Louise herself, and payments to the gas, light and coke company. Each quarter too there were the payments into the account from another that Edward recognised as being the company account Herbert Grace had created in his wife Rose's name, which had briefly been frozen when she had died. He riffled through the cancelled cheques accompanying the statements. 'Is this everything?'

Louise rummaged through the writing desk drawer once more. 'Only these.'

'These' turned out to be letters from the bank's head office in the City advising of payments it had made 'according to your instructions'. They included her daughter Grace's school fees until they too had been frozen – Edward had already decided to pay them out of his own account. Another payment 'according to your instructions' had been made at six monthly intervals, and very much looked like the lease renewal on Caroline Crescent. It was in the form of a transfer to another account with the same bank, an account only identified with a number. If Edward had been hoping to see the name of the Antwerp Trust's London agent, he was disappointed. And since this account, he assumed, hadn't been in Rose's name he would have little chance of finding it out.

He finished examining the accounts and satisfied himself that Louise was now receiving regular quarterly payments again, although he did not tell her that they were now coming from the money he had inherited. At their first meeting, and smitten by her sad circumstance, he had assured her that the regular payments, which had been frozen by probate, would resume. Then he had had no idea how he would manage to fulfil that promise from the meagre funds at his disposal. Now he wrestled with himself over whether he should tell her they would come from the very considerable fortune he had come into as a direct consequence, as he saw it, of the incarceration of her protector, the father of one of her children. In the event he persuaded himself that the fact of the money appearing to come from its accustomed, anonymous source was sufficient comfort for her and that he would not wish her to feel beholden to him for it. He thought he remembered telling her on his first visit to Hove, of Rose's bequest to his mother. But then he had had no idea how large the legacy would turn out to be. So he said nothing more about his inheritance nor of his acquisition of Hillcote Grange. Still, his silence on the matter was to nag away at him. Not, he knew, because of the deception, so much as his really wanting her to feel free of Herbert Grace and – yes – if not exactly beholden to him, at least under his own protection instead.

As Louise locked the accounts back in the writing desk, the sun came flooding through the bay window. 'Oh, what a lovely afternoon it's turning out,' she exclaimed. 'Shall we stroll out to the lawns? We could go for some tea along the front. Shall we though?' She looked a little doubtful. Edward guessed she was worried about the propriety of being seen alone with an unknown man. But it was a lovely day.

'I can be your cousin, if you're worried about the neighbours.'

'Yes – we're almost family after all – in a way. I mean he's your uncle so that must make me something, mustn't it.' She laughed and blushed deeply and he, too, felt himself colouring up. 'Silly,' she said, her Irish lilt coming to the fore as she tried to brush away her thoughts and in doing so, getting herself in deeper. 'I meant if he weren't in prison and he weren't married, I might be his wife now, mightn't I? But that's a lot of mights and might-nots. I don't know what I'm saying.' And it dawned on Edward that she was more concerned about his own reputation with the crescent than hers.

'Come on,' he said. 'Let's get our hats and go for tea. The neighbours can go hang. This *is* nearly Brighton after all.' But he had realised as she spoke that there were some awkward explanations still to be made which in his heart of hearts he had been quietly avoiding.

On the way out a thought occurred to him. 'One of the mews stables at the back must belong to this house, mustn't it?'

Louise said there was one although no-one lived over it now. 'May and her husband had it until he went to France, and then after a while she moved into the house with me. Said she found it too worrying on her own without him. Herbert's motor car is still in the stable – garage I suppose that would make it.'

'Really? Can we have a look at it?'

'If I can find the key we can. I assume it's on the board in the kitchen.' She called through to May who brought it out.

The cobbled mews at the rear of Caroline Crescent was fairly quiet. The stables themselves appeared to be empty of horses, the Crescent residents probably being unable to obtain sufficient feed because of the war to keep one, as well as there being a lack of men to groom and care for them. Those few stables that had become garages for motor cars were locked up too, the fuel to feed them also being in very short supply.

Louise stopped outside her garage and handed the key to Edward. 'You'd better do it – I haven't been able to look at it since he went away.'

Herbert Grace evidently hadn't driven himself up to London as Mr Kirby had suggested, he'd left his car here in Hove. But then of course, Kirby wouldn't have known that. 'Is it on blocks?' Edward asked. He was rather more conversant with cars and their needs now. Louise said she thought it was. 'May's man was going to do it. He said it should be done if…it wasn't going to be used for a while.'

Edward pulled the garage door open, letting in the sunlight which revealed Herbert Grace's missing Vauxhall touring car reposing on blocks in one of the two former loose boxes. Its wheels had been removed and were stacked in the adjacent one.

'Is it all right d'you think,' Louise asked anxiously. 'I haven't had anything else done to it. Should I have done?'

Edward wasn't sure either. 'I think they're meant to be drained of oil, maybe. But I should think May's husband will have seen to it. Is there anyone who could look it over – maybe put the wheels back on?'

'Why? Do you want to use it then?'

'I was thinking I might,' he said, mentally already ensuring his own passage to France by shipping two much-needed vehicles over.

They walked together along the seafront – or as near to it as they could get, as the beach and south side of the promenade had been strewn with barbed wire loops and other obstructions against an invasion – towards the Brighton end. Most of the groups out taking advantage of the sunshine were in military uniform; many were recovering from injuries and amputations. A largish number were Indian soldiers in their turbans. Louise explained that the Pavilion had been turned into a hospital especially for them. Edward's sense of his incongruity as a civilian amidst all this physical weight of evidence of what was happening barely seventy miles across the Channel, deepened as they made their way slowly towards the relative sanctuary of the Grand Hotel, although here too the public rooms were mainly filled with officers in field brown.

Probably for their different reasons, therefore, they were glad to find a table suitably obscured from curious observation by potted palms and a pillar. As they drank their tea and nibbled on a sparse plate of fish paste sandwiches and dry cake decidedly lacking in sweetness Edward said conversationally, 'I've had an interview with something called the Graves Registration Directorate. I'm hoping they are going to send me to France.' Louise was the first person he had confided in since the meeting and for him, of course, he was announcing good news. It hadn't occurred to him in the excitement of being within reach of a goal that had eluded him for best part of three years, that others might not see it that way too, especially not Louise. The words were scarcely out of his mouth when he saw the affect they were having. He had casually inflicted a cruel blow on her in the midst of their pleasant *tête à tête*. Her face went white and her teacup rattled in the saucer as she made an effort to put it down. Edward's first thought was that his mention of going to France had brought to the surface her worst fears about Cornelius whom she had to pretend was still alive while she really grieved for his death. He put his hand over hers on the table and started to mumble an apologetic excuse for his thoughtlessness. She shook her head.

'I've only just found you and now you're going there too. You're the only man in my life, now. Do you realise that? Don't you see there are women in almost every street, who have no men left in their lives because of this horrible, horrible war. And I thought I had you at least. But if you go there I'll lose you too. Don't I lose all my men?'

Edward was horrified at what he had done and taken aback by the unadorned rawness of her outburst. What did she mean? Was she making a declaration of the sorts of feelings he kept trying to leave unformed?

'It's just a desk job. I'll be perfectly safe, I'm sure,' he stammered. But the words sounded like just another incantation so many men must have invoked on parting from the women in their lives, doubly deceitful because he was not looking for safety. He still hoped for something more from this war: he hoped to be freed from this sentence of imprisonment for a disease he did not have.

After that there was a silence between them. Edward made a sign to the waitress for the bill, paid and they left. As they walked back along the Lawns to Caroline Crescent he could tell from Louise's demeanour that they had crossed a boundary. They had moved on from their developing friendship into an uncomfortable, premature intimacy because he had ripped open the buttons on her inner emotions and she had let him see she was now counting him among the men she could not bear to lose. For some unaccountable reason he remembered her blaming their loss on her not having been to confession. He wondered whether she would go now – before he went to France.

Louise let them back into the house with her own key. 'May's night off,' she said flatly. 'She'll be going to the picture house with her friend, I'll be bound.'

'What's on?' Edward asked, trying to sound matter-of-fact: they were the first words they had exchanged since leaving the Grand Hotel.

'I think she said she was going to the Tivoli to see this new heart-throb they're all talking about – Ronald Coleman is it? She'll have left us some cold supper, if that's all right?'

'Well, I really ought to be getting back – assuming there are any trains for civilians at this time. You never can tell…'

'I thought you wanted to stay. Didn't you say? May's made up the guest bedroom. I asked her. I'll take you up if you like.'

There it was, thought Edward: his postscript. He tried to persuade himself it had just been an innocent request on his part. But how had Louise read it? And now, after tea at the Grand: how was she reading it now?

'Well if you're sure it'll be no trouble. I wouldn't want to…'

She had preceded him into the entrance hall and had gone into the hall closet to remove her hat and coat. She emerged re-arranging her hair with her fingers. 'Wouldn't want to what? Compromise me? Are you still thinking about the neighbours? I thought we owned them anyway.' And she put her fingertips to his cheek to soothe away the obvious embarrassment on his face.

'Didn't want to put you to any trouble, I was going to say. But since you put it that way – no, I wouldn't want to compromise you,' he stammered.

'I'm not sorry I said what I said back there at the hotel. Not sorry at all. I'm suddenly tired of trying to behave as if nothing in my life has changed. It has been a lie for so long – there, that old platitude, living a lie – and now even the lie has fallen to pieces. Herbert is in prison and has forbidden me to see him. I'm no kind of comfort to him there. And what is he in prison for? A lie, a monstrous lie about his money and his businesses – about his whole life really, and me just another bit of his lie. And Gee, now. Part of the lie. Her real father who couldn't acknowledge her in public any more than he could me, and a pretend father who's long since disappeared on the other side of the world. I don't know. I don't know any more.'

She looked down at the hall floor. Her eyes were full of unshed tears. Edward knew he wanted to hold her, to kiss her. But he did not: he told himself he would be taking enormous advantage of her even if she did not resist. And if she did resist him, in spite of everything she had said? Well then an awful confusion would blight anything there might be between them.

'And now there's my sweet Cornelius. Another one. *Missing*. What's that if it's not a lie?' A tear made its way down her face.

Edward didn't know what to do. He knew that words would never be enough. He stood helplessly with his hands at his sides, staring down at the top of her lowered head. 'I don't know what to say, Louise. What should I say? Tell me.'

'Tell me you're not a lie, Edward. Tell me you're not just a messenger of false hope. Because you give me hope, Edward, real hope for the first time for I don't know how long. Tell me truthfully that if you go over there, you will come back. You know, if you don't, I won't even get a telegram will I?'

'I'm not a lie, Louise. I am real. I *am* here, and I shall come back.'

She took both his hands in hers and put them to her lips. Then still holding one of them she turned as if leading him up the stairs. Suddenly at the half landing he needed to cough. He dropped her hand and reached hurriedly for his handkerchief. When he took it away from his mouth, for the first time in months he saw a tell-tale spot of blood beginning to spread like a careless scarlet ink blot. He hastily folded the handkerchief, hoping Louise had not noticed it. If she had she said nothing. They continued on up but Edward made no effort to retake her hand.

She opened the door to his bedroom and stood aside to let him go in. 'There,' she said. 'And I'm just at the end – if there's anything.'

Later after they had eaten and Louise had played some soulful Irish ballads on the piano, when he finally turned in for the night, he gently turned the key in his bedroom door locking himself away from her with his secret.

# Part Two

*Acts of Contrition*

# 10

THE mass of khaki rippled as though it were a single, flexing muscle. Occasionally it sparked like struck matches as brief bursts of December sunshine found metal in it. The mass hummed underneath like a hive, or the drone of the pipes, while above it individual voices rose up, swearing, laughing, and calling.

Here were more soldiers gathered together than Dereham had ever seen in one place at one time. It was barely a month since the armistice, but the sight of all these men poised to go home did not lift his own spirits. He felt only a dull ache of guilt that he was not part of it, that he was too late, just a voyeur in spite of his newly acquired subaltern's rank and his general service uniform still emitting the expensive fragrance of the Saville Row fitting room. He gripped the *Elizabeth's* rail to steady himself as she made final contact with the Boulogne dockside and waiting hands heaved the mooring cables over the iron bollards. It was then his eyes became fixed on those more passive lines of men; men swathed in bandages, men propping themselves on crutches, men with their heads and eyes wrapped in dressings holding the arms and shoulders of their sighted neighbours; motionless forms of men as well, on ranks of stretchers seemingly laid at regulation intervals as if dressed on parade. These were the *Elizabeth's* return passengers, waiting for embarkation to

Folkestone by one gangway as Edward and his fellow able-bodied arrivals prepared to disembark by another, as if to spare them the embarrassment of their paths having to cross.

Once ashore, he struggled with his heavy leather valise through the crowd which barely parted at the sight of his single pip. These men were finally going home to demobilisation, they had little time for any deference to a junior officer not even dignified with his own regimental insignia. However, his invisibility suited him very well. He did not sit comfortably in his uniform, despite its perfect cut. It reminded him every time he glanced down at it beneath his unbuttoned great coat that he was still no soldier, no matter how hard he had yearned to be one. He made his way with difficulty to the street at the back of the harbour and, without much hope, stood looking for some guiding light in the perpetual coming and going all around him.

It appeared in the shape of a corporal with a military police armband who appeared from a doorway to the left, pinching out a partially-smoked cigarette end and placing it in the top pocket of his tunic. His eyes met Dereham's. With only a hint of reluctance he came to attention and saluted. 'Need some help, Sir? You look a bit lost.'

Edward looked at him thankfully, uncertain whether he was supposed to return the salute. He half gestured towards his cap peak. 'Thank you – ah – corporal, I have to report to somewhere called…' he rummaged in his greatcoat pocket for his instructions, '…somewhere called Hesdin.' He pronounced it *Aydan* in his best schoolboy French. The corporal looked puzzled.

'Can I have a look, Sir, begging your pardon?' He took the letter and scrutinised it. 'No Sir. That's *Ezdinn* that is. Are they sending you transport? There won't likely be a train, not now. What unit is it?' He looked at the reference heading at the top of the instructions: 'Directorate of War Graves Registration? What's that when it's at home – Red Cross or something?'

Edward grimaced slightly. 'Something like that, Corporal. No-one seems quite sure. They've put me in the army though.'

'So I can see, Sir. Well, you could try at the movement office over there, but they're mostly doing AT transfers to the hospitals here and they've precious few lorries. Anyone as can has to walk – there's four thousand men a day coming through Boulogne for demob since the armistice; they won't have much going to Ezdinn, I shouldn't think. It's on the way to Amiens.'

'Any chance of a taxi, would you think?'

'If you're made of money, Sir. You could try in the main square, three streets back by the big church.'

Edward thanked him. 'And are you going home soon, Corporal, now it's all over?' he asked.

'Not me, Sir. I'm regular. Second Battalion London Irish Rifles. Been in since Loos. High Wood, Vimy Ridge. Should've gone to Mesopotamia by rights, but I landed in hospital and missed the boat. So here I am. Still, must get on, begging your pardon Sir.' The corporal came to attention and saluted.

As Edward watched him go he wished he could have made a better job of returning the salute, but as yet no-one had shown him how. The significance of the Corporal's brief geography of action he had been part of, was not lost on him. It spoke of survival against all odds of bloody horror for more than three years; something to his constant regret Edward had not shared. 'I say,' he called out recalling that Louise's son Cornelius had been in the London Irish, but the corporal was out of earshot

Still flowing with men, the streets leading to the main square reminded him of the crowds spilling out from the cup final, but at least not all were heading in the opposite direction to him. There was one ancient French taxi standing by the church. It looked as though it had seen some action itself at the front line. When he said where he wanted to go the driver shrugged and said that it would take perhaps three or four hours, what with all the military traffic and the state of the roads; even supposing he could find sufficient fuel the fare would have to be considerable – he suggested a hundred and fifty francs at least. Edward worked out that would be getting on for ten pounds: even with his recently acquired wealth, it seemed exorbitant. He hesitated. Perhaps he should offer gold – say five sovereigns? Would that be too much? But he mentally shrugged too. He needed to get to his destination before nightfall, come what may. 'Five in gold, Monsieur?'

The cab driver demanded to see the colour of the money, but he already had a gleam in his eye. He bit into one of the proffered sovereigns, trying to judge how many more there might be in Dereham's coin holder 'Six,' he growled, trying to hide his eagerness, 'and ten francs for the extra fuel I will have to find.'

Edward agreed grudgingly. He had still not come to terms with his financial position and the circumstances of his having achieved it. He found it very difficult to begin think like a rich man being shrewd with his money. Regarding the money as mostly ill-gotten made him all the more reluctant now to disburse some of it on another rogue. However, he did insist on half now and half on arrival. The cab driver went off in search of fuel, returning surprisingly quickly, lugging a large petrol can, making Edward think he must have had it stored nearby already. When the taxi had been filled up they set off on the road east out of Boulogne along the river, laboriously negotiating the incoming military lorries, ambulances and columns of marching men. As a consequence it was very late in the day and already dark when they eventually crept into the ancient market town of Hesdin. Edward had found out as much as he was able about the place he was being sent to and knew it had been a staging post for the front lines as well as its chateau being turned over to house a field hospital. So while it showed plenty of evidence of the wear and tear that goes with military occupation it was pretty much intact.

Neither Edward nor, needless to say, the driver had the slightest idea where the Graves Registration Directorate was located. Enquiries of locals and military passers-by alike drew a blank until one soldier, with a hint of black humour, suggested they should try the military hospital, it being only one step from the grave for many of its inhabitants. The cab driver's limited patience lasted just about as far as the gates to the chateau, but there he unceremoniously dumped Edward and his valise, having demanded the balance of his fare. By now Edward was in no mood to argue and anyhow felt rather glad to see the back of him.

He trudged unhopefully up to the main door of the chateau and stood in the entrance hall wondering which of the staff scurrying back and forth he might usefully approach. He was acutely aware that he only had a hazy knowledge of military correctness, basic officer training had not been too much to the fore in the induction he had received from Captain Baker in St James's Park. Baker had not gone into much more detail than a vague suggestion of which tailor he might try in Saville Row for his uniform. But he had gathered enough to know that he should return a salute if he was wearing his cap but only come to attention if he was not. So he was relieved when a medical officer wearing an open white coat over his captain's uniform, a stethoscope round his neck, but no cap, checked his stride and asked Edward if he was being looked after.

Edward explained that he was looking for the Graves Registration Directorate. The doctor replied that he didn't think it was part of the hospital. 'I think they're in the woods somewhere, beyond the station. Along by the river.'

'Can I walk there?' Edward asked.

The doctor looked at him curiously. 'Walk? Bit unusual even in these straightened times. Junior officers are only meant to walk in front of the men when they go over the top.' He gave a wry smile. 'Just got off the boat have you?' He looked down at Edward's valise. 'No-one coming to meet you? How did you get from Boulogne?'

Edward explained.

'Graves Registration – are they on the telephone?'

Edward didn't know.

'Let's see if we can find out.' He led the way to an office where a Voluntary Aid Detachment nurse was sitting behind a desk with a telephone on it. 'Do we have a number for the…what was it? The Graves Registration Directorate.' The nurse said she would ask the switchboard. 'They're trying. They'll call back.'

While they waited the doctor began to quiz Edward about his role. 'General Service Officer, I see. So you're new to it are you? Seen any service already? You look a bit old, if you don't mind my saying so, to be newly called up.'

Edward explained that he had been deferred in 1916 on medical grounds. 'But I've been given the all clear now,' he added quickly.

'Bad luck – I don't mean about getting a clean bill of health. But you'd have thought the army would have left you out of it now there's the armistice. They mostly can't wait to send people home. What was it?'

Edward thought for a moment what to say. He was hardly likely to be sent home now, was he? But how much should he confide to a doctor? Still, it might be an idea to try out the tentative diagnosis Carradine had proffered at St Mary's. 'Personally, I'm fairly convinced it's not TB,' he had said, when Edward had with trepidation taken him his blood-spotted handkerchief from Hove. 'Whether that would pass a second opinion is another matter although I'm the one usually giving the second opinions around here. And seeing as it's the Red Cross that want you and not the army, I'll find you a non-infectious explanation, should anyone ask you. I still think you're mad to go, but there you are.'

Edward decided to give Carradine's diagnosis a go. 'I had recurring haemoptysis from scarring on the lung. I had whooping cough and a go of pneumonia when I was a child, which may account for it or possibly I have a tendency to sarcoidosis.'

The doctor was impressed. 'Well done. Never come across sarcoidosis. It's not my field. Who diagnosed that for you?'

'Dr Carradine at St Mary's.'

'He's a good man. He produced an x-ray machine for us from absolutely nowhere – out of a top hat. We sorely needed it. I suppose the army just assumed you had consumption and left it at that, did they?'

The telephone rang and the VAD nurse picked it up. 'It's the GRD,' she said.

'Ask them if they can send some transport for Lieutenant…?'

'Dereham,' said Edward with a start, realising the doctor meant him.

After a few moments it was clear the VAD was having difficulty prevailing on them. The doctor took the telephone and spoke to them himself. After some huffing and puffing he said, 'Well, we can hardly put him up here. He'd better go to the *estaminet* across the road and you can pick him up from there in the morning.' He hung up. 'I don't know what kind of an outfit they are. They say all their vehicles are still out somewhere and they have no drivers. I'm not too sure they're expecting you. Perhaps you can get a cab tomorrow if they don't turn up. Corinne at *La Vie Est Belle* over the way will find one for you if anyone can. A bit late now though. I should get a half decent bed there if you can, before you get lumbered with a hut in the woods. Nurse, would you see about an orderly to take Lieutenant Dereham's luggage over and show him the way.'

In the entrance hall the doctor shook Edward's hand goodbye. 'What are you going to be doing at this directorate, then?'

'Legal work I think. I'm not too sure. The set-up is still changing now that the war is over and the new cemeteries can be laid out.'

'And the bodies still out there? Thousands of them. Will you be bringing them in?'

'That's the plan.'

'Good God! What a thought.'

Corinne at *La Vie Est Belle* made Edward very welcome, restoring his faith in the French after his experience with the cab driver. She found him a bed for the night with sheets that had hardly been slept in, which he assumed was normal in France, as she made no apology for them. However he was rather taken aback, when she asked him if he had any rations *'pour le petit déjeuner'* assuming his breakfast would be included. With his schoolboy French and her landlady English he was able to gather that the British soldiers were generally expected to provide their own food in the garrison towns, so as not to deny their French hosts their own scarce resources. Edward tried to explain that he was still *en route* to his posting and had not been provided with any rations for the journey. So in the morning he found himself seated at a table in the bar sipping a rather watery coffee and chewing on a stale bread end spread, fairly liberally it has to be said, with a kind of dripping from an earthenware jar and containing occasional stringy morsels he hoped might be pork. When Corinne came to replenish his coffee cup, he thanked her and asked what was in the crock. '*Rillettes,*' she told him, but he was none the wiser.

After the VAD's telephone conversation with the reluctant GRD the previous evening Edward didn't hold out much hope that any transport would arrive to collect him. He went up to the bar to pay, making up his mind to return over the road to the hospital to make another call or at least get some proper directions to the Directorate's HQ. Madame handed him a large glass of cognac, which he thought it would be churlish to decline, even though it was not yet half past eight. But as he was breathing it in and sipping it, a soldier entered and approached him.

'Mr Dereham, Sir?' He stood to attention and saluted, seemingly surprised to have come upon a uniformed officer.

Edward's cap was sitting on the bar, so he was relieved not to have to return the salute, gesturing airily instead. 'Have you come to take me to the GRD…Private er…?' He could see no stripes.

'Pilgrim, Sir. I'm sorry I wasn't here last night Sir. The Albion was playing up on the way back from Béthune and they'd all gone back to billet from here, so I didn't get the order until this morning.'

'The Albion?'

'Yes Sir, we've got three and some box cars besides.'

Edward divined that the Albion was a vehicle. 'So is it all right this morning then?'

No, Sir. They're working on it at the garage in Hesdin. I've brought one of the new motors,' he added proudly. 'Arrived yesterday, unexpected. Just sitting there at the gates when we got back. Someone must've signed for them, else the army would've nicked them back.'

Private Pilgrim picked up Edward's valise and turned towards the door. Edward knocked back the remains of his brandy and putting on his cap and straightening it gave Madame Corinne a pretty fair salute.

'*Au revoir, Monsieur.* You can have a room here if you need a *billet de logement.* I would be happy to have the rations.'

He thanked her and followed Pilgrim outside inwardly beaming because of the salute, his improving recollection of the French tongue, and the cognac. Outside Pilgrim had already stowed Edward's luggage in the parked car and was holding the passenger door open for him. 'Will you be coming in the front sir?'

Edward was flabbergasted and delighted. The last time he had seen this car had been in the mews garage behind Caroline Crescent. It was Herbert Grace's Vauxhall. The fact that it had turned up here in Hesdin on the same day as he had, felt like an enormous portent of good fortune and a testament to Captain Baker's determination to get his hands not just on Lieutenant Dereham but more importantly on his gift of two vehicles.

'Is the other motor a Sunbeam by any chance, Private?' Edward asked as he elected to sit up front.

'I believe it is, Sir, yes. This one happened to be in front, that's why I brought it. Do you know about them, then, Sir?'

'I spoke to Captain Baker about them a few months ago, now. Do you know Captain Baker? He said he was getting the army to requisition them and get them brought over.'

'Can't say as I do know him, Sir. But whoever he is he's done us a big favour, and no mistake.'

They drove to the edge of the town, crossed over the railway line and turned right along a wooded river valley. In a short while they came to a large, partially cleared area with a fence and gates through which were several large wooden huts with metal or asbestos roofs.

'Here we are, Sir. GRD HQ.'

'Does it have any other name?'

'Not really. It was a French camp before. That's why these are Adrian huts, not Nissens. Still just as draughty as Nissens. We just call it Hesdin.' Pilgrim pronounced it like the corporal at Boulogne harbour had although he did manage not to drop the aitch.

'Where do you suppose I'm meant to go?' Edward addressed the question as much to himself as to Pilgrim. The private looked at him sympathetically.

'Begging your pardon Sir. But you're another one who's not done much of this, have you?'

'Much of what?'

'Soldiering Sir. See, I didn't know this morning whether I'd be picking up an officer, or just a civilian gentleman. Some are and some aren't, here. They've mostly got temporary commissions, but they haven't actually done any soldiering. Not that there's many of us here who have. I'm one of the few and I got a piece of shell splinter in my back at Mailly Wood they can't shift, so I got invalided back out of the line. I can drive, but I don't dig. You'd better see Lieutenant Scarsbrook. He's a temporary like you Sir. He's in the drawing office. Hut Three. Red Cross he was, but we're all Graves Registration or Commission – I can't keep up. In the end we're all in the army. That's the way I see it.'

That was the way Lieutenant Dereham saw it too.

Lieutenant Scarsbrook, 'call me Scarsie', turned out to be a middle-aged draughtsman from an architect's office in Horsham. 'I'm meant to be working on designs for the new cemeteries. But I'm mostly scrounging supplies and stores. It's all hands to the pumps here I'm afraid. Not that there's many hands. Still you're another one. What are you supposed to be doing?'

'Legal work I think…with the French. Land acquisitions, that sort of thing. I was told to report to a Lieutenant Colonel somebody or other.' Edward rummaged in his greatcoat pockets for his letter.

'Not here, I'm afraid. That's generally the case. There's so much to be done and so few of us. I think the Colonel has gone over to Albert to see about transport. Getting hold of vehicles is the devil's own work and sometimes a bit of rank needs pulling.'

Edward told him about Pilgrim and the broken down lorry. 'He collected me in the Vauxhall.'

'Yes. I've no idea where they came from. I just signed for them sharpish last night. If I'd looked as though I wasn't expecting them the army would have whisked them back. You see it's all very well me sitting here drawing plans for the new cemeteries, the big problem is getting the bodies back to them in the first place. Some of the poor wretches have never been properly buried at all. Still lying where they fell. I heard that the front line casualties at Loos have only just been recovered and that was 1915. Do you have a billet?'

'I assumed I'd be sleeping here. Aren't I?'

Lieutenant Scarsbrook pursed his lips. 'I wouldn't if I were you. The men do – the gardeners we have. But they go out with the mobile units mostly anyway, so a bed in the huts here is just a temporary respite for them really. And they prefer to save the money and rations. The officers and the civilian staff have digs in the town. But then there are less than a dozen of us.'

'So why do gardeners go out with the mobile units? They're surely not…' Edward hesitated: 'Not searching for bodies?'

'Well, supposedly not. That's still the army's job – exhumation. Mostly volunteers, you know. A lot of them do it almost as an act of contrition. They survived. Their comrades didn't. Survival breeds guilt. But our mobile gardeners have to be there too, bringing some semblance of order to those cemeteries that are going to become permanent. Preparing the ground, marking out plots for the bodies that are being brought in daily to add to those already there. It's bloody grim work, especially with winter coming. Some of them are living out on their own at their cemeteries all week. I've heard of one chap living in a dugout. The bigger mobile gardening parties go from site to site, usually the more isolated ones. They get back to base camp for the weekend with any luck. Anyway you'll see all that. I shouldn't think you'll be here in Hesdin for long, if you're doing the rounds of the French authorities.'

Edward wondered what he should do now in the absence of any instructions or the Colonel.

'First things first, I've learned that in my short time here. Get your billet sorted out.'

Edward said he thought he could put up at the *Vie Est Belle*. A thought struck him. 'What about rations? The lady owner said she would welcome my rations.'

'You give her a chitty. I can let you have those. She takes it to the army paymaster in the town. She'll know. But it only covers the basics. If you can dip into your own pocket, life gets a little more tolerable. She's bound to have access to the black market as she's running a pub.'

Edward wondered if he should make the acquaintance of the other officers and staff first before disappearing back to the town. Scarsbrook wasn't sure who might be around. 'As I said, there's only a handful of us and sorting supplies is the priority, so they're mostly out on the scrounge.'

This proved to be the case, there being only two others in the camp, one of whom had just returned with a small detachment of men from the pioneer corps who were busy unloading an assortment of hardware, mainly picks and shovels, which were clearly surplus to the army's requirement. The scrounging officer was obviously delighted with his haul, particularly as he had been able to get the army to deliver it. 'We've got enough picks and shovels to be going on with. What we need now is men to wield them.' He waved at the pioneers who had finished unloading and were now standing around smoking. 'I tried to talk this lot into volunteering for the gardening, but they're all on their way back to Blighty and their families. Their NCO was quite straight with me. He's to deliver them to Boulogne for demobilisation after this – extra half-crown a day or not.'

The pioneers and their NCO clambered back into their lorry and departed; Scarsbrook had disappeared on a mission of his own: and Edward found himself standing awkwardly next to his valise outside the hut, still wondering what to do next. Secure his billet seemed to be the only instruction he had been given, but he had little idea how to make his way back to the town. Some bicycles had been included with the picks and shovels. Edward eyed them nervously, not certain whether he was allowed to commandeer one and not at all certain he would be able to manage it and his luggage. As he was sizing up one of the machines he heard someone whistling round the back of the hut. On investigation he discovered Private Pilgrim in shirtsleeves and braces in the process of washing the Vauxhall. For some reason the sight made Edward feel slightly aggrieved: it seemed that here was neither the time nor the place to be washing a car, regardless of the state it might be in; it was disrespectful to the task that they were about, of finding and burying the dead, the task from which Pilgrim himself had so recently returned. Yet here he was washing Herbert Grace's motor car and whistling *Till the Clouds Roll By* very badly.

Edward cleared his throat to draw attention to his presence: it sounded apologetic, as if he didn't wish to disturb the chauffeur at his work. The private looked up but continued with his leathering. Edward straightened his shoulders.

'Who asked you to do that?'

It may be Pilgrim detected the sudden sharpness in Edward's tone, but he came instantly to attention, at the same time dropping the leather into his bucket. 'Sir? No-one sir.'

'Finish it later. Fetch my luggage round and take me back to the *estaminet.*'

'Yes sir. Very good, Sir.'

It was the first order Edward had given and he felt surprisingly good about it. He was damned if he was going to have Herbert Grace's motor car taking precedence.

## 11

THE Lieutenant Colonel, who it turned out was a civil servant administrator in his fifties, also now a general service officer, returned from pulling rank with the army over men and supplies a few days later. Remarkably he had some prescience of Edward's arrival. Much to his relief it seemed that he was not expected to conduct tricky negotiations in French with recalcitrant local mayors: it seemed that French and British powers further up the chain had already reached agreement about the perpetual status and location of the cemeteries and in a very French way edicts had been issued. Instead Edward was to be part of the process of correctly establishing the identities of the dead, work the colonel considered for some reason to be appropriate to a small, country solicitor.

Edward was to have use of the Vauxhall, which rather surprised him, knowing that transport was so difficult for the Commission to come by. But although he did not actually say so, the colonel seemed to have knowledge of its provenance. Edward was to base himself at the Commission's southern sector HQ at Doullens, which covered two base camps, at Arras and Albert, from where the mobile gardening parties went out to their temporary camps in what had been until very recently the communication sectors and the front line itself.

'There is a small problem,' he told the colonel, who had asked him if he had any questions, 'I haven't actually ever driven a motor car.'

'Neither have I,' the colonel replied, his tone implying that it was no occupation for a gentleman. 'But there's not much to it from what I can see. Anyway it won't be much use to you at the front. You'd be better off with a horse if you can get hold of one. I take it you ride.'

Edward said he could ride, at a pinch. 'I mostly get around on a bicycle to be honest.'

'Well put one in the back of the motor, then. And get one of the drivers here to give you a quick lesson with your Vauxhall. By the way, where's your billet?'

Edward told him.

'Well I should hang on to it if you can. You'll be needing to come back here from time to time and you won't want to sleep in one of these damn huts if you can possibly avoid it. You'll have enough of that at Doullens.'

Edward asked if that was possible. 'Aren't the chitties meant for people who are actually occupying the billet, Sir?'

'Quite so. Quite so, Dereham. But I should have thought that someone who can afford a Saville Row cutter like that might find a way. You could probably buy *la Vie Est Belle* for the price of that uniform.'

Suitably chastised and wishing he had tried his normal tailor in Kingston rather than listen to Captain Baker, Edward went in search of Private Pilgrim for a driving lesson, only to find he had been dispatched to Doullens himself with the repaired Albion. As usual there were not many people around; he could only see two in the drawing office and they were hard at their work and it was plain not to be disturbed.

It was a pleasant day, so Edward decided that he should walk into Hesdin and at least carry out the rest of the colonel's instructions regarding his billet. Collecting his greatcoat on his way out of the camp he set off along the woodland path running between the river and the road leading to the town. After about fifteen minutes he came in sight of the railway crossing. A Studebaker touring car was straddled across it and its driver was struggling furiously with the starting handle at the front. Edward quickened his pace and then as he heard the distant whistle of a railway engine approaching although not yet in sight, he broke into a run. The car's driver heard the whistle too, stopped trying to start the engine and went to the back to try and push the vehicle off the crossing. Edward put his shoulder to the other side and between them they managed to shift the obstinate machine off the crossing just as the train was coming into view. The driver straightened up and took a moment to recover his breath. He looked about thirty, perhaps a little more, and was wearing a French flyer's uniform greatcoat, a leather flying helmet and goggles pushed up. Edward was surprised therefore when he was addressed in perfect English.

'Many thanks old man. Not sure I could have shifted her on my own. I rather think I'm out of petrol judging by her refusal to restart.' He thrust open the bonnet of the car and peered at the small glass reservoir inside. 'Hmm. Not much anyhow. Do you know where I might get some?'

Edward said it would be difficult. 'We have fuel for our own vehicles at the camp. Otherwise I think you have to know somebody if it's not official. Are you on official business?'

'Good Lord no. I've just been demobilised. I thought I might take a look at Paris before heading home. So do you know somebody who might help – with the petrol?'

Edward thought for a moment. 'Madame at the *estaminet* might. I'm on my way to sort out my billet if you want to walk with me and we can ask her.' Looking at the French greatcoat he said, 'Your English is very good. I mean you sound English.'

'That's because I *am* English. But my mother's French. I've been serving in the French air corps. I was living over here when the war came so I volunteered here.'

'Are you a pilot then?'

'Not really, no. I can fly at a pinch, but I was mostly an observer and sometimes rear-gunner. Taking photographs you know. My name's Burnell – Maurice Burnell.' He pronounced 'Maurice' in the English way, like the dancers.

Edward introduced himself too and they fell in step together. So by the time they reached *La Vie Est Belle*, Maurice Burnell had discovered most of what there was to know about Edward's path to the Directorate of Graves Registration, although curiously Edward was not much the wiser about his companion. Burnell was the kind of person who could coax answers out of others while only giving snippets of information back about himself. He readily charmed Madame Corinne in fluent French, she clearly taking him for a Frenchman. When she asked him where he was from, and he had told her his family was from Lille, she said with an air of satisfaction that she had detected as much from his accent. The subject of finding petrol was raised in a roundabout way and Madame Corinne said 'it was possible'. After she and the kitchen maid had had a whispered exchange, the maid was dispatched with a message.

Edward then set about broaching with Corinne the delicate matter of keeping his room available even though there would be no chitty for rations.

Burnell listened to his attempts to negotiate a fair price with interest. 'You'll need to promise something on top when you return to make sure the room is free when you want it. Otherwise she'll take your money and let the room while you're away. She will anyway, of course, but you want vacant possession and clean sheets.'

Edward took the point and had a stab at making his wishes known. Burnell lent weight to the discussions rather more fluently, with the result that Madame Corinne agreed to hold Edward's room for fifty francs a week with a single payment of another fifty to ensure an empty room and clean linen whenever he should return. Burnell said it wasn't a bad deal considering the obvious dearth of accommodation so close to the recent front lines.

They sat at one of the little scrubbed tables and had bread and some tolerable *saucisson*, Madame Corinne still under the impression she was serving a fellow-countryman, while they waited for possible news of petrol.

'I gather from all this that you are moving on from here?' Burnell quizzed.

Edward explained he was going to Doullens to begin identification work. 'I'm hoping to find someone to show me how to drive otherwise I shall be in some difficulty. Unfortunately for me, our drivers are mostly out in the communication sectors most of the time. I was hoping to get one of them to teach me.'

'What motor have you got?'

'A Vauxhall.'

'Well I've never driven one, but I can give it a go,' Burnell offered. 'They're all much of a muchness.'

Edward was about to decline the offer, but something made him think that perhaps fate had thrown them together. 'Don't you have to be in Paris, though?' he said half-heartedly, not wishing to have the opportunity withdrawn.

'Oh, Paris will always be there.'

'What about your mother? Won't she be expecting you?'

'I shouldn't think so – but she isn't in Paris. She's nursing my married sister, Florence, back in England. Mother's sold up and moved in with Florence's family. So there wouldn't be room for me, I shouldn't suppose. Anyway I'm rather *persona non grata* with my brother-in-law. My sister has TB, sadly.'

Edward felt as if he had received a blow to the stomach. Since quoting Carradine's possible explanation of his own condition to the doctor at the military hospital in the chateau across the road, he had managed to put any doubts he still had about it to the back of his mind. Nor had he mentioned the matter of his medical deferment to his new acquaintance. But it only needed a mention of the loathsome initials to bring them to the front again and have him furtively reaching for his handkerchief.

A man driving a trap pulled by a sorry-looking horse arrived at the front door with the kitchen maid beside him. Burnell went outside and spoke to the man who pulled aside some sacking in the back of the trap. Burnell came back in.

'Shall we go back to my motor together? We can fill up and you could have a go driving her – why not?'

Edward's first driving lesson was not a roaring success, although he did manage to start the engine without dislocating his thumb with the starting handle. However, changing the gears was a manoeuvre he found difficult and he was constantly stalling.

After a while Maurice Burnell told him to move over. 'I'd better drive you back to your camp and we can have a go on your Vauxhall. Does it have a cone clutch?'

Edward didn't know.

'Well if it's got a cone clutch you're going to find the gears a lot easier than on this. Otherwise I can see I shall have to come to Doullens with you.'

'You're not serious?'

'Why not? I've nothing better to do. It sounds to me that you are going to be doing something rather important. I hadn't really thought about it.'

'About what?'

'This monstrous war being over. But it's not over, is it? Not with all those men's bodies still out there. We cannot just walk away from them and say "well that's that". Here I am heading for Paris and the *Folies Bergères* while you are about to head back into no-man's land in an effort to bring it all to some kind of an end.'

'I'm not heading back into no-man's land. I've never been there. You have. When did you volunteer – 1915? I should say you've done enough.'

'Well, I have been lucky to come through it. But I have lost plenty of friends who might still be out there waiting to be found. And their mothers, their wives, waiting for them to be found. Peace? What does peace mean to them?' What will it ever mean to them?'

They arrived at the entrance to the camp. Burnell pulled over and turned the engine off. 'Do you need a photographer? I kept some of the apparatus – it's in the back.'

Edward couldn't tell if he was being serious and he did not feel he had any kind of authority to recruit this chance acquaintance to the Directorate, still less to the Commission. He stepped down from the car. 'Perhaps I could mention it to the colonel,' he suggested doubtfully. But Burnell didn't seem quite so keen on this. 'I thought I might just come along with you, for the ride. I hadn't really thought about joining up again so soon after being demobbed. Anyway, I've only offered to take you to Doullens.'

However, the colonel inadvertently resolved the matter himself. When Edward reported in to him for further instructions the colonel asked him about his driving lesson. 'I need you in Doullens before the end of the week, are you going to be able to manage that? Well – not *are you* going to manage – you'll have to.'

'Actually, I've got a driver who'll go with me to Doullens and give me lessons on the way, If that's all right,' Edward said.

'One of ours?'

Edward told him more or less truthfully that he was a French aviator who was heading in that direction.

'Officer?'

'NCO I think Sir. Observer he told me.'

'Sounds all right. Don't think we could take on a French officer without referring back to St James's, but a sergeant shouldn't pose a problem.'

Edward was about to explain that he wasn't proposing they should recruit Burnell and that in any case he was English, but thought perhaps in the circumstances he did not need to complicate matters further.

Now of course there was a problem. They would need to take the Vauxhall back to the *estaminet* for the night in order to make an early start in the morning, but Burnell would need to drive his car as well. They decided to have another shot at getting Edward to drive before nightfall made it unwise but although he managed not to stall the Vauxhall as much as he had Burnell's larger Studebaker, neither of them felt confident that he could yet drive it by himself in the dark. The feeling that he was a fraud began to assert itself in him again. After all it was his donation of two motor cars that had opened the door of the Commission to him: he should at least master how to drive them. He felt sure that if he could have Burnell with him in the Vauxhall, by the time they arrived in Doullens he would have accomplished it sufficiently. Doullens was only about thirty miles from Hesdin in theory, but Edward knew the nearer one got to the front a journey began to be measured in time taken rather than miles covered.

His despondency communicated itself to Burnell. 'Cheer up, old man. I've an idea. Your lot here are desperately short of transport, aren't they? So why don't they buy the Studebaker from me and we can go on to Doullens in the Vauxhall.'

Edward was completely taken aback by such a radical proposal. He had not yet begun to come to terms with the compromise and inventiveness that years of war at the front had made second nature to men like Burnell. He, by contrast, was still thinking like the uniformed non-combatant he was. Nevertheless he could see a flaw in the suggestion, welcome as the Studebaker would be to their transport pool: the Directorate scrounged from the army, it did not buy from private sources if it could help it.

'What would you want for the car?' he asked.
'Do you pay in Francs or sterling?'
'Sterling,' said Edward.
'I should say a hundred, wouldn't you? And I'll throw in the driving lessons for free!'

Edward told him to wait outside while he went in to talk to Lieutenant Scarsbrook. 'He does chitties and so on,' he explained.

Scarsbrook was in the drawing office at his board. 'What do you think of this, Dereham? It's a layout for the cemetery at Loos. We've only just managed to get the surveys back.'

Edward looked with interest at the board. Here at any rate something was taking shape out of what was still to him a senseless confusion. 'I've managed to scrounge another car for the pool. The Studebaker out there. Do you need to sign for it or anything?'

Scarsbrook gave him a receipt from the book in his drawer. 'You can fill this out, seeing as it's your scrounge. It's not pinched is it?'

'Good Lord, no!'

Edward waited until he was outside before quietly pocketing the receipt.

'Well?' said Burnell.

'They want to know if it's pinched.'

'Not exactly. Liberated, you might say, from the Americans. They're just abandoning anything they can't carry on their backs now they are going home too. Does that count?'

Edward wondered whether stealing by finding could be applied to the litter of war.

'Shall we say seventy-five pounds then?' He thought that would a reasonable sum for getting him to Doullens with driving lessons thrown in, and a very appropriate transaction for Herbert Grace's money. He reached into the inner recesses of his greatcoat and produced a fistful of five pound notes as if the price had been agreed.

However, Burnell did not quibble at the price but at the sight of the money. 'That's a good deal of cash to be carrying around.'

'I've just drawn it from our paymaster,' Edward lied.

'No, I meant for me to be carrying around, really,' said Burnell. 'But then, we don't have much option in the circumstances.

I can hardly pay it into the bank in Hesdin – I don't believe there is one. Still, I'd take a banker's draft – I'm sure the Commission is good for that sort of money until I get back to England.'

Edward thought quickly. 'I think a draft would need the colonel's signature as well as the paymaster. I should take the cash if I were you, while it's available. I should think we're safe enough so long as we carry it on us.' He held out the sheaf of notes which after a moment's deliberation, Burnell thrust away into the inside pocket of his own coat. But he was obviously still thinking about the transaction as he transferred his sparse amount of luggage and the photographic equipment from the back of the Studebaker to the Vauxhall.

They spent the night at *La Vie Est Belle,* Burnell's French and his good looks having already secured him the promise of a bed from Madame Corinne. Early the next morning, with Edward nervously at the wheel of the Vauxhall they lurched eastwards along the road that followed the River Canche in the general direction of Doullens and the final front line, where it had been abandoned by the armistice.

## 12

AT first their way was relatively easy: the country road was in a reasonably good state, considering the heavy use by military traffic for the last few years had obviously tested it to its limits in places. When his improving progress permitted him occasionally to tear his gaze from the road in front of him, Edward could also see the fields to either side were being cultivated. Lumbering dung carts were depositing manure in heaps for farm workers, mostly old men, women and boys, to spread along the furrows prepared for next year's sugar beet. By some field gates there were cows patiently chewing the cud where heaps of hay had been left for their winter feed; sheep too in their thick winter fleeces getting what grazing they could from the wet December ground.

Burnell remarked grimly on these familiar seasonal signs. 'Hard to believe we are only a stone's throw from the front. You'll see, Dereham, you'll see soon enough. In a few miles there's ground France won't be ploughing any time soon. What did we call it, what the Conqueror did? The harrying of the north? You'll see harrying hereabouts and no mistake. A blessing in a way this is such a vast country. At least they'll be able to feed themselves from elsewhere. If they can find the men – I mean, look at that old fellow there, muck-spreading. He should be tucked up in a bath chair!'

Most of the other traffic was heading back in the opposite direction to the Vauxhall; small columns of marching men and horses making for the coast and demobilisation; ambulances destined for the coastal hospitals and the Red Cross ships still shuttling to and from Dover and Southampton. The sight of them made Edward very solemn. It seemed wrong, didn't it, the war was over and still there were wounded men on the move, many who would probably never make it back home at all. Eventually their headstones in the Commission's new cemeteries, he thought, would have their death dates months after the armistice and unrelated to a battlefield. Did these, and those of them who had taken this route before the end, feel cheated to have died under the surgeon's knife in Boulogne or Etaples, or from septicaemia in Stationary Hospital 14 in Wimereux, and not from the instant oblivion of combat? He put it to Burnell, as a recent combatant, when they stopped at the wayside to change places at the steering wheel.

The aviator eyed him curiously. 'You're an odd fellow, and no mistake, Dereham. What are you really here for?'

Edward sensed what might be coming. He tried to be evasive. 'What do you mean? You know what I'm here for. You are taking me to Doullens so I can get on with it.'

'Well, I don't mean to pry,' said Burnell, indicating that he had every intention of doing just that, 'but I reckon you are still young enough to have been called up. So why weren't you? Medically unfit – or the other thing?'

'What other thing?'

'You know – prison. Are you a conchy? I assume not a regular villain.' Burnell laughed off-handedly to show that it was all one to him.

Edward bridled at this suggestion: Major Rees had inferred something of the sort might have accounted for his civilian status, but he had not made the next logical assumption that Edward should be behind bars. Perhaps he had assumed Dereham had bought his way out by offering Hillcote to the War Office. No, Edward could not allow Burnell to think that he had managed to delay serving until after the arrival of the armistice on the pretext of genuine or faked conscientious objection. So he told him about his medical deferment and that now he had at least been acquitted of tuberculosis, if not exactly given a totally clean bill of health. But he could tell that Maurice Burnell was only partially convinced.

'So you would have joined up even if the war had carried on, would you? You weren't to know they'd post you to this War Graves outfit.' Burnell had assumed because of Edward's General Service rank, his posting to the Graves Registration Directorate had been a random decision by the army. Edward did not disabuse him. He didn't wish to be drawn further into his recent past than he absolutely had to. He grunted non-committally.

Still Burnell persisted in his quest for information. He apologised for suggesting Edward might have been in prison for the duration of the war. 'After all, you've obviously got plenty of brass – for a country solicitor, I mean. You might have embezzled the clients' funds and ended up in jug.'

Edward asked him what made him think he had money, if it was any of his business anyway. But Burnell was not to be put off. 'Because, old man, you quite obviously bought my car this morning with your own cash. Military outfits, even odd ones like yours, don't just give out wads of cash like that. Especially sterling. A few francs for the local baker maybe. Be honest, it came out of your own pocket, didn't it? Although I'm damned if I know why.'

Edward wanted simply to deny it, to tell him he was wrong and leave it at that. But yet again he could feel the sly conspiracy of Herbert Grace's wealth conniving with him to cloak it with respectability. Buying Burnell's Studebaker for the Commission had been another act of contrition for the money, he told himself. While he wanted no thanks for this, any more than for those x-ray machines, he still did not want to feel as though he was colluding with his uncle by keeping its source a secret and at the same time appearing to aggrandise himself by his own phoney generosity. In any case he was forming an opinion of Burnell that suggested that likeable though he undoubtedly was, he was a man with an eye to the main chance, unlikely to share or understand Dereham's scruples. He had already observed that Burnell was adept at extracting information from him without reciprocating the confidences too much, the kind of man who probably regarded other people as there to be used. But if that were the case, then why offer to take him to Doullens? Wasn't that simply a selfless act? Edward wondered.

'I don't want to talk about it, if it's all the same to you,' he said, realising that this was a response only likely to store up trouble for him with someone like Maurice Burnell.

Although Doullens could be said to be on the western edge of the devastation that lay beyond it, the town had not been totally obliterated like many of the villages further to the north and east. There seemed at first to Edward little reason why it should have been selected as the location for the southern area headquarters until he realised it had for a long time, when the front had hardly moved, been a hub for the lines of communication which led from it. Maurice Burnell made little reference to the sight which met their eyes, other than to insist that he took over the driving as the road became more and more difficult to negotiate. Since the armistice there had been little maintenance carried out beyond ensuring the way to the west and the coast remained passable. This town, like larger neighbours, and the battered remains of the outlying villages dotting the miles of churned battlefield and shattered woodland running more or less south to north, would be left to the French authorities to pick over and recover in the fullness of time.

It was a hopeless landscape Edward glimpsed beyond the edges of the town, for which he was unprepared. The Vauxhall lurched along the main street, in places only lined by the rubble of its former buildings now heaped to either side. It was, thought Edward, like a camel ride he had been on at the zoo as a child and he felt instantly contrite that such an image should have entered his head. But he had no other experience to draw on in the middle of such an alien place. He made an effort to see and hear this as it would have been to men, more worthy of his uniform, only two months earlier, but the land gave back nothing that would help him place himself there. It lay silently nursing its hurts, wishing Edward and all men dressed like him would go away.

The Directorate's southern headquarters turned out to be a mixture of army huts and tents. An area had been cleared to house the transport for the mobile parties as the number of available vehicles was beginning slowly to increase. Edward was delighted to run into Private Pilgrim here, as usual with his head stuck under the bonnet of his Albion. Pilgrim told him his party was currently working around a place called Auchonvillers where a permanent cemetery was being created. He called it by the tommies' name, Ocean Villas. A great many temporary graves were dotted all around it, as this section of the front had seen a great deal of action in the summer of 1916 in the first battle of the Somme.

'We're bringing them into Ocean Villas now, but it won't be long before it's full. I reckon we'll need dozens of cemeteries along the road from Albert before we're done,' Pilgrim said. 'Are you coming out with us, Sir? Our identification officer is due to be going up to Saint Omer so I suppose you'll be taking his place won't you?'

As usual Private Pilgrim was right, seeming to know the Directorate's mind before the Directorate had actually made it up. Edward made himself known to the senior officer-in-charge, by the name of Banks, who had last fought in South Africa and had now come out of retirement for the Directorate of Graves Registration. He informed Edward he was to accompany the current identification officer to the sites where exhumed bodies were being brought in for reburial, currently at Auchonvillers, but then to move on when that site was full to the other battlefield cemeteries along the Albert Road which were to be made permanent resting places. 'Anywhere where there are already ten or more graves is being turned into a permanent cemetery. We'll have hundreds, maybe thousands in the Somme alone, Dereham, so we'll need to get cracking. The army cannot be expected to take responsibility in the longer run. Sooner or later they'll have to hand over everything to us.'

When he came out from his briefing he found that Maurice Burnell had found himself a billet in the town. He told Edward he had fixed one for him too. Edward said he had been allocated accommodation at the headquarters. 'In any case it looks as though I shall be camping out a lot of the time. That's if I can't find an *estaminet* for the night or even at a pinch a *cabaret*. Private Pilgrim says that would be my best bet. Better than a tent. Apparently they are beginning to open up again already. People cannot wait to return and take up their lives again, although when you look at what a complete shambles it all is, it's hard to fathom why.'

'They have nowhere else to go. Nothing else to do, I expect,' said Maurice. 'They will have been flowing backwards and forwards behind the lines, always hoping that they might return to their homes. You'd be surprised how tenaciously these stubborn people hung on to their homes and land even when the shells were almost whistling overhead. If the line only moved a few hundred yard towards them they'd carry on ploughing. And if they were forced to up sticks, you can bet they were only an hour or so in front of the advance. Don't forget, Dereham, in this part of the world, until last March the line hardly moved for two years. So yes – find ourselves a *cabaret* for the night. We should.'

'*We* should? I thought you'd be moving on to Paris? There's not much to keep you here, by the look of it.'

'Well I'm rather stuck without a vehicle until I can get a ride out. There's an airfield not too far from here. I might be able to get a rear seat in a Farman to somewhere useful while I'm still wearing the uniform. In the meantime, I thought I might take some pictures. You never know, someone might buy them. And you could probably use a spare driver for that Vauxhall. Who's to know? Your colonel said you could take on local labour, didn't he?'

Much to his own surprise, Edward could see nothing wrong with Burnell's proposal. He was already learning that 'compromise' and 'improvise' were the keys to surviving here. When he looked out over the town and beyond to the broken, empty landscape, he understood there were few if any rules and regulations with any point to them. In any case as far as he could see, Baker was unlikely to object to another driver, especially one who did not appear to be a drain on Doullens' slender resources and appeared to have the colonel's blessing back at Hesdin.

The next day, a Monday, Edward and Maurice Burnell set out in the Vauxhall for Auchonvillers, following behind Private Pilgrim in the temperamental Albion with its small work party of mobile gardeners. As well as being the driver, Pilgrim was also their cook. They had supplies for the week as well as tools and equipment. This included a shotgun which Pilgrim said was for 'conies for the pot' if they were lucky, as well as for 'keeping down the vermin.' He added darkly something about 'not getting the two confused, as they knew what the rabbits had been eating, which was more than you could say for the rats, although you'd a pretty good idea.' In good time Edward came to understand what Pilgrim had meant.

He discovered that he was effectively in charge of this reburial sector for the Graves Registration Commission, although his relationship with the men in the small details bringing in the bodies they had exhumed was rather blurred as they were still serving soldiers and under the army's jurisdiction. The job of identification officer which he took over within a couple of days was to check the names, ranks and regimental details of the bodies being brought in for re-interment and the position of their new graves. Until this time the only dead bodies he had come into contact with had been his mother's and the occasional shrouded corpse waiting to be moved to the mortuary when he had been at the sanatorium. Here at Auchonvillers as many as a dozen bodies in a day were being brought in from the now silent, blasted fields of battle, recovered from the hasty graves dug for them in the intervening years since the first months of the battle of the Somme, when most of them had fallen.

The village had been largely destroyed although the church and some buildings around it had remarkably survived: the road to it from Albert was passable only with difficulty. They had abandoned the Vauxhall a mile or so from the outskirts and continued on foot. Burnell took the precaution of taking the starting handle with him and removing something from under the bonnet to immobilise it, although the road was devoid of other traffic. The only other sign of life was a small work detail in the distance, busy with another exhumation.

Pilgrim's party in the lumbering Albion had pressed on to the village. Some of the evacuated inhabitants had returned and had begun to patch up their homes where their destruction had not been complete. To Burnell's glee one of these was a small *estaminet* close by the church where he was able to negotiate at least a roof over their heads for the time they would be there before returning to Doullens. Food was another matter and they had to rely on Private Pilgrim's efforts for their sustenance. Strangely there seemed to be no shortage of wine at the *estaminet,* some of it of excellent quality. Over several glasses of a very good prewar vintage, Burnell's French managed to extract from the *patron* that it was wine from the cellars of the chateau at neighbouring Mailly-Maillet which had been abandoned by its owners as the front line for much of the time had run through its grounds.

During the days that followed, Pilgrim's mobile gardeners spent most of their time preparing new graves for the bodies being brought in by the exhumation team. To start with they were still being given temporary crosses with brief inscriptions identifying them stamped on tinplate strips, like the luggage labelling machines at railway stations; the uniform white headstones being planned by the Hesdin drawing office would eventually replace them, making Edward's job of ensuring the record was accurately maintained during the transfer all the more critical. It was made easier where the soldier's body was accompanied by the temporary cross that had marked it on the battlefield. With any luck the pencilled inscription scored into it would still be legible and miraculously would tally with the record that had been kept at the time by his comrades who had hastily laid him to rest, perhaps still under fire.

Other arrivals at the cemetery did not yield up their identities so easily. As they moved from one group of crosses to the next, the diggers would come across other remains, often only partial and unmarked by any cross. Perhaps they had never received even a cursory burial or had been separated from their markers by the passage of later fighting, or the sudden upheaval of a barrage. Edward would try and find out if there had been an identity tag, or a regimental badge discovered by the diggers, and he soon came to experience a huge feeling of achievement whenever the pitiful pieces of what had once been a young man contained a scrap of regimental identity – a button or a cap badge.

In the weeks that followed his first at Auchonvillers his emotions fought inside him like warring creatures in a sack. He felt pity and anger at the same time; admiration too. A small group of bodies brought in together might mean they had died together on a single day probably in the same moments in that summer three years ago. Edward wanted to believe they were saying to him, 'we died hard and brave, and it wasn't pointless.' He still needed to share something with them that he himself had been denied, but as time passed those conflicting emotions became duller and blunted. Daily familiarity with the dead meant his stomach turned less frequently, and when he searched for how he really felt now, increasingly he found only emptiness.

When he was not taking photographs, Maurice assisted with the identity recording and, where it was possible, drove Edward to the other cemeteries along the Albert road, some of which had been designated to be permanent and others which were too small and would need to be, as the Commission referred to it, 'concentrated.' Some of these were some way off the road and only accessible with difficulty on foot across the remains of old plank roads that had been part of the lines of communication. Their isolated gardeners welcomed visits from the two of them, knowing they would get a ride back in the Vauxhall to the comparative comfort of Auchonvillers, instead of more nights under canvas or in some cases in old, partially collapsed trench dugouts.

Maurice Burnell stopped talking about moving on to Paris or the coast and Edward stopped asking him. Like those around them, Pilgrim and his gardeners, and the army grave diggers plodding quietly in from the wasteland with their day's burdens, the two of them were as if self-ordained into a kind of holy office. Out there in that landscape redrawn by death, the dead were depending on them to bring order, to provide perpetuity. It felt like a calling. So no-one questioned Maurice's presence there or what his role might be (or come to that, whether any pay or rations might be due to him): he was simply a member of the Order. As part of that brotherhood, too, he had started calling Edward by his first name rather than Dereham or 'old man' much to Edward's relief.

Fortunately, everyone was able to put aside these articles of faith and let their hair down when the time came round at the end of the week to retreat back to Doullens. It was, Pilgrim said, like being stood down from the front line again, for a week's respite at the rear. But there was a grim edge of resignation in his comment which made Edward realise that in Pilgrim's head the guns had not yet fallen silent and that after a weekend in the Doullens bars he would return to a personal horror which had not ended with the armistice.

As the year turned and the winter frosts and rains set in, work along their southern section of the front necessarily slowed. Edward was called back to Hesdin HQ partly to be debriefed and partly to help with preparations for its closure as the camp and its drawing office were to move in the coming months to a chateau near St Omer.

The Lieutenant Colonel who was on one of his own flying visits to Hesdin took Edward on one side and suggested in a friendly way that he might need to think about getting hold of a fresh uniform. 'We'll very likely be getting some visits this year especially as the concentrations are coming along so well. You know the sort of thing. But we're still desperately short of men and resources, so we'll need, you know, we'll need to…'

'Impress people?'

'Just so, just so. Scarsbrook's going home on leave very soon. Why not ask him to drop in to your tailor and pick something up?'

Edward said he would. But he privately had no intention of asking Lieutenant Scarsbrook to drop into Savile Row for him. Three months negotiating the mouldering plank roads and collapsing communications trenches either side of the Albert Road had cured him of his physical need for the uniform. He had very soon swopped his cavalry boots and breeches for scrounged fatigues and wellingtons, dressing practically, like the gardeners. Remembering what Captain Baker had told him at his interview about the army needing to put people in their right compartments, he still wore his General Service cap in case any officers came by to inspect the army reburial parties, which they did from time to time. Maurice Burnell had quietly shed his French air corps uniform too, apart from the sheepskin flying helmet and the goggles, which stood him in better stead in the Vauxhall than Edward's service cap. He had somehow managed to put together for himself a collection of clothing which still gave him a military rather than a civilian look. If you examined it closely it was a mixture of British and French tunics and trousers with any insignia carefully removed. They had both kept their greatcoats against the weather, but here again Burnell had carefully removed his insignia.

The Colonel's mentioning the state of his uniform, however, made Edward aware of how much his mind was changing about his need to wear one at all. He wondered if in truth he had been forced to feel a fraud when he had been prevented from being in uniform but that now he was able to wear one, he really *was* a fraud. Where had it gone, that compulsion he had had? Perhaps the armistice, the cessation of hostilities, the emptiness and silence that remained were leaving him exposed for what he was – just a fraud. The uniforms he saw now were mostly on dead men; some rotting fragments of cloth, but some, like the men who were wearing them, were still remarkably intact. The more he saw of them the less he felt like wearing his own.

He tackled Scarsbrook in the drawing office which was gradually being packed up. 'D'you mind telling me where you had your uniform made, Scarsie? The old man thinks I'm looking a bit of a scruff.'

'Not like yours in Savile Row, Dereham, that's for sure. I got it ready-made, I'm afraid – Marshall and Snelgrove's.'

'Would you get me one when you're on leave? We're much of a size wouldn't you think? Would ten guineas cover it for now?'

'Five I should think. But why don't you telegraph your tailor and I'll pick one up for you?'

Without thinking Edward said he would prefer not to look so ostentatious and then made matters worse by apologising.

Maurice Burnell, who by now was inseparable from Edward, had accompanied him back to Hesdin. He claimed that he preferred to spend a few days at *La Vie Est Belle* to enjoy some of Madame Corinne's black market offerings from the kitchen, rather than stay on his own in Doullens waiting for Edward's return. 'We'll have to settle up with *Madame,* in any case to make sure of the beds for next time – clean sheets remember!'

It occurred to Edward that Burnell's true motive in accompanying him back to Hesdin might be to put in a claim for his daily local recruitment payment from the paymaster. But he had never mentioned being put on the payroll – indeed he had seemed very reluctant to countenance the idea when they had first met and Edward had not pursued the Colonel's suggestion at the time. Now of course three months later a daily local allowance would have mounted up. Might not Burnell think it would be worth having after all? Edward had never questioned where his companion's money was coming from. Naturally Maurice never mentioned money; a gentleman – and Edward thought him as much a gentleman as himself – would not unless he found himself in difficulty when it came to paying his share. But he never lacked for cash to pay his bills in Doullens or out at Auchonvillers, which, given the need to service the struggling local French economy there, might be considered a little eye-watering at times. Edward didn't mind, of course. For his own part he regarded that kind of disbursal of Herbert Grace's funds as paying his dues. But all the same, he wondered about Maurice Burnell.

Thus, with some nervousness, he had raised the matter in the Vauxhall on the way to Hesdin. As they began to leave the war-torn areas behind them and retraced their way through the relatively untroubled farmlands of the Canche valley, his reticence in enquiring about Maurice's future plans began to seep away.

'I never did anything about putting you on the payroll, Maurice, in the end.'

'I didn't suppose you had.'

'I thought you were going to move on – you know – Paris, England, home…'

'Are you trying to get rid of me, then?'

'No, it isn't that.'

'The Directorate then? Am I too…too informal for them?'

'Not that I know of.'

Maybe there were regulations about civilians wandering over the former battlefields: Edward didn't know; moreover he didn't care; the place was making him mentally anarchic. A few months ago that sort of thing would have bothered his solicitor's mind, but not now. He had been working long enough now, trying to glimpse some future order in the cemeteries – sacred gardens in a violated landscape which rules had otherwise forsaken; landscape as far removed from the idea of countryside, as mud banks and treacherous quicksands would be when revealed only once in a generation by the pull of a blue moon.

So no. No-one questioned where Maurice Burnell fitted in or whose responsibility he was, with his imprecise military appearance and his official-looking photographic apparatus. Should a British military inspection group turn up at one of the emerging cemeteries Maurice would address them only in French if spoken to. With his camera and plates they generally assumed he was something to do with the French Emergency Works Service overseeing the task of surveying and clearing the battlefields to return them to their former agricultural use.

Etiquette or not, Edward felt a measure of guilty responsibility for Maurice's finances. He returned to the subject again that evening as they sat over a bottle of Madame Corinne's pre-war raspberry *eau de vie* for which Maurice had handed over a sizeable wad of francs without batting an eyelid.

'You're…you're still all right for cash then, Maurice?'

'Still got the money you gave me for the Studebaker, haven't I? It *was* your money wasn't it?'

'That was pounds sterling, Maurice. But we're spending francs in the main, aren't we? I'm being paid by the Directorate, but you aren't.'

Burnell held his glass in front of his face, turning it as if trying to focus on Edward on the other side of the table: he was a trifle inebriated – they both were. 'I'll tell you what. I'll tell you where my money comes from if you tell me where yours comes from first.'

'You know where. I've told you. I inherited it...'

'From your mother...yes. But where did she get it from? I can tell you're not used to money. Makes you really uncomfortable. And the two cars you've given the people here. They weren't hers. You can't even drive. Come on Edward,' – he reached forward and topped up his friend's glass – 'spill the beans.'

Suddenly, perhaps it was not only the *eau de vie*, Edward wanted to tell him, to disgorge the hard stone that had been stuck in his chest for months and months. For the first time since the shadow of Herbert Grace's money had descended on him he was faced with someone – maybe even a friend now – who did not have a part in its history, someone who had no need to be lied to; or protected from it. And a vision of Louise Bolden filled his head, adding to his intoxication, making him all the more desperate to let Burnell be the one to unbolt his prison door, so that she might be part of his release. He drained his refilled glass, cleared his throat and started to speak.

When he came to an end he had left out nothing of any significance. 'Your turn now Maurice.'

'Oh yes! Mmm. I liberated mine.'

'Pinched it, do you mean?' Why wasn't Edward surprised?

'Well it was in the Studebaker.'

'Which you liberated from the Americans. I thought you said it had been abandoned by them. Surely they didn't just leave it with money in it? Quite a lot judging by the way you've been getting through it.'

'I didn't know that until later. They were in a bar. I took it on the off-chance.'

'In a bar. Leaving a car full of money outside.'

'Yes. Criminal isn't it?'

'How much?'

'About twenty thousand.'

'Good God! That's over a thousand pounds.'

'Don't sound so outraged. It's a drop in the ocean compared with yours!'

Edward wanted to say that was different, but he knew it was not. He may not have been the one to steal Herbert Grace's fortune, but he had accepted it knowing its illegitimate provenance and made it his own. Oh yes, he had persuaded himself that the money could not have been returned to its rightful owners, or that he was disbursing a deal of it on philanthropic gestures. But even those were acts mostly designed to smooth his path into a uniform he no longer needed and a war that was supposed to be over. His riches had placed him in the company of the dead and the survivors, yet he was neither one nor the other: they were free to declare it was they, the living and the dead, who were victorious; not death; not the grave. All that he could do was to see to the plots which would eventually stand for the world's unending conflicts.

Burnell cleared his throat in a questioning way, bringing Edward back to earth. 'What am I supposed to say to that, Maurice? That we're both thieves? There – I've said it. But I did rather have mine thrust upon me nevertheless.'

'So did I – I only took the car. The money was incidental. And in any case the Studebaker is being put to good use by our lot, isn't it? I bet the Americans would have sold it off to some fishmonger on the dockside at Dieppe by now. They're not taking anything home but themselves.'

'Their dead. They're taking their dead home with them.'

'So why aren't we, then?'

Edward wasn't sure he knew the answer to this. 'Politics, I suppose. Some people would be able to afford to bring their sons home, but many could not, could they? I don't know – something to do with unity in death regardless of rank or station. I mean we're not burying the officers separately are we? They died together and now they'll lie together. Our cemeteries are mostly close to where they all died. We bring in the isolated ones, I know

– but hardly more than a mile or two. Look at those who were brought in from Mailly-Maillet Wood to Auchonvillers last week – barely two miles, would you say? But some of them were in bits, weren't they. It wouldn't be right to send them home to Suffolk or Cambridge or wherever they were from, for their mothers to deal with. Can you imagine it? Thousands of them. A week on the boat, on the train, and summer coming. Waiting around in sidings. And then what would you do about those bodies we can't put a name to? They'd all have to go somewhere.'

'Yes, you're probably right. They'd have to be in closed coffins, but families would want to see them and there'd be hell to pay if they couldn't. Mind you they won't be able to see them here either, will they?'

Edward had seen the plans being drawn up at Hesdin. 'When it's finished they'll look as if they're all still on parade. Rank on rank. For those that do come it will be a bit like going to the boy's passing out. We might even pay for visits, if they can't afford it, who knows?' Edward paused as a thought crossed his mind.

It must have crossed Maurice's too. 'There you are – something else to do with your ill-gotten gains.'

'Yes, well, when it comes to ill-gotten gains, I'm no longer surprised that you are prolonging your stay here with half the American army looking for its mess funds or payroll or whatever it is you've run off with. I cannot believe they were just in a bar leaving it unattended. Someone must have been for it when they came out and found it gone.'

It occurred to Edward that once again Burnell had managed to extract far more information from him than he had from Burnell. As much as their friendship appeared to be deepening so too did the aviator's mystery. He had volunteered nothing to Edward about his past before the moment they had met on the railway level crossing, other than his mother in England was French. In the time since then he had divested himself of his incriminating motor car and, little by little, of his identifying uniform; and whenever they were in habitation, as now, Maurice always found them digs away from the barracks and regular company – although Edward had no problem with that, even if there was an ulterior motive.

He stood up a little unsteadily. The raspberry liqueur had sharpened his curiosity and blunted his natural reticence. 'Another one before turning in, Maurice?'

Burnell nodded his assent. 'Cognac. Had enough of this pop.'

Edward helped himself to a bottle from behind the bar – Madame Corinne had already gone to bed herself and was sufficiently sure of the depth of both her lodgers' pockets to sleep peacefully above. Edward smiled nevertheless as he poured two glasses. 'She wouldn't be half so trusting with the brandy if she knew what a couple of crooks she had in the bar. Are you a crook, Maurice? I mean generally a crook. Not just the francs in the Studebaker. I mean, don't get me wrong. I make no judgements. I'm just curious. That ghastly wasteland we are spending our lives in at the moment, the remnants of human beings it is grudgingly offering up from one grave over there, only for us to put in another one over here, none of it fits with the old morality, our old right and wrong. We sit here, you and I, in the relative comfort of *La Vie Est Belle*, and tomorrow we will cross a line somewhere and the world will be transformed again, just like that, back to the wasteland. It has no shape, no dimension. Out there where the plank boards end. The shattered stumps of trees – what's it called?'

'Like Mailly Wood, you mean?'

'Yes Maurice, Mailly Wood for God's sake! How can any morality, anything we live by, anything we try and put a meaning to, make any sense at all when we call those pitiful stumps a wood. Pitiful stumps, just like we have done to ourselves!'

'It didn't seem like that when it was all under fire. Certainly not at first. Communication trenches, full of men going up the line, coming back from the line. Horses and men heaving the artillery pieces into position. It seemed full of purpose then – and noise.'

Edward pursed his lips thoughtfully. 'Perhaps that's it. Now there's just silence. Not even birds singing. Have you noticed how many of us whisper when we are out there, in no-man's land? It's as if our ability to make the ordinary sounds of life has been eradicated by what's been done. As if, when peace came and they all started to go home, a gigantic soundproof door closed behind them. And I came too late to go home with them, like that. And too late to stay behind.'

They both stared silently into their glasses of brandy. After a few moments Burnell spoke. 'I remember once, when we were flying on a recce a bit to the north of here. Over our lines – the French lines. I was in the rear cockpit taking pictures – I had the camera mounted on one side of the fuselage and the gun on the other side. My pilot made a wide turn to come back over our front line – and the engine cut out. Not an infrequent occurrence. We had reasonable height and were able to glide while the pilot tried to restart – no immediate panic, although I prayed we wouldn't meet a Boche plane – we hadn't done so far. But I remember a moment of serene silence. I couldn't recall anything quite like it before – and it was so wonderfully extraordinary in the midst of everything going on below. But for those few moments all the guns for a distance either side were quiet – and a skylark started to sing above us as we descended, as if he had been waiting to seize the moment to remind us that the sky and everything below it still belonged to him. Then our engine cut back in and guns started up again. I wonder if that bird went on with his song, how long before he was driven away for good?'

Shortly after, they both decided to call time. As he was going up the stairs Edward wondered if Maurice had really heard the skylark or had he all the time been avoiding to Edward's pointed question about a criminal past. As usual he was none the wiser.

## 13

ALTHOUGH Christmas leave was not actually stopped that first year of the armistice, very few of the Directorate staff and gardeners, or the men of the burial parties, chose to go home. Their grim work did not have any less urgency because it was the season of goodwill; on the contrary, it seemed to increase it, as if those dead waiting to be reclaimed were demanding still to be home by Christmas as they had once been promised. In any case Edward could see no point in making a difficult journey simply to spend a brief time alone in Lower Sunbury, and after his last awkward visit he dismissed the idea of inviting himself to Caroline Crescent. Maurice simply didn't acknowledge the approach of Christmas, other than to say, 'Is it?' once when it was mentioned.

So Christmas and New Year came and went with bit of a shindig round the piano in Doullens and a black market *coq au vin* at their *estaminet* in Auchonvillers, made with a bottle of the Mailly Chateau vintage Bordeaux. Maurice grumbled that it had probably cost more than dinner at the Ritz in Paris.

As the spring of 1919 began to turn to summer, Edward and his constant companion found themselves moving to cemetery sites in a more northerly direction from the sector base at Doullens. When not having to share canvas or ruined dugouts with Private Pilgrim's gardening party, either because of the remoteness of the day's location, or the dire effect even half a day's rain would have on the churned up roadways, they had managed to exchange the limited comfort of the *estaminet* at Auchonvillers for what seemed to be a more promising nightly billet, a bar café on the road to Vimy, in the now partly ruined village of Souchez and conveniently close to the cemetery named after another café, now destroyed, *Cabaret Rouge*. The proprietor of the bar in Auchonvillers was crestfallen when they announced they would be moving on: their generous custom had enabled him to make great strides with several buildings in which he had an interest and to set himself up as the *de facto* mayor in the absence of an election or indeed a significant populace to vote one way or the other. In addition to his own private enterprise being financed by Edward and Maurice he had managed to get the French departmental authority to allocate him some German prisoners of war to set about clearing what had once been the surrounding farmland of shells. Much of this ordnance was still live and consequently took some toll of the workforce.

Although destroyed by shell fire and no longer open for business, the *Cabaret Rouge* had survived in name only because it had been an assembly point for the communications trenches up to the Lorette and Vimy sector front line. These had not been overrun by any German advances, lying as they did below the redoubt at Colline de Lorette, which the French had never given up. As the location had been designated the site of a principal cemetery, reburials from isolated outlying graves were being brought there, and to the nearby British cemetery below Vimy Ridge, although Edward understood the Canadians were to have the main ground there. So, much of his identification work meant that he did not have to move very far from the billet. It also suited Private Pilgrim who was also able supply his gardeners camping further afield, and bring the Albion back to Souchez some evenings, so avoiding having to sleep out himself.

One morning Edward was in the cemetery hut reviewing his records from the previous day's re-interments two of which had been unidentified bodies. He heard Pilgrim struggling to start his lorry and went out to catch him before he left for the day.

'What happened to the two unidentified yesterday? Have they already been reburied?'

Pilgrim stood upright from the starting handle. 'Not yet, Sir. They're in together still.'

Edward knew what this meant: still under fire, perhaps fearing an imminent counter-attack, their comrades would have hastily buried two bodies together, probably because neither of them was then distinguishable from the other. Indeed sometimes the gardeners would find some remnants of several others in what had first been thought a battlefield grave for one or two. At first these, what he could only think of as collections of unknown soldiers, had been immensely troubling to him. It was not because he was particularly squeamish about checking over the pieces to ensure that no clues as to the number of bodies and their identities had been overlooked by the exhumers, unpleasant as the task was. It was more the pictures they created of how the end had come. Some, he could imagine, had died instantly only to lie shattered beside their more complete comrades for whom death had only come later to remove their pain. These grotesque foetal groups more than anything taught him that this was not the experience he had so recently longed for and been prevented from joining, even when he had seen the wounded arriving in London and had still managed to persuade himself he could imagine being part of that. What he saw and visualised here in front of him now was nothing he could have dreamt of then, and so the fate of these young men had redoubled his sense of being an outsider.

He had confessed these feelings to Maurice, who had probed him about his melancholia, and was increasingly putting himself in the priestly role.

'My God! You must banish these demons, Edward, before it's too late or they'll take up permanent residence. I've known some men driven mad by the noise, others by what they have seen. If they were lucky and had an enlightened medic, they'd be given some understanding and respite. But the ones who often suffered the most and sank deeper and deeper into the mire were men who could not come to terms with the horrors in their own imaginations, couldn't get rid of the idea. They would often be dismissed as cowards, which they weren't, any more than you are.'

Edward heard what he said and he knew a little about what was being called psychiatry by people like Dr Carradine. He asked Maurice what he should do when confronted with one of these troubling groups of remains.

'Simple. Call them Brothers-in-Arms.'

It had probably saved his sanity for the time being.

There was another temporary shelter for bodies brought in too late in the day for immediate reburial or because the plots the gardeners had prepared were not immediately useable, perhaps too full of rainwater. There Edward found the remains of the two which had been brought in the previous day just before nightfall. One was recognisable as a young man, a corporal from his still visible stripes, although he had been in the ground for over a year according to the record of his name, regiment and date of death, provided by his first burial party on that occasion. The other set of remains, which the latest burial party had not yet separated, had also been recorded as those of a private in the same regiment, the London Regiment. These remains were not a complete body, so not as easily identifiable. Edward called out to Pilgrim who still had not left.

'Did you speak to the burial party that brought these two in last night?'

Pilgrim came to the hut entrance. 'I spoke to the padre, Sir. He said they would be back later today for the reburial. He'll get his men to finish separating them, Sir, if you don't feel up to it. I know it's not our job, properly. Smithy, our gardener has marked out the next row, where they're to go – over there. If you wouldn't mind telling him. You'll be here on your own for today, if you remember, Sir? I'm taking Smithy with me when I can get this wretched vehicle to go.' He pointed across to a new line neatly pegged out in front of an existing row of plots already filled and marked with their wooden crosses. The gardener had made a start planting these with calendula marigolds, their vivid orange shouting out at the wild cornflowers and even at the scarlet poppies which had already sprung up unbidden, their seeds having lain dormant beneath the churned soil, perhaps since the first years of the war. The waiting crosses for this new row were stacked together at one end against a boundary fence post.

'Did the chaplain say anything about this one – the private, London Regiment?'

'No Sir. Only the usual, you know – he's all bits and pieces, poor sod. They're both together, but they'll separate them now. Why? Do you think they've got them mixed up? It happens.'

Edward wasn't sure. Something about the remains of the private was puzzling although he couldn't put his finger on why. His copy of the burial record from London seemed clear enough, London Regiment, 1/18th Battalion. He heard Pilgrim give the Albion an almighty swing and it sprang into life. 'First brigade eighteenth battalion, Pilgrim? Any idea?' he shouted above the engine racket.

Pilgrim heaved himself up into the cab. 'One of the London lot – London Irish Rifles, sounds like. I know they were at Eaucourt L'Abbaye for a while, back end of '16. But that's a fair way south of here. But that doesn't necessarily signify. They were probably here in reserve some time waiting to move up. Where was the burial party yesterday?'

A small hand seemed to clutch at Edward's stomach: there was that regiment again, following him around – or was he following them?

'Shouldn't they have gone to the cemetery at Vimy then, rather than here?'

Pilgrim shrugged. 'Depends, Sir. They might have been at this end of the Lorette line so the burial party would have been heading back in this direction as it was getting late.' He let out the clutch and the Albion was on its way.

171

The army chaplain in charge turned up with his burial party shortly afterwards. He confirmed that the two bodies had been found in a single grave on the Lorette line. There were several more which the burial party would be disinterring next and bringing in to the *Cabaret Rouge* cemetery. He asked if Edward had any objection to the choice of cemetery, but as two were already brought in, it made sense to put all the little group together rather than split them up. Edward asked him if he had been happy with the identifications, to which he said he had although the second body in the grave had been in a mess.

'Would you mind having another look with me, Padre? Something doesn't feel quite right.'

One of the army burial party was detailed to undertake the gentle separation of the second body remains from his more complete companion, while Edward and the chaplain watchfully supervised. As far as the identity of this body was concerned, all Edward had to go on was the copy of the record that had been sent through to the Graves Registration Unit, as it was, back in September 1916. Neither soldier had been found with an identity disk. The corporal had been identified by his stripes and regimental insignia at the time – and quite possibly by the fact that he had been buried by comrades who knew him.

What remained of the other body had no distinguishing marks evident other than regimental insignia and an absence of rank markings, indicating he must have been a private. He had no head or face so it would have been very difficult in the immediate post-battle circumstances to give him a name. The soldier with the chaplain was clearly well-used to the delicate and sickening task of separating the dead from one another: Maurice Burnell's description of them as 'brothers-in-arms' had not been far wrong. He slipped a strip of tarpaulin between them and underneath the corporal's body so that the three of them could lift him into the canvas sheeting they had laid out for him. This act of lifting caused the remains of the private left behind to move slightly. Part of one of his arms rolled to one side and revealed some small pieces that, they all could see, did not belong. The army grave-digger voiced insensitively what all three of them were thinking.

'If them's what I think they are, this poor bugger shouldn't 'ave three!'

They were evidently looking at the vestiges of a third body. Further careful exploration turned up a scrap of uniform and a single crown.

'So,' said Edward, 'does this mean this man was an officer and not a private? Or does the crown belong to the third man?'

The grave-digger was well-used to solving little mysteries of this kind, however. He pointed out that the predominant uniform material on the pieces they had was that of a private, which accorded with the record of his burial. The crown indicated an officer, but there was little, if nothing, else to elaborate on this.

'Three bodies then – not two,' said the chaplain. 'You'd better put one down as an unknown officer. We can't even be sure what regiment. Not enough to go on. Although one might assume the same as the other two given the…er…close proximity.'

But Edward was reluctant to accept that the possible third body had necessarily died on the same day in the same action. The ground had been fought over on more than one occasion; much of it had suffered repeated bombardment. Such a small piece of evidence they had unearthed was not nearly sufficient to make any assumptions. An image came to him, as it often did now, of a grieving mother eventually visiting the cemetery and finding nothing to relieve the constant nagging pain of not knowing. This small fragment of a young man's body would in time be consigned to a grave to itself with the common epitaph they would give to yet another unknown soldier of the war.

'Did you say there were several others to bring in from the same area today, Padre?'

'That's right.'

'I'll come with you, then. We can have a check around to see if there's…any more of him, before we mark him unknown.'

The chaplain was surprised but had no desire to stand in Edward's way. 'By all means, Dereham. By all means. Very difficult terrain though, you know.' Edward did know. But something was pushing him to go, or perhaps pulling him there.

There wasn't room for them all in the burial party's vehicle with Edward too: it would have meant one of the soldiers bicycling as far as the road would take them, and that would probably have taken him all morning. Edward went to look for Maurice and found him in the improvised dark room he amazingly managed to set up whenever they stayed long enough in one place to make it worthwhile. This one was in the outside privy at the café which, given the ravaged state of what had once been its garden, was not much used anyway. Edward knocked on the door and Maurice told him to hang on for five more minutes for the plates.

'I'm taking the Vauxhall out to the Lorette lines – or as near as we can get. Want to come?'

'Go and fill her up. She might need some petrol if we are going any distance. I'll bring the apparatus. Might get some good shots.'

Their way took them lurching painfully along what had once been the Arras to Bapaume road – and still was in parts – until they reached the remains of a plank road leading to the Lorette support trenches. This was clearly as far as vehicles could go because the burial party had already abandoned theirs at this point. They followed suit; Maurice went to unload his camera and tripod, but taking a look at the churned terrain that lay before them thought better of it, muttering that he would come back for his stuff if there was anything worth photographing.

The two of them set off along the shattered plank road, but this soon gave out and they were forced to descend into the crumbling remains of the communication trench. Picking their way with difficulty over the fallen sand bag reinforcements and ducking under broken wooden props they eventually caught sight of the burial party above them and clambered out. 'Over the top!' said Maurice to himself as he heaved himself up from the firing step and then cursed as his hand encountered a strand of rusting barbed wire.

The chaplain a few yards away heard him. 'Mind the wire,' he called a little unnecessarily. 'This is the spot where we finished yesterday for the night. You see…it's to the rear of the communication trench and perhaps twenty or thirty yards from where the front trench starts at right angles. Another three graves according to the record. That's right isn't it?'

Edward looked at his copy of the GRU record, but he was uncertain having rather lost his bearings after struggling through the trench system below ground level. 'These d'you mean, Padre?'

The chaplain peered over his shoulder. 'No – over the page. These four here. One we've done and three more.'

Edward asked to see where the double grave had been from the day before. It wasn't very deep.

'None of them are very deep. They were probably in a hurry. Expecting that they would be shelled again pretty soon and destroyed, shouldn't wonder,' said the chaplain. 'They're all on the edge of a largish shell crater as it is, although I couldn't say which was here first – crater or graves. Quite possibly the graves, since there's no record of others in this place.'

Edward didn't voice the question he had constantly asked himself. He had pretty soon stopped wondering why soldiers had taken precious time and trouble to bury their dead comrades, especially as their efforts would often be rewarded by these temporary resting places being blown to kingdom come sooner or later. Yes, they were under orders to bury their dead: but it was more than simply that. It was what his colleague Scarsbrook had called them – acts of contrition, penance for the sins they had committed and had been committed on them. While the army, the politicians, even the church had collectively absolved them in the name of king and country, families and their children, this personal labour by one living man for a dead one was perhaps the nearest he would come to forgiveness. Perhaps, too, in the same way, the laying out of the cemeteries was a huge collective plea for forgiveness. Edward wondered. So simply by being here, being part of it, was he also one of the forgiven? And forgiven for what? Because assuredly something was telling him every day he spent alive in this country of the dead, that some of it must be his fault.

'Can you dig down a bit?' he asked, indicating the grave they burial party had already exhumed. The senior NCO glanced questioningly at the chaplain. They clearly thought they had enough work to do.

'Yes, do as Lieutenant Dereham says, Corporal, there's a good fellow,' said the chaplain. The corporal seemed surprised to hear that this man in overalls, gumboots and filthy cap was in fact an officer at all. It was evidently news to him. He detailed the other two men to start what they obviously regarded as wasted effort. By the time Edward was beginning to agree with them, the gravediggers were standing more than waist deep. What had previously been a fairly shallow grave was, too late for its purpose, in danger of becoming a decent size. Maurice was standing on the side of it opposite Edward and the chaplain. He leant forward to peer in and in so doing a sizeable piece of the grave's rim gave way under his feet pitching him into the excavation on top of the two diggers. When they had finished cursing and dusting themselves down, the collapse revealed what on inspection were revealed as more remains of a body, although by the look of them not one that had been properly buried.

'What do you think?' Edward asked.

'Me, Sir?' said the Corporal, thinking he was being addressed. 'I think this one copped it from the shell that fell here afterwards. Not directly though. He looks more or less all there to me. Could have been blown sideways, mebbe.'

'Stray shell, Sir,' one of the other two soldiers volunteered, sounding anxious to make up for any offence he might previously have given this man who had turned out to be an officer. 'Otherwise these others would have been blown up as well.'

An air of respect returned to the burial party as they realised their labour had borne fruit after all. Very gently they cleaned round what could be seen of the corpse. It was difficult to say how long it might have been in the ground, although the young man they were gradually revealing had been thankfully well-preserved in the wet clay. After a while they were able to lift him clear of the collapse and lay him on canvas sheeting on the surface. One sleeve of his tunic with a length of the arm and most of its hand were missing.

'That accounts for the lieutenant's pip we found with the others,' said the chaplain. 'And the...er...other bits. I'll just say a few words as they won't have been said at the time...before we move him again.'

They all stood with heads bowed for a moment and then the burial party lifted him on the canvas sheeting onto their stretcher. The corporal wiped the clay from the other sleeve 'London Regiment. Like the others.'

Edward asked if they would look for an identity disk. He was conscious of the fact that the body wasn't yet technically his responsibility.

'Not as far as I can see, Sir. The others didn't have them either did they? No wait a minute...it's underneath. Gone round the back of his neck.'

'Leave it for now,' said the chaplain hastily. 'There's been enough disturbance already. We can look when he's reburied. Mark his position as the same as the other two.'

While the burial party moved on to begin the remaining exhumations, two of them were told by the corporal to carry the stretcher back through the trenches to their vehicle. On an impulse Edward said that he and Maurice would take it so that the two soldiers could stay where they were more needed.

Carrying the stretcher was extremely slow and arduous. Maurice grumbled most of the way until the effort reduced him to silence. It took them about half an hour to cover a distance of about a hundred yards as a crow would have flown if there had been any, but which seemed considerably further as they followed the switchback line of the communications trench, frequently having to clamber out over the fallen parapets when the stretcher could not be negotiated round a partially blocked corner if it was not to shed its precious load. When they reached the plank road again, their progress speeded up and Maurice resumed his grumbling. 'It's a good job I didn't bring the apparatus, although it would have been easier than this. This is no work for officers, Edward.'

'Are you an officer then, Maurice? I thought I was the only one here.' Burnell grimaced but made no comment.

As they were depositing the stretcher on the back of the army vehicle it occurred to Edward that the burial party might have further need of it: nothing had been said; he could not remember whether they had other stretchers with them out there. He shared his thought with Maurice, who was not at all happy at the prospect of making the journey again.

'I'll go,' said Edward. 'It was my idea to bring him back. You wait here and take some pictures. We'll have to lift him off between us though.'

'Poor devil!' said Maurice. 'There he was…resting in peace and he's been on the go all day.'

'Not funny, Maurice!'

'Wasn't meant to be funny. But you have to ask yourself, don't you?'

'He's got a mother, a wife, a sweetheart at least. Someone who needs to know.'

'Only if you can find out who he is.'

'I thought you were here out of some kind of finer feelings – there being no peace for those left grieving for those not found, and all that. Or are you just here hiding, after all?'

'Well that would make two of us, wouldn't it?'

Their words grew angry and their raised voices echoed across the empty waste of no-man's land which they had just left.

When Edward had eventually made his way back to the vehicles he was filthy and exhausted, but nevertheless elated. He forgot the altercation with Maurice. 'There you are, see. At least I can say I was a stretcher bearer on the western front.'

Maurice too was happy to get things back on an even keel. 'I'll give you my *Croix de Guerre* – it's in my pocket somewhere.' And taking Edward entirely unawares he clasped him by both arms pinning them to his sides and embraced him three times on both cheeks, French style. '*Voilà, mon ami*! Consider yourself well and truly invested.'

Edward was speechless with embarrassment; he even looked round furtively to see if anyone from the burial party might have seen their antics, despite that being impossible with several hundred yards of shell craters between them. But not wishing it to appear he couldn't take it in good part, particularly when he had started it with his stretcher bearer joke, he straightened his cap, stepped smartly back two paces and executed one of his best salutes to date. Then they both laughed: something they never did out here, yet somehow it didn't seem to Edward as sacrilegious as he might have expected, amid the desecration and with a young man's corpse on the army lorry a few yards away, his face turned away from them.

Maurice must have shared Edward's thought too at the sound of their laughter because they both glanced across to the body lying on its canvas sheeting at the same moment. 'I shouldn't worry about Second Lieutenant Bolden, Edward...'

For a moment Edward did not register what Maurice had said. It was as if a name, any name had simply been hanging in the air waiting to be used. But then the name took shape, became flesh. He stopped laughing. 'Why did you call him that?'

'Because that's who he is – Second Lieutenant C. Bolden. I managed to extricate his identity tag while you were returning the stretcher – I say, are you feeling all right? You look as though you could do to sit down – been a strenuous day so far.'

Edward did feel suddenly exhausted; light headed. He sat down on the running step of the Vauxhall and rested his head in his hands with his elbows on his knees. Maurice rummaged in the boot. 'There's cold coffee and a flask of brandy – I should have both if I were you. I'm going to. And here's some hard tack. We've had nothing since what passed for breakfast this morning.'

Edward accepted the drink and the biscuit and for a while they both munched in silence. Then Edward said: 'I know him.'

'You do?'

'Well his mother. She's the lady I think I may have mentioned – in Hove.'

'The one who's…involved with your uncle?'

Edward felt his conscience prick him. He'd said quite a lot to Maurice hadn't he? As he sat there with the remains of her son only a few yards away he regretted having mentioned Louise to him at all. Even though he had been spare with the details Maurice had clearly put two and two together regarding the precise nature of her connection with Herbert Grace.

'His name is Cornelius. He was posted missing.'

Maurice did not immediately reply. He must have guessed at the causes of the change from laughter to silence and was sensitive enough to the need for tact. But Maurice being Maurice it didn't last; his urge to ask for more as a means of avoiding silences he might have to fill with his own revelations soon reasserted itself.

'So…er…was he your uncle's boy, then?'

Edward needed to make some pretence at propriety, if only to make out Louise had a good name to protect: he owed her that at least in this place where such things had virtually been stripped away. He lifted his head from his hands and looked levelly at Maurice.

'What makes you suppose that?'

'Well, forgive me. I just assumed because you had taken over the old man's responsibilities…'

180

'Perhaps you shouldn't assume. Mrs Bolden is a widow. Cornelius is her late husband's son.'

'I'm sorry, Edward. Forgive me.'

'Bolden was employed by my uncle. He disappeared in America, presumed dead as no word has been heard for more than seven years. He was in some fairly rough and ready places by all accounts. Grace took her under his wing as an act of charity.' Edward felt satisfied at having paraphrased Louise's circumstances in this deft way: none of it was untrue although the lawyer in him knew that it was by no means the whole truth and would not stand up to probing cross-examination. As that side of him rarely put in an appearance out here in no-man's land, having become an irrelevance a while ago, he experienced a feeling of reassurance that the discovery of Cornelius Bolden had served to reconnect him a little, if not to home, at least to Hove. He even felt home-sick for Caroline Crescent, but much more he knew he wanted to be the one to tell Louise he and her son had found one another and to staunch the wound that it would re-open. They were interrupted by the sound of the army grave diggers trudging back, carrying the other bodies they had recovered, on stretchers. Edward announced to the chaplain that they had managed to discover the identity of this one they had unearthed earlier.

'Yes, Padre. And Dereham here knows him, would you believe?' Maurice announced. 'Son of friends of his, posted missing in '17,' he added hastily, to spare Edward another round of questions – he had evidently grasped the sensitivities, even if he did not yet entirely go along with Edward's explanation.

The chaplain went over and looked thoughtfully at Boden's body on the back of the lorry. Edward and Maurice joined him. 'That's remarkable Dereham, isn't it? You were the one who elected to come with us today. Made us look again. The men were about to give up and then your colleague here – I'm sorry, Mister, or is it M'sieur? I don't think I know your name – grateful to you anyway, it was your unexpected dislodgement turned him up. If you were superstitious you'd almost believe we'd been brought here wouldn't you? However I don't hold with superstition – I prefer divine providence. So that being the case, and as we know who he is and moreover can claim some kind of kinship in the absence of his poor family, I propose to say a short prayer more befitting what has been revealed to us. Off caps please, Corporal.'

Edward and Maurice bowed their heads too as the chaplain prayed for Second Lieutenant Cornelius Boden and resurrection and eternal life for them all. Edward, who had begun lately to question the presence of the Almighty in a place He surely could have had no hand in creating, still took comfort from the thought that he would at least be able to tell Louise the Lord had moved in a mysterious way for her son, and she herself might find reason to go once more to confession.

## 14

THE following day Cornelius Boden was buried at *Cabaret Rouge* alongside his fellow men from the London Irish Rifles. Edward and Maurice had an earnest conversation about photographing the grave for his mother; whether or not it should be pictured before it was filled in or after. Maurice said that the Irish were accustomed to having their loved ones' bodies on display before the burial, weren't they? But Edward argued that a body just in a canvas winding sheet at the bottom of a grave was a different thing entirely to one in an open coffin set up in the best parlour. In the end they agreed that a picture of Edward, the chaplain and the burial party at the graveside would be the thing, and another after the grave was filled in, together with its temporary cross. As they were due back at Doullens for the approaching weekend Edward asked the gardener to plant some calendula marigolds and cornflowers all along the row, for the photographs, even though strictly speaking it was not its turn for planting. From Doullens he would be able to telephone the Commission HQ which had now moved to Longuenesse, to ask for leave.

He wondered what Maurice would do with himself if he was given leave to return home. Strictly speaking he was a free agent and could come and go as he pleased. 'We could travel back to England together, if you like. Isn't it about time you went to see your mother and your sister? The war has been over for months now and your sister's not well, is she?'

Maurice was decidedly cagey about this suggestion, Edward thought, but he did not immediately push the matter, knowing that his friend only had conversations like this when it suited him. In any case, Edward reasoned, if he went home on leave shortly Maurice would have to make up his mind what to do soon enough. Not that Edward was entirely convinced that he would be given leave of absence so soon, after all he had been out in France less than a year, and Graves Registration still very stretched.

However, events took an unexpected turn when they both arrived back in Doullens. First there was a message waiting for him from the colonel, now in Longuenesse, instructing him to get himself there by the end of the week. He would be given papers and be briefed for an important meeting in London, 'where your recent experience in the southern sector will be invaluable.'

When Edward had digested this he turned his attention to the other two communications Lieutenant Banks had handed him. The first was a letter from the War Office. It was from Partridge telling him that the military convalescent hospital was vacating Hillcote Grange and everything would be put in order. It had been sent there, dated about a month earlier and had been forwarded several times since then.

The second was a letter from Louise in Hove; its contents filled him with alarm, especially as it was dated some weeks earlier and had clearly also had difficulty running him to earth here in Doullens.

*'You should know,'* Louise wrote, *'I have received a letter from Herbert. His sentence is coming to an end and as his health has deteriorated they are releasing him early on compassionate grounds. What should I do if he comes to Caroline Crescent, Edward? This news should make me happy but I am at a loss and there is Gee to think about.'*

Edward felt numb. His suppressed emotions for Louise resurrected themselves, helpless anger battling with the spectre of having to put himself back in the role of legal adviser both to her and his uncle. It had been one thing to manage the poisonous substance of Grace's wealth and property and preserve Louise's dignity and separateness while he was safely incarcerated in Brixton. Now that the evil was to be let out of its bottle it would be a different matter. He looked again at the letter's date – perhaps he was already out – how long did it take? Wasn't a solicitor meant to know things like that? Standing outside the hut looking out to the desolation which had become his own prison, he ground his teeth when he realised that now Herbert Grace could take him out of one prison in an instant, only to lock him up in another.

He asked the clerk to get him the lieutenant colonel on the telephone at Longuenesse and after what seemed an interminable wait he came on the very bad line. He gave Edward more information about the London meeting which would be at the Commission's office in St James's Square in less than a week's time.

'So you'll need to look slippy. Have you got that new uniform by the way?'

Edward had not seen Scarsbrook since giving him the commission and had not made an effort to do so, a new outfit seeming to be less and less important in no-man's-land. He assumed Scarsbrook would have it with him at Longuenesse if he was there now.

'After the meeting, Colonel, do you think I could stay on for a week or so? There's some urgent family business come up.'

The colonel said grudgingly he could have ten days and no more. 'I'll need to be briefed on the meeting, so we can't have you hanging around, family business or not. You can pick up a leave chitty here at Longuenesse.'

Maurice was washing the Vauxhall in the absence of a more willing pair of hands; he had more or less managed to discard his military status by now. He looked at Edward questioningly.

'How do you feel about driving me up to St Omer tomorrow and then on to Boulogne? I've to be in London before Friday for some kind of top level meeting.'

Maurice hissed through his teeth while he leathered the car, as if he were grooming a horse. 'This old lady is in dire need of an overhaul. We've rather punished her out there in the last few months, y'know. I'm not at all sure we'd get to the coast, if you're in a hurry.'

Edward wondered to himself why Maurice was washing the car now if he knew it needed to go into the workshop. It almost looked as though he was making an excuse not to go. 'Perhaps we could take another one from the motor pool and leave the Vauxhall in exchange.'

The only other vehicle in the workshop which could be ready turned out to be none other than the dubious Studebaker. At the sight of it Maurice looked particularly unhappy. The mechanic was also unhappy about Edward's proposal to swap it for the Vauxhall which he said would need at least three day's work on it, assuming he had parts, and the Studebaker was due out on Monday 'with Mr Skillman'. Mr Skillman was one of the Commission's travelling architects; Edward had encountered him from time to time at some of the cemeteries in the southern sector, working up plans for their final appearance. He was not to be put off. 'I'll have a word with him and see if we cannot work something out.'

They went in search of Skillman, Maurice trailing rather disconsolately behind Edward. 'We cannot pinch his car, y'know Edward. Not if he's due out at the same time. Wouldn't be right.'

'Strictly speaking, Maurice, it's not his car, or the Commission's. It's mine, as you well know.'

'That's as may be. But you're hardly going to explain that to him, now are you? It's much too late in the day.'

'We'll see.'

To Maurice's obviously increasing misery, fate took another hand. They found the architect in his hut, looking extremely sorry for himself and evidently in no fit state to set off on his travels for a bit. He was only too relieved to be told by Edward that he needed to commandeer the Studebaker to get to St Omer on urgent Commission business. 'I'm not going anywhere for now. The MO's dosed me up with something but it hasn't solved anything yet. I had some dodgy rabbit stew at a cemetery near Bray. I was stuck for the night with the gardener. He was living in an old dugout there on his own. To be frank, I'm not sure he was too fussy about what he'd shot for the pot. I'm just hoping it was nothing worse than cat. Yes, you take the Studebaker by all means, Dereham. I'll wait for the Vauxhall. Nice motor. Not sure about these American machines. Now you'll have to excuse me!'

Edward and Maurice took themselves off to the café in Doullens where once again they had taken the precaution of keeping a room and two beds available for the weekends. As a rule Edward was now picking up the bill for the retainer, as he reckoned his funds were at least legal, if not actually moral. Since their mutual exchange of confidences about the origins of their respective monies, Maurice was inclined not to argue so much about the strict division of expenses, although he did comment ruefully on the occasions when he did take his turn that this room in Doullens was probably costing the equivalent of a flat in South Audley Street.

Over a repast of endives in a white sauce containing rumours of cheese, washed down with an on-going bottle of cognac, Edward deliberately behaved as if Maurice could have no difficulties with the planned trip – even though it was entirely obvious he did.

'Look, you can come back to England with me or you can stay in Boulogne or somewhere and wait until I return. We could even get hold of another car in England if you want to go your own way and leave me with the Studebaker – although I should be very sorry to see you go – you're a free agent, after all.'

It was then Maurice Burnell finally took a big step forward in their relationship. 'It's going to be rather difficult for me to get back to England.'

'Why's that?'

'Because I have no discharge papers and a British passport. I'll be stopped at the port by the army and arrested as a deserter.'

'But you fought with the *Aeronautique Militaire* – as you were entitled to do because of your mother being French.'

'Yes, that's true. But I'm afraid I didn't wait to be demobbed when the armistice was announced.'

Edward waited. Maurice paused, took his cigarette case out of his pocket and lit a fag from the candle on the table. He tipped back on his chair and taking a deep drag, slowly exhaled it up to the ceiling out of the corner of his mouth. He offered one to Edward although he knew by now he didn't smoke. 'I left England in rather a hurry on the eve of the war. I'd ended up owing some interesting people rather a large sum of money for some goods I was unable to deliver. Not my fault entirely. But these were men you don't default on. Just to be on the safe side when I joined up I used my mother's maiden name and a birth certificate I obtained with the help of a man she knew over here.'

'Forged you mean?'

'Not as such. The certificate is actually genuine – a replacements for one I'd supposedly lost. My mother's friend knew that some personal records for a couple of years in the 1890s had been destroyed in a small fire in one of the northern department's prefectures. It fitted with my age give or take a couple of years, so there were very few questions asked.'

'That was handy – your mother's friend having that kind of information, I mean.'

'Not really surprising. He was in fire insurance so he had access to records of fire claims and so forth all over France.'

'But fancy her knowing that.' Edward, the lawyer, was intrigued by level of coincidence: it smacked of being more than met the eye; shady dealings. For some reason it came into his head that it was the kind of inside information Herbert Grace would have had access to.

'My mother knows all sorts,' said Maurice. 'That's why I wrote and asked her for help. In her younger days she was in one of the grand Parisian salons – not *that* kind of salon, I should say. It was mainly eating and gaming. She's a wonderful cook as well as being able to cut cards and spin the wheel. After the siege of Paris by the Prussians she ended up in one of the big casinos along the coast here.'[1]

'Where?'

'Not sure – might have been Boulogne or Le Touquet, one of those. Anyway, she would have known the insurance man there or in Paris. He was somebody important, a director not a twopence-a-week collector.'

This was more than Maurice Burnell had disclosed in the whole of their acquaintance so far; it must have cost him a great deal to divulge this much and Edward did not want to staunch the flow by asking too many questions or the wrong ones.

'I still fail to see why the British would be able to arrest you as a deserter if you have French citizenship.'

Maurice gave an exasperated snort. 'If I have no discharge papers I cannot prove my military status nor my right to leave France. And if I use my British passport they will also want to know where I have been and what I have been doing. I'll almost certainly be on a list of British deserters because they came looking for me at my mother's in Billericay. She just sent them away with a flea in their ear. Anyway I'd already signed up with the French army by then so I had no desire to reveal my English identity. Besides, I'd told them about my knowledge of cameras and photography so they transferred me into the *Aeronautique* almost immediately. Balloons at first.' He took another long drag on his cigarette before dogging it in the tin lid that served as an ash tray, and said thoughtfully, 'My mother knew a thing or two about balloons from her time in the siege. Bloody things. Sitting ducks.'

Edward could see by now that there was going to be no way he would persuade him to attempt a crossing to England. He gave voice to his frustration. 'I cannot fathom for the life of me

---
[1] See *The Middle Room*

why you bunked off without waiting for demob. It was surely only a going to be a matter of days or weeks, wasn't it?' Then a thought struck him. 'Or had you been AWOL for some time before our paths crossed – is that it?' It was one question too many; Maurice just shrugged and poured another brandy.

The atmosphere in the morning was strained, although they hadn't exactly fallen out the night before. But the evening had relapsed into the kind of silence neither person knows how to break comfortably. After breakfasting alone Edward packed his things for the journey, and with a sinking feeling set off to locate the Studebaker. He half hoped he might find a driver at the motor pool whom he could order to take him to St Omer. Despite his uncertainty about the likely pitfalls on the journey he had put on his full, shabby uniform, not wishing to arrive in front of the lieutenant colonel in overalls and wellingtons; he still hoped Scarsbrook would have come up trumps with one to replace it. However, even thus attired he felt he could if necessary issue a command. But, inevitably, there was no-one he could reasonably take away from their duties, so with a heavy heart he set about cranking the Studebaker. Much to his relief it burst into life at only the third swing. He stowed the handle, climbed in and letting out the clutch moved out cautiously onto the roadway. His way led him back the way he had come. As he passed the bar Maurice appeared at the door, carrying his own valise. He had evidently been looking out for the car. Throwing his stuff into the back and jumping onto the running board without giving Edward a chance to come to a halt he shouted, 'don't stop or you'll stall it. D'you know the way?'

Edward breathed an inward sigh of relief at Maurice's change of heart, but he thought it best to wait for an explanation. He was simply very glad to have his company.

'I've a rough idea from the map, but you never know what the roads will be like. I thought we should head back towards Hesdin where they're better and head up towards Boulogne.'

Maurice said he could get them to St Omer airfield. He'd been there several times by road and he was fairly sure the chateau now housing the Commission at Longuenesse was not far from there, adding, 'I've decided to head up the coast and make myself scarce. There's a seaside place called Wimereux…used to be very popular before the war.'

'But aren't all our military hospitals along that stretch? Not the kind of place to…er…lie low.'

'I told you. My mother has some good friends around Wimereux and Boulogne. From the old days. If they're still there I'll be all right. If not I'll just have to see.'

'The man who helped you over the birth certificate?'

'Amongst others. Now, how about leaving me the Studebaker – and a bill of sale in case I get pinched?'

Edward sensed he had been given as much information as he was likely to get; the curtain of silence was beginning to drop down again; already Maurice's expansiveness from the night before and today's further embellishment were not quite tying up: nearly, but not quite. It was obvious to Edward that he was much more familiar with that part of the channel coast than he was letting on.

'What good will a bill of sale do?'

'Something to show the car belongs to the Commission. I can talk my way out of having it then. Delivering it or something. God knows, we've scrounged enough dubious stuff in the last months to equip ourselves. Who's going to be bothered to track it back? Now, pull over and I'll drive for a while.'

They reached Longuenesse without incident towards the end of the day. The roads away from the front, while still in a state of disrepair, were far less congested with military traffic than they had been when Edward had made the journey from the coast the previous year, and they had enough spare cans of petrol with them to see them as far as the motor pool at the chateau.

The lieutenant colonel was decidedly unimpressed with Edward's turnout, however, and wanted to know where his new uniform was. 'You cannot possibly turn up to the meeting looking like that. From the agenda I think the Prince of Wales might be there. I thought you were having a new one brought over.'

But there had been no sign of the Marshall and Snelgrove's ready-made, nor of Lieutenant Scarsbrook who had been spirited away to the northern sector base at Poperinghe. Edward explained this lamely to the colonel, leaving out the ready-made part.

'Well, you'd better send a telegram to your tailor and have it sent round to your club.'

Edward said he would. He did not wish to start explaining that he did not have a club. The question of accommodation had completely passed him by. When he had been dismissed he went and sought Maurice's advice.

'Good God! You haven't worked it out yet, have you Edward? You are a very wealthy man. They've got a couple of secretaries here now: I've been talking to one, Miss Hibberd. Get her to book you into a suite at the Savoy and send another telegram to the hall porter telling him to have a few general service uniforms, nearest fit, send your measurements, waiting for you from their own tailor – Moss's, I assume – and someone on hand to make the alterations on the spot. Suggest fifty to a hundred guineas – that'll make the concierge sit up, that and booking a suite.'

The next day they drove to Boulogne. Once again Edward was sailing on the *Elizabeth*. There were not so many demobilised men boarding as when he had arrived in Boulogne, but there were still plenty of walking and barely walking wounded. It was less than a year ago, but it felt as though it had been in a dimly remembered previous life; as if someone else, not him, had disembarked then, and now that person was being absorbed back into the shape of Edward Dereham like a wraith resuming its body.

'Where will I see you when I return?' he asked Maurice. 'Are you coming back to the cemeteries with me?'

'I'll find you, my friend, never fear. The delightful-but-no-nonsense Miss Hibberd at Longuenesse will know where you are, I'm sure. And I still have the Commission's Studebaker, don't I?'

'That reminds me,' said Edward; he reached into his coat pocket and produced the blank chitty Scarsbrook had given him in Hesdin all that time ago. He signed it and handed it to Maurice. 'There, you fill in the rest.'

## 15

MISS Hibberd's no-nonsense telegrams, emanating from the War Graves Commission's prestigious-sounding chateau in France, had worked the oracle at the Savoy – that and, Edward soon discovered, the hint of golden guineas. The assistant manager barely glanced at his appearance, even more dishevelled after nearly twelve hours by boat and train, than it had been when he had left Boulogne. He was shown to his suite where, as he had requested, there were three uniforms of slightly different sizes waiting for him. Realising how much he needed a hot bath and a shave before trying them on, he inquired if the tailor could be available in an hour's time. While the water was running he picked up the telephone and gave the switchboard Louise's number in Hove. After a short while the operator called him back to say that there was no reply and should she keep trying? Edward said no: he would try again later.

 He had not contacted Louise since receiving her letter. He told himself a reply would have taken too long to arrive, and that another telegram from France might reopen her still fresh wound. But the truth was he had to speak to Louise on her own, face to face. In the few letters they had written since his going to France they had exchanged little information of any importance. Edward had deliberately kept from her the gruesome nature of his work and anything like a truthful description of the desperate desolation in which he carried it out. Until the chance finding of Cornelius's remains he had thought it kinder not to plant further imaginings in her grief in that way. For her part, she did not enquire. She said nothing to invite any exchanges of emotion, as if all that could be said and done, had been, on the stairs that last night in Hove. So the contents of their letters and their infrequency were a reflection of the personal distances they both needed to put between them. But all the while Edward could tell himself that she, like him, wanted desperately to say more. Then, when this last communication from her had come, he saw in it what he wanted to see; a short, clear cry for help, a declaration of her need for him, not his uncle.

The tailor came and pinned the uniform that was the best fit, promising to have it back by noon the following day – by now it was already past seven in the evening. Edward's meeting was at eleven the next morning and his face must have registered a look of panic. The tailor shuffled a little and picked a stray thread from Edward's new tunic, saying that it might be possible to have it back first thing, if he could catch the seamstress before she left for the night. He shuffled again and Edward realised he was being asked for money. 'Please,' he said hurriedly, 'I'll pay whatever is necessary to have the uniform back in time for breakfast.' The tailor bowed graciously, helped him out of the tunic and picked up the breeches. 'Within reason, that is,' Edward added, immediately wishing he had not, as the tailor opened the door to leave.

Whatever it had cost, his perfectly fitting uniform complete with his General Service insignia, shirts and a new cap, was delivered with his morning tea the next day. His boots and Sam Browne had been cleaned and polished every bit to the standard one would expect from a grand hotel. The assistant manager rang up to enquire if everything was satisfactory and would he require someone to pack for him as he understood Lieutenant Dereham was leaving them after breakfast? Edward had taken the decision to take the train to Brighton as soon as the meeting ended, rather than waste more time and money at the Savoy.

'No thank you, I can manage. I should like you to burn any of my things I leave in the wardrobe. Discreetly, if you don't mind.'

'Very good Sir. We were well used to that instruction from officers fresh back from the front, although it's been a little while now.'

After breakfast Edward retrieved his almost empty valise from the hall porter and settled his account, trying not to gasp physically at its size. He actually felt ashamed at the amount of money he had spent and felt that the eyes of the assistant manager must be boring into him accusingly for being a wastrel and an imposter. He braced himself as the quietly intimidating figure behind the desk addressed him.

'I beg your pardon, Sir, but I couldn't help seeing from your secretary's telegram that you are with the War Graves Commission.'

Slightly startled Edward said he was indeed.

'And do I assume from the…er…the condition of your uniform when you arrived that you…you are in the field, so to speak?' Again Edward confirmed this was so.

'Then may I thank you from the bottom of my heart for finding my son? About a month ago now, it was. He was a gunner, artillery. Wipers salient – Ypres, you know.'

Edward said he was glad his son had been found after this time. He was about to add 'and been identifiable' but managed to stop himself just in time. 'But I had nothing to do with it, I'm afraid. I'm not operating in that sector. Further south – the Somme.'

'Makes no odds, Sir. I just think it's magnificent that you are still out there in no-man's-land doing all this, when nobody would blame you for wanting to come home. It must have been a long time, Sir. I suppose you must have been in several years, judging by your, forgive me, but judging by your age. You'll have found other father's sons, I'm sure.'

Edward wanted to say that it was the army that had found his son; that he was only making sure he and all the others had a decent grave; that he hadn't been out there in the fighting, because of a phantom medical condition he did not believe in. But standing there in the Savoy's majestic entrance hall, he could see that he represented something to this father who needed to give voice to his gratitude. It was nothing personal.

The meeting in St James's Square was like nothing Edward had ever experienced. If he had not just spent a night at the Savoy Hotel he might have felt even more out of place than he actually did. The permanent committee members were seated around a long, highly polished oval table, whilst various invited advisors on different aspects of the agenda sat behind them in an outer circle against the wall. Edward discovered he was one of these and was shown where to sit. As the committee members were beginning to take their places one of them, also in a General Service uniform like Edward, but with a major-general's ranking came over to him. It was the Director General, clearly now elevated from brigadier.

'Dereham isn't it? I'm Fabian Ware. Thanks for coming at such short notice. Just speak up when I ask you and if the Prince of Wales addresses you, just call him "Sir". He's not a stickler. Any questions before it gets going?'

'What am I to speak up about, exactly, Sir? It's all been a bit of a rush getting here and the Lieutenant Colonel wasn't able to give me much to go on.'

'I asked for someone who was currently in the field, rather than someone who's just part of official inspections. Tell us all what it's like now we're coming up to nine months into the armistice. Wait up – here's HRH and that's Kipling with him, the poet. Stand to.'

The meeting began. Much of the business, as far as Edward could tell concerned progress on various contracts for the new headstones and similar financial issues. While it was all interesting to him, involved from the other end of the operation, as the clock ticked by and so too the agenda items, he did start to wonder if he would be ever called on to speak, and if so, what about? The headstones sounded like a good idea, but there again what would be written on the graves of all the unknown men; all those bits and pieces he had been dealing with?

The room was warm and his chair was directly in the sunlight streaming through the windows on the other side. Perhaps the accumulated fatigue of the recent months in makeshift accommodation had barely begun to be undone by a few hours' sleep in a suite at the Savoy. His consciousness started to wander away from the exchanges around the table. Inevitably he had thoughts about seeing Louise again, but in the warmth of the sunlit room they were vague and disconnected. That they had barely communicated with one another since his leaving for France did not enter into them, or lead him to consider the awkwardness, distance or even anger he might well have to face when he turned up unannounced in Caroline Crescent.

It may have been his vague awareness of the discussion round the table, where the thorny issue of the design and supply of headstones had strayed into planting and the supply of flowers and shrubs in sufficient quantities, which put Hillcote Grange into his mind. It was only a matter of time now before the War Office would give it back. He hoped they would have been as good as their word and looked after the garden, but what would Mr Kirby do now without the convalescing officers to look after the roses? His under gardeners had died at Ypres too but one could only hope others from the villages around would have returned. Edward had not warmed to the house: it lacked serious character, but nevertheless he had begun to feel an affinity with the garden. For a moment he speculated it might be worth thinking about getting Mr Kirby to provide nursery shrubs – rose bushes – for the cemeteries. But it would be too far away wouldn't it? And besides the gardeners in France were starting to do that. Perhaps, though he could reinstate the Hillcote garden parties and raise funds.

He became aware that the eyes of the table had turned to him. Fabian Ware was asking him to describe the daily work in the field. 'How would you characterise it, at the moment, Dercham? Give His Royal Highness the benefit of your very recent experience.'

Without thinking he began to tell them about Maurice Burnell dislodging the edge of the excavation and uncovering Second Lieutenant Cornelius Bolden who otherwise might just have remained missing in that wasteland; how they had struggled back with him on a stretcher as bearers might have done two years earlier, but not now to a forward dressing station but to a final resting place. And how they had identified a young man whose mother might have had nothing but a fading scrap of telegram, '…missing. Letter follows.'

The image of Louise came to him as he said that, making him pause involuntarily, becoming part of the wrapt silence that had by then fallen round the table, as if it had been called for as a mark of respect. Oblivious of them all, a Hamlet confronting only darkness beyond the spotlights Edward resumed his personal soliloquy. 'We are giving the men who cannot come home somewhere to call their own in the foreign land they died for. Whether we know who they are or whether we cannot know, each has a place in the gardens we are making. We are the gardening parties for the dead, and when the mothers come looking for their sons, the wives for their men, they should feel that is what they have come to – a garden we have made for them, that is their own too.'

The silence continued as if everyone round the table was holding his breath. Then it gave way to collective murmuring; papers were shuffled and the business moved on. The committee secretary touched Edward's sleeve indicating that he should go now. He stood up, wondering how best to make his exit. He put on his cap, straightened it and saluted the table. It was his best yet: Fabian Ware nodded approvingly as he left and that was that.

Outside in the corridor he felt an old familiar sensation and, making sure he was unobserved reached for his handkerchief and spat. Glancing at it and the tell-tale scarlet stain he saw nothing to cause him alarm. It had become irrelevant with the passage of time and events. It must be getting on for two years since the last time he had spat blood on the stairs at Caroline Crescent. Carradine at St Mary's had given him another six months hadn't he? And that was well passed. So what had triggered it now, one reproachful spot, less than a small nose-bleed? Had it been the strain of that meeting or was it the anticipation of seeing Louise again? The last time the blood had marked the way they had parted; so was it now to colour his return?

Before he had even reached for the doorbell, the front door at Caroline Crescent was flung open, not by May but by a bright-eyed young girl of about fifteen or sixteen – Edward was never very good at determining women's ages, young or old. This sudden, unexpected apparition took him entirely unawares and they both gazed at one another in silence, uncertain what to do or say next. The girl spoke first.

'I saw the uniform as you came down the crescent. I knew you were coming here. Are you bringing any news?'

Edward was still feeling nonplussed. Doorstep civilities seemed to have been bypassed. 'News? What news?'

'About my brother. He's still missing. I thought you must be from the War Office.'

'You must be Grace – Gee – is that right?' It hadn't entered his mind that she might also be here. Until now she had been simply a name, a person away at school, someone who had appeared on the invoice for fees to be paid for by the bank in his absence.

'I'm Edward Dereham, Grace. Does that mean anything to you?'

The girl shook her head doubtfully. 'Are you something to do with my guardian?'

'Your guardian?'

'Uncle Herbert. He's a friend of the family. I think of him as my guardian. He's rather wicked I think and all girls like me without their own father should have a wicked guardian, don't you think? It helps at school when my friends want to know where my real father is. But he died in America before I was born.'

This was already a great deal of information to be imparted on the doorstep, thought Edward. He asked if her mother was at home, but he assumed as she had not appeared by now to see what was happening, that she was not. Fortunately at that moment May, the maid, arrived belatedly from upstairs. She apologised profusely for not having heard the bell, and scolded Grace for having left Lieutenant Dereham on the step.

'Mrs Bolden is out walking on the Lawns, Sir. They went out about half an hour ago so I should think they'll be back shortly.'

'*They* May?'

'Yes Sir. Mr Grace has been back about a week now, Sir.' May failed to meet his eye and it wasn't possible for him to tell what her feelings might be on this situation.

Until now the distinct possibility that Herbert Grace would gravitate to Hove upon being released had buried itself out of sight at the back of Edward's mind. He had busied himself with the practicalities of his own return to England. The difficult journey, the state of his uniform, coping with the Savoy, and his presence at a meeting in the company of the Prince of Wales had left him little room to consider seriously what other realities might need his attention. Even his daydreaming in the meeting hadn't produced any sharp focus on what might be coming next. Whenever his thoughts turned to Louise Bolden, as they had at the meeting, they blended into one another; the hard facts of his responsibility for the mundane necessities of her daily life, stirred in with a reverie of them both instantly being in a state of bliss without effort on either side, unspoiled by a bloody handkerchief on the staircase. His contemplations became a thick soup with indistinguishable ingredients. While he had been away in France and experiencing another set of realities so far removed from anything that had impinged on the world of an unsuccessful country solicitor, he had been able to put it all to one side. Now, in the hallway of the house in Caroline Crescent and at the foot of those stairs, the soup had suddenly boiled away, leaving its unappetising dry components in plain view.

May brought him some tea in the drawing room which Grace poured for him in a very grown-up way. Edward cudgelled his brains to recall what she did or did not know about her and her mother's situation. She had referred to Herbert Grace as a friend of the family and as her guardian – her 'wicked' guardian. Was that just schoolgirl romanticising or did she have some inkling of where he had been for the last few years?

He took the cup from her. 'I'm your er…Uncle Herbert's solicitor,' he said tentatively.

'Not from the War Office then?'

'No, not from the War Office.'

'But you're in uniform. How can you be his solicitor?'

Edward said that he could still be his solicitor even if he was in uniform. He mentioned the War Graves Commission. 'Not proper army,' he said.

'You didn't have to go away with Uncle Herbert, then?'

'Away with him?'

'Yes – in South Africa, looking for diamonds.'

Edward very nearly wrote himself into this fiction, but caution got the better of him. 'I knew he'd been away…a long time…but fortunately I don't have to look after that side of things. I'm more to do with his business here.' He wondered whether Herbert Grace had devised this South African explanation of his absence or whether it had been Louise's doing. He couldn't imagine that several years in Brixton had given him the look of a man who had spent them in Africa.

There were sounds of arrival in the hall. Edward braced himself for the confrontation that was to come, wishing now that he had simply left a note for Louise saying he would telephone later. He heard May say that Lieutenant Dereham was in the drawing room with Grace. Evidently, he thought, May had kept Herbert Grace's secret from his daughter at any rate.

Still in her outdoor coat Louise entered the drawing room on her own and in a great flurry, with no greeting or preliminaries. 'He's gone upstairs to spend a penny. You didn't let me know you were coming.' Then, becoming aware of her daughter's presence, 'Gee, will you take yourself off upstairs for a while too. Lieutenant Dereham and I have some rather dull things to discuss with Uncle Herbert. Better still, you can take yourself down to the lawns for half an hour. Here – buy yourself some hokey-pokey, I saw the young boy with his trike on the front.' She ferreted in her bag and handed Grace sixpence. 'Go on with you now,' she added, as Grace seemed inclined to argue.

Herbert Grace was taking his time upstairs. Edward guessed it was deliberate: he too would have been taken by surprise at Edward's presence and would need to consider how to handle it. Knowing Herbert Grace, he would certainly endeavour to take control of the situation. Edward wondered if he would be looking for a row. He looked miserably at Louise who was now taking off her coat. Since dismissing Gee she had not uttered a word or met his eye.

'How long have you been back?' she asked flatly in a tone which conveyed rebuke by an apparent lack of interest in the answer. His recent reverie of a reunion enveloped in blessed harmony were dashed away. He was instantly ashamed that he had not tended to her emotionally; he cursed himself for being too ready to assume that the fewness of the letters between them and their bland practical contents was how they should both really have been talking to each other.

'Only a few days. I had a meeting to attend in London. I've been given another week's leave, though.'

'Oh yes?' Her voice was still flat and uninterested. Then she said, 'Did you get my last letter?'

'Yes, eventually. But I was on my way...'

'I told you Herbert was being released early, didn't I?'

'Yes. But I didn't have time to...' His awkward attempt at explanation and apology was interrupted by the drawing room door opening abruptly and there stood Herbert Grace himself.

'Didn't have time to do what, Dereham? Tell her to ignore me, just like you've been doing since we last met? Typical lawyer if you ask me.'

It was said as a hearty jest, but there was no doubt it was meant seriously. Still, Edward said nothing, just shook the gnarled, nail-less right hand Grace extended towards him. He was remembering suddenly that the main thing he had not had time to do was to break the news to Louise that her son was found and buried. But he felt this was not the time. The telegram she had received on that day of their first meeting had been a shared grief between the two of them. So, Edward told himself, breaking the news of his death had to be just between them, too. And he remembered how she had clung to him on the stairs that last time, willing him not to go to France. He had been her solace then and would be now: Herbert Grace's crimes and punishment had removed *his* right to give her comfort.

It might have been the case that the prison authorities had succumbed to a rare moment of compassion when they decided to release him early. More likely, Edward thought spitefully, as he let drop the hand deformed by years of picking oakum, much more likely, they had decided to spare the taxpayers the cost of a funeral within the prison walls. This once imposing figure of a man now stooping in front of Edward had shrunk even more since they had last met in Brixton. He already had the pallor of death about him; it put Edward in mind of some of the young men they had been bringing out of no-man's land – this colour. He would not have believed it could apply to the living.

Louise murmured something about him probably needing to sit for a while after their walk out. As she took her protector's arm and gently steered him towards an armchair, it was blindingly obvious to Edward that their roles had been well and truly reversed and the protector was now to be protected. It was plain that whatever time he might have, Herbert Grace was not long for the world and equally plain that Louise would be there night and day to see him out of it. The panicked question she had asked in her letter to Edward, *'what should I do if he comes to Caroline Crescent?'* had been well and truly answered, if not by him.

## 16

As he leaned on the taffrail of the Le Havre ferry watching the eastern end of the Isle of Wight becoming a darkened silhouette against the setting sun, a great burden of care slipped from Edward's shoulders as if going down with it too. For the first time since registering at the Savoy just over a week ago his mind was free from the anxieties, which had haunted him, of questions still waiting to be answered.

His worst fear – imparting the news of Cornelius's death to Louise – hadn't resulted in the reaction he had been dreading. Herbert Grace had declined supper that evening; the walk along the Lawns towards Brighton had been more exercise of that kind than he was used to, his hard labour having been at least sedentary during his years of incarceration and, in any case, latterly much reduced by a combination of compassion and bribery. So Edward ate alone with Louise. She still behaved coolly towards him at first but eventually began to ask him a few questions about his work, gradually thawing out sufficiently to reprove him openly for his lack of letter writing rather than persisting with the cold shoulder. It was not an attitude she would have been able to keep up for long – Edward could tell that her naturally warm heart was getting the better of her as usual. Thus by the time May had cleared away the coffee cups the distance had closed between them.

'Louise, there was a particular reason I could not reply to your last letter, even supposing it would have reached you before I got here in person.' As he had said it he knew it was all humbug, but it enabled him to broach the subject. 'It's something I needed to tell you face to face and alone.'

But Louise had intervened. 'It's Cornelius, isn't it? He was always dead, wasn't he? Not in some prison camp or some old hospital. I haven't dreamt about him since…since the letter came – did I tell you they'd written? But I dreamt about him just about three weeks ago now for the first time. I was standing by a grave and he was there beside me looking at it too.' She'd paused and reached in the pocket of her skirt for a handkerchief but found none. Edward had handed her his and she quietly dabbed her eyes. When she was composed again, she said. 'I asked him if he was there – in the grave. He didn't say anything but I knew he was at peace. I went to mass the next day, it was a Sunday. I asked Father Twomey to say a prayer for him. So whatever you're about to tell me, I *know* my son is dead even if he's still missing.'

Edward reached into the side pocket of his uniform and took out a small envelope. 'Yes you're right Louise. He is dead and he is not missing. My friend Maurice Burnell found him at a place called Lorette. We buried him at the new Cabaret Rouge cemetery. I got him to take a picture – here.' He handed her the envelope.

Louise gazed at the photograph Maurice had taken for a very long time. 'Did he have a service when he was buried?'

'Yes. And we said prayers when he was found. The padre was there.'

'There's already flowers.'

'Yes. Cornflowers and calendula. You know, those big orange marigolds. They seem to do well. The French call them *soucis* – cares – but I like to think that, on the graves, it's because they've taken them away from those young men – the cares of the world. Poppies will come, too, of their own accord. They do where the ground has been disturbed.'

'Is that what you've really been doing? Making gardens in that terrible place?'

Edward had cleared his throat: a sudden lump had come into it. Louise refolded his handkerchief and handed it back to him. 'Here, you'll need this now, won't you? Still, at least there's no blood on it this time.'

'You weren't supposed to see it. Anyway my doctor says it probably isn't what you think. More likely some old scarring left over from the whooping cough. It just seems to come when I've been put under particular pressure. It's odd.'

'So you were under pressure, were you? Here, at the Crescent that time?' Her question was so ingenuous it made Edward question whether she had harboured the same hidden feelings for him that he did for her. He tried to think what he should say, whether he could say anything now. But Louise continued. 'So that makes the two of you spitting blood and trying to hide it from me, although I don't think his is to do with the whooping cough. I would think it's the real thing.'

'Good God! Do you mean...my uncle?' Edward still had difficulty acknowledging that accident of marriage to his aunt.

'Of course, your uncle. It's why they let him out early, I would imagine, although he's said nothing, his poor health was the consumption. He'll have got it in there, I'll be bound.'

'So is he seeing a doctor, now?'

'He refuses. He just says, Time heals all, and he doesn't want a local doctor knowing who he is and where he has been – for my sake, mainly.'

Edward found his emotions were torn. He had a sudden guilty surge of elation at the thought that Herbert Grace's days were even more numbered than he had supposed – yes, and let's face it – had hoped: the man had been sent home to die and to avoid infecting those around him in prison. It was much the same official logic as had kept Edward out of the war. Compassion had little or nothing to do with it. His realisation that here was something else he and his uncle now shared, as well as his misbegotten fortune, was yet another constricting coil around him from which there was no extricating himself.

But his other side had felt sudden alarm for Louise herself and for her daughter. He'd searched for the right words, but she had intervened yet again, saying she was managing to keep Gee at arms' length. 'You might have noticed this afternoon. And to be fair to the man, he's not been over-demonstrative with her. He must know and he's always had a decent care for both of us, whatever else he might have done.' She had shot him one of her level looks. 'And I'm not sharing his bed, if that was what you were not so bold as to ask.' Edward had breathed an inward sigh of relief at this declaration, trying not to feel too triumphant.

'I was just wondering what was happening to his handkerchiefs if he's trying to keep it a secret?'

'I'm burning them, myself. I've ordered a fresh supply every week from the town and told May Mr Grace is very particular. I expect she's noticed things but she says nothing. This family's business is safe with her. Anyway, I wouldn't want the laundry refusing our custom.'

He had been too late to book a single cabin for the crossing, so was faced with the prospect of passing the night in the discomfort of the passenger saloon. Deciding he should delay taking a seat there for as long as possible he went to the dining saloon to see about something to eat. It too was crowded with men, mostly in uniform like himself, but rather to his surprise a fair scattering of women not all of whom were in uniform. Edward managed to get the last table which had been laid for two. He placed his uniform cap on the seat opposite in the hope that it would deter another officer from seeking to join him. The waiter came with the card offering to start a choice of brown Windsor soup or an egg salad, followed by liver and onions. Edward asked what was in the egg salad and was informed it was with liver sausage and a gribiche dressing but that it had all gone. So he ordered the soup and the liver and a bottle of beer. When the beer eventually appeared the waiter announced that the liver too was finished and had been substituted by bloater and mashed potatoes. Edward further resigned himself to an uncomfortable crossing.

By now he had gathered from the conversation going on at the adjacent tables that a number of these passengers were on a Cooks Tour of the battlefields, which accounted for the preponderance of women. Edward had mixed views about the wisdom of these newly organised visits, knowing as he did, first hand, what the condition of most of the cemeteries still was. Nevertheless he could understand that families, wives and sweethearts had a deep need, a solemn right, to visit the graves of their menfolk who, it had been decreed, were never to come home for burial and to gaze across the fields where those who would never be found had met their end. At least, he could see, that vulgar and unwelcome as it might appear to some in authority, organised groups were better than individuals wandering unescorted in an unimaginable world for which most would be totally unprepared.

Louise herself had asked him when, not if, she would be able to visit Cornelius' grave at Cabaret Rouge. Edward had long ago anticipated this event in his imaginings of their being together. He would take her there himself as a holy duty; the practical idea of her going on a Cooks Tour could not have remotely suggested itself in his reverie. Coming face-to-face with one on the boat made him horrified to think of her as a part of it. But now of course there was the spanner in the works in the very real shape of Herbert Grace.

Edward had stayed the night at an hotel – a better one than on his first visit to Caroline Crescent – there being no room for him there with Gee and her 'guardian' each occupying the available bedrooms. In any case Edward would not have wished to spend the night under the same roof as Louise and Herbert Grace, whatever their sleeping arrangements. He put in an appearance the next morning at breakfast to say goodbye before taking the train for Portsmouth. His extended furlough was very nearly over and it would be touch and go whether he would report back to St Omer at his allotted time, especially as he had to cross to Le Havre, there being nothing available from Dover to Calais.

Herbert Grace had looked up from his eggs and waved a proprietorial fork at the spare chair. 'We haven't really talked. I cannot stay here indefinitely I've decided. I shall take Louise to Hillcote. Better for me there than here in Hove. Proper gardens to sit in. I suppose I have to ask you, do I?'

Edward was taken aback by this announcement. 'I let the War Office have it for officers' convalescence. They've gone now, but I don't know what kind of state it's in.'

But Herbert Grace was not to be put off. Now that he was out of prison he made it subtly clear to Edward that if he could not have his money back he was determined to occupy the real estate at Edward's continuing expense regardless of the fact that legally it was no longer his to enjoy. There was enough in the funds to make good any predations by the military, wasn't there? Grace's inclusion of Louise and presumably Gee when she was home from school was like taking hostages to guarantee Edward's acquiescence – a declaration of his ownership of them. It occurred to Edward at that instant that his uncle suspected that as well as acquiring his wealth Edward had also removed Louise's affections from him; and what else besides? Well, he thought, he had earnestly wished for that to be the case, hadn't he? But that had been in those lonely moments in France when he conjured up an imaginary blissful state to blot out the awful emptiness of the western front. And what was any of it based on? A fleeting moment on the stairs on the eve of his departure, when she had briefly touched his face with her fingers to make light of her earlier outburst of emotion in case it had been too embarrassing for him – no more.

The soup arrived and he had just made a start on it when the waiter came back to ask whether he would object to sharing the other place at his table as it was the last one left and there would not be another sitting. Edward felt put out as he was not in the mood to make small talk with a stranger who would more than likely be a regular officer himself and would be bound to ask about his military role. However, it would be churlish to refuse point blank, he supposed, so he reluctantly agreed and told the waiter to hang up his cap for him. To his surprise it was not an officer who arrived at the table, but a woman, clearly on her own. Edward stood up, rather clumsily scraping the chair, which was rather heavy as a precaution in rough weather, and managing to drop the corner of his napkin in the soup in the process. As the waiter had not accompanied the lady to her seat, Edward came round to pull it out for her.

'That is most kind of you, Sir. I'm sorry to put you to the inconvenience of dining with a stranger, especially as you have already started your meal. Please, please, ignore my intrusion, if you wish. I shall not take offence.'

Mightily relieved not to have an inquisitive regular officer to deal with, Edward was instantly all smiles and good manners. Apart from Louise Bolden he had had no female company for a very long time, other than brief exchanges in schoolboy French with Corinne at the *estaminet* in Hesdin. Finding himself suddenly face-to-face with another woman in a situation requiring social exchange, particularly a woman with an aura about her, a soft beauty and a look that spoke of an open heart, reminded him with a pang what a monastic life he had been leading since he could not remember when. There had been Ursula, but that seemed so long ago now the memory of their relationship had ceased to have any reality left.

He introduced himself, without mentioning his military status, such as it was, although his uniform was plain to see. In turn the lady, who looked about ten years older than him, perhaps early fifties, introduced herself as Mrs Annie Turner of Icingbury. When he asked where that was, she said with a laugh that that was an interesting question. 'The village green at Icingbury is where three counties actually meet, Suffolk, Essex and Cambridgeshire. So in my time I have lived in all three counties without moving more than a mile. Since being widowed I have moved back to my father-in-law's house in the Suffolk part. He's a farm bailiff who should have given up long ago, but of course, there's no-one to take over now most of the young men...have gone. Fortunately my husband left us well provided for, and the land army girls have been a great help.'

Edward's first thought was that Mrs Turner's husband had been killed in the war and that she might be going to France for that reason. He would have been older perhaps but senior officers often were. Tentatively he asked her.

She smiled a little wistfully. 'Well, Henry was killed in the war in a manner of speaking. He was a passenger on the *Lusitania* when it was sunk by the Germans in 1915. He had business interests in Kentucky and travelled back after we were married in 1914 to settle them up. He was a naturalised American citizen. I would have gone too, but my son joined up almost as soon as the war was declared and I felt I should not go. Henry was coming back for good when the *Lusitania* was sunk so I never saw him again. We only got married so that my son Reuben could be there, before Henry had to go back. I suppose that was fate, really.'

'So your son...Reuben, did you say...?'

'Was killed a year later in France. He was with the Suffolk Regiment of course — that's where the farm was. Some of the village boys joined the Essex Regiment. And I believe some went into the Cambridgeshires. I'm afraid it hasn't stopped too many of them being killed — being spread around the counties I mean.' Edward wondered to himself if she had been married before, but there again, her late husband might still have been her son's father, mightn't he?[2]

He was struck by a thought of Louise; her fear that all the men in her life would be gone: her husband, her son Cornelius,

---

[2] See *The Equal Sky*

Edward himself once, and now even her sickly charge, Herbert Grace, cruelly for her sent home to die, their roles reversed, her keeper kept. Now here opposite him was another with no men left in her life, just a wistful smile.

'So are you with the Cooks Tour then? Visiting his cemetery?' he asked.

Mrs Turner looked round as if surprised at the question. 'Is that who they all are? I wondered. I didn't know you could do it that way. We're a little off the news I'm afraid, in Icingbury. Do they take you wherever you need to go then? To the different cemeteries, I mean?'

Edward confessed he didn't know how it worked. 'I suppose they go to different areas with different groups. Would you like me to ask? Where exactly do you have to go? Do you know?'

'A place called Auchonvillers, I understand from the Enquiries people in London. Well, they couldn't exactly say because…' She caught her bottom lip '…because he was buried somewhere else. On his own. So he will have been reburied, they think at this Auchonvillers. Do you know where that is?'

Edward said he knew it well.

'Were you in the fighting there then? Is that how you know it?' she asked.

He took a breath and began to explain to her how he came to be in uniform and what he was doing with the Directorate of Graves Registration which now came under the new War Graves Commission.

'So you have been doing this at Auchonvillers, have you? They told me that Reuben was killed at a place called Mailly something – is that how you say it?'

Edward smiled. 'Close enough. The fighting was at a place called Mailly-Maillet Wood – although there's not much of the wood left now. And there's a chateau there which is a bit of a ruin needless to say. Rather a good wine cellar though which the locals managed to save.'

Mrs Turner said she had tried to look it up on a map of France in the public library in Cambridge but hadn't been able to locate it. It hadn't crossed her mind to write to the Commission and ask where it was. Edward asked her how then she had been intending to find her way to Auchonvillers all alone.

'I have assumed I could enquire at the train station where the nearest big town would be and then take a taxi. But you did very kindly offer to ask about the Cooks Tour. Perhaps I could go with them if they are going in that direction – if it's not too late. I have money.'

She spoke as if she were about to buy a day railway ticket to Cambridge on market day. How little she, and the thousands of rural dwellers like her who rarely saw anything of the world beyond their own horizons, could comprehend of the western front in France. How could they be expected to visualise what more than four years of terrible conflict could do to the towns and villages, the good farmland, the roads, and the railways?

Coming from a village probably not unlike Auchonvillers had been, she would have been, as she put it, 'off the news, cocooned in a rural backwater. Even when the telegrams arrived bearing curt messages of yet another young farm boy who would never return, they were never accompanied by a picture of where they met their end. Authority put an official brave face on its losses both to protect people like Mrs Turner from imagining too much and to prevent their knowledge becoming a nuisance. So as a result, now that it was all over she felt able to embark on a journey into a great unknown that no-one had described to her. Edward had an overwhelming desire to protect her from what she was about to see. She needed at least to have the company of these others in the dining saloon if that could be arranged. Perhaps Cooks had found a way of explaining it all to their customers.

Edward looked around the other diners and lighted on an older man whose manner suggested he was probably in charge.

Excusing himself from Mrs Turner he went over, apologised for interrupting his meal, and explained her dilemma.

The Cooks group leader confirmed what she had feared. The tour was fully subscribed. 'Perhaps she would care to return and book a later visit?' he said half-heartedly. It was obvious that this was unlikely to appeal to her as they were already half-way across the Channel. 'Which sector is the lady needing to access? It's not easy to go unaccompanied, as I expect you know, Sir, as a military man. Certain formalities with the French authorities and so forth.'

She needed to go to the southern sector beyond Doullens Edward said. The Cooks man shook his head emphatically. 'We are heading for Ypres and Passchendaele, so I am afraid we cannot help your lady friend even if we had space.'

Edward felt piqued. It was a clumsy description of the woman at his table, although probably not intended to be insinuating. He wanted to say that she was a chance acquaintance brought about simply by lack of dining space: certainly not his 'lady friend'. However he knew that such an explanation would be seen as protesting too much. In any case, the fact that Cooks could not help her suggested that she might have to be his responsibility, for the time being. He should at least help her find a train at Le Havre although where trains might be going was anyone's guess. Paris, more than likely, but where then? Looking across to her waiting expectantly at their table he was again aware of the soft aura seeming to surround her. The prospect of having to offer his assistance was not entirely an imposition even though he was only too conscious that his furlough was fast running out. Making his way back to his chair he tried to tell himself that his desire to help her was not simply due to being attracted to her, and as if to counteract any such feeling he imagined himself asking Louise for permission which made it worse. He told himself severely to pull himself together.

The fact that he had drawn a blank with the Cooks Tour leader did not come as a surprise to her. She had watched the conversation across the saloon even if she had not been able to hear it. 'Oh well, never mind. I'll just have to get there by myself. After all I managed to get myself from the station at Great Duster to London and then to Portsmouth. I have a tongue in my head.'

'Is it a French tongue though?' said Edward. 'I'd be happy to help. It might not be as easy as all that. The French railway system is still suffering considerably. You know – after the war. But you might be able to get from Paris to Albert by train now. That's about twenty miles from Auchonvillers. You could get a lift from there, I would imagine – if you have enough money. Everything like that is very expensive, but that's hardly surprising.'

Neither of them really fancied their bloaters and mashed potatoes, but they continued to sit at the table for a while after the barely touched dishes had been cleared and most of the other passengers had retreated to their cabins or the passenger saloon. Edward was in no rush to take his own place there and was anxious in any case to try and give Mrs Turner some idea of what to expect when visiting the battlefields. But memories of Louise and how she had taken the news that Cornelius was missing made him reluctant to paint a truly honest picture. At least if Mrs Turner managed to get to the cemetery at Auchonvillers there would be some semblance of order, possibly flowers round the graves even though the crosses were still temporary.

She had managed to secure a cabin, so eventually, stifling a yawn, she declared herself ready to turn in for the few hours of the crossing remaining. 'I don't think I shall undress,' she said candidly. 'Well, perhaps just my dress. I made sure to wear something which fastened at the front as I was travelling alone.'

Hearing this Edward felt himself blushing. She must have noticed and smiled reassuringly. 'Still I don't suppose you want to hear about my personal arrangements, now do you?' This made his confusion all the greater. He felt he knew nothing about women now. His assumptions about them were those he had acquired at the beginning of the century, already a period that seemed to have passed into the mists of time. He wondered whether his instinct to protect her was misplaced. Country women like Mrs Turner would always have been self-sufficient; the men in her life would have deferred to her in many respects although probably without acknowledging the fact. But the demands of the war and the absence now of many of those men meant that her self-sufficiency had become plain to the naked eye, not cloaked by men's convention. She could simply pack her bag, put on a dress and coat which buttoned up the front and set out alone to find the grave of her dead son without anyone remonstrating with her – at least not with any conviction.

As he settled himself uncomfortably on a bench in the passenger saloon next to a young woman, not much older than Gee, and her grumbling father, he couldn't help comparing Louise with his new acquaintance. Both had lost their sons, but he had not until now imagined Louise setting out on her own to find Cornelius's grave. Since knowing her he thought of her as a woman under protection. She had no need of Mrs Turner's self-sufficiency, did she? Even when Herbert Grace had gone to prison, his money had kept his mistress at arms' length from a critical world. Edward had continued that by proxy. Now Herbert Grace had reclaimed her; his sickness demanded her attention even when her most pressing need was the same as Mrs Turner's – to find her son.

The boat docked in Le Havre soon after sunrise. Edward shuddered at the breakfast offering which was the repeated bloater with toast rather than mashed potatoes. He took his valise and went to stand at the top of the gangway waiting for the gangplank to be wheeled into place on the waiting dockside. He was also keeping an eye open for his previous night's dinner companion, to offer his services at the harbour station. Mrs Turner came on deck carrying her own luggage and endeavouring not to be jostled by the Cooks party who were all anxious to be together and not get left behind.

Catching sight of Edward she gave him a wave and made her way to him through the throng. After they had said their good mornings she said, 'I've been thinking about what you said about maybe needing a French tongue at the station. Would it be very rude of me to ask you to…?'

'Not at all,' Edward said, anticipating her request. 'Only too delighted to be of assistance. I may in any case be going in the same direction. It depends if I have to go back to St Omer or straight on to my sector. I'm supposed to telephone from here.'

There were several bars and cafes along the harbour side and one hotel. Edward suggested they might look there for some breakfast and he could find a telephone. They took a seat in the dining room where they were treated to fresh croissants and halfway drinkable coffee. Things had certainly looked up here, in Le Havre at any rate, in the last year, although Edward anticipated he would have to pay well over the odds for the *petit-déjeuner*. When they were nearly finished he excused himself and went to search out the guest telephone. There was one in a booth with a folding door at the back of the lobby but it wasn't working. In fact it didn't look as though it had ever worked. He went to the reception desk and asked the ancient concierge if he would get him the number he wanted. In this department of the hotel, however, things had not looked up. The concierge pushed the instrument towards him and told him to do it himself. Edward waited nervously for the operator to come on the line and asked her in his best, halting, French if she could put him through to the Chateau de Longuenesse, near St Omer. She said he would have to wait: she would call him back. Reluctantly, the ancient concierge said he would fetch *monsieur* when the operator called back and Edward thankfully went back to the dining room to finish his breakfast with Mrs Turner. She was getting anxious about not missing a train if there was one, so Edward went to enquire if the concierge knew about trains to Paris. Apparently the Paris train waited for the night ferry to come in, so it might already now have left. While this dispiriting exchange was taking place the telephone rang. The concierge answered it and after a deliberate pause handed the receiver to Edward without comment.

When the operator put him through to the chateau, to his great relief he recognised Miss Hibberd's voice at the other end. 'The colonel is in Ypres for a few days. He hasn't left any instructions about you,' she said. 'By the way, there's a letter for him from General Ware about you. You must have made a big impression at that meeting in London. The colonel hasn't seen it yet. There might be a promotion in the offing.'

Edward wasn't at all sure about this news. While he was keen to continue with his work on the cemeteries and the recovery of the dead from the battlefields, he was not certain he wanted to become any more elevated in the new Commission. The prospect of promotion made that more likely. He would have to think carefully about it if a new role were offered to him. He knew only too well that his work directly with the dead was an expiation of his deep guilt at not having been there with them. His hands were still in the earth where they lay; perhaps it wasn't yet time to wipe them down and excuse himself from his labour. A promotion would involve new insignia on his uniform too, wouldn't it? He had quietly come to the conclusion some time ago, picking through the shreds of khaki for some intimations of the identity of another unrecognisable body, that the uniform he had thought would initiate him into that brotherhood was not the General Service one he had acquired. Indeed he had gradually been shedding it in favour of his fatigues. He felt comfortable in those; they were not a pretence at something phoney; they gave him a role in the service of the dead. That was where he needed to be, not writing reports in Longuenesse or worse still, St James's Square, recording and regurgitating the platitudes of committee meetings, a piddling solicitor from Lower Sunbury. Essential though that work was, it was not what he needed to be doing.

He did need breathing space and not allow himself to be swept along by a tide of events, as he had been so often. The colonel's absence was a stroke of luck. Bravely he told Miss Hibberd, 'I'd better go back to Doullens, then, and talk to Lieutenant Banks about what I should be doing. I shall probably have to go into Paris first for a connection regardless, anyway. Thank you very much for the Savoy, by the way. They were expecting me.'

'Did your new uniform come?'

'Yes. Very good. Thank you. I'd better be going now to see about the train.'

'Oh, before you do – your friend gave me a telephone number to pass on to you. It's here. Just a second.'

'My friend? Do you mean Maurice Burnell?'

'Yes. The French pilot. Is he French? I'm never sure. Here it is. Have you something to write with?'

Edward fished in his pocket for his notebook and pencil. 'You've seen him then?'

'No. He telephoned. A bit odd. He asked me not to give this number to the military police if they came asking for him. Was it a joke d'you think, Lieutenant?

'Probably not.'

'Oh dear,' sighed Miss Hibberd, in a way which suggested she'd heard it all before.

## 17

As predicted by the gloomy concierge, the Paris train had already departed. The next through one would not be until the next day, but the booking clerk at Le Havre informed them they could take a slow train to Rouen and try their luck from there. Edward asked if there was anything going to Amiens; he was thinking he might get to Albert from there, which would also suit Mrs Turner. Having failed to get her on the Paris train, he felt more than ever that she had become his responsibility. As he had reported in to Miss Hibberd at Longuenesse and, in the absence of any other instructions from the colonel, had announced his intention of resuming his duties in the southern sector, he considered he was free to use his initiative about how to get there. The clerk sucked his teeth and shrugged: services to towns in the former battlefield zones were still very hit or miss. The best advice he said would be to wait another day for the Paris train and take it from there. 'There is a good hotel at the harbour, Monsieur.'

Edward relayed this to Mrs Turner. 'I am to return to my duties at Doullens, anyway,' he said. 'So I would be happy to accompany you that far. It's not too far to Auchonvillers from there. If we can make it to Albert on the train I will be able to arrange some transport. You would be well advised to find somewhere to stay in Albert. Doullens is not exactly a ruin, but the facilities for a...for a civilian lady, are rather lacking.' Then he added awkwardly, 'That's if you have no…er…no misgivings about throwing in your lot with a complete stranger.'

The night before on the boat, Mrs Turner would probably have protested that his offer of help would put him to too much trouble. But now that they had actually landed on French soil it looked as though she was beginning to understand what her quest for her son's grave might entail. She accepted thankfully and with a good grace. 'Well Lieutenant Dereham, if I am to have an adventure like this I should take it as it comes – Good Samaritan into the bargain. I didn't suppose it would be easy.'

With a sudden jolt Edward knew he no longer wanted to be called 'Lieutenant Dereham' by people like her, people who were friends or on the way to becoming friends. His military rank might still be unavoidable in the surroundings of the Graves Registration Directorate or the Commission, but he knew now he wanted to shed it in the way he had been shedding his uniform in those outlying cemeteries.

Still, he could hardly expect Mrs Turner to call him 'Mister Dereham' could he? 'If I am to stop being the complete stranger, and as we are likely to be together for a few days at least, by the look of things, perhaps you would call me Edward.'

'Only if you call me Annie, then.'

Denying his military status to himself was another step towards expunging his guilt. He thought about Maurice Burnell gradually changing his French Air Corps uniform into something that blended anonymously with his surroundings, like a chameleon. Maurice wasn't exactly doing it for the same reasons though, was he? Edward smiled inwardly; perhaps he should try and telephone him as they had time on their hands.

Back at the hotel on the harbour, he managed to secure two rooms for that night. The concierge evidently found this ridiculous. 'There is a perfectly good room with a large bed. Why pay twice?' Edward had had enough of the man's surly familiarity and found enough instant fluency to speak sharply to him. He was, however relieved that his companion had not followed this exchange. Feeling himself in command of the lobby for the moment, Edward curtly demanded to use the telephone again. The concierge pushed it along the desk, demanding payment for the rooms in advance, as he did so. Edward produced his pocket book and took out sufficient notes from the quite considerable sum contained in it. He had learned by now that a half-way comfortable life on the former western front required plenty of cash, beyond the meagre expenses paid by the Commission and the army and he had returned prepared. Both the concierge and Mrs Turner could not help but see the bulging wallet. She of course said that she hoped Edward would let her pay her way, while the concierge became instantly more obliging, although it was not a pose he could keep up for long, no matter how large the wad of money a guest was carrying. The operator once again said she would call back when she had the number. She must have recognised Edward's French from earlier, because she told him he would have to be patient as the call was out of the region and would need more than one connection.

While Mrs Turner went up to her room to make her belated toilette before lunch was served at eleven, Edward sat in the small front bar where various locals and the postman were sipping cognac and ordered one himself. He heard the telephone ring in the hall and went to see if it was his call, which it was. The operator spoke to her counterpart in another exchange, saying she had her caller ready to be put through. After some delay Edward heard Maurice's tones speaking in French.

'Maurice it's me, Edward. You can drop the French. Where are you?'

'I'm in Wimereux like I said. You were right. There are still a lot of hospitals here, although the military are shutting them down just as fast as they can. The one in the old casino where my mother was has just been cleared out.'

'So are you going to stay there – in Wimereux?'

'No fear. Too many MPs for my liking. And my mother's old friends seem to have moved away – or died. Where are you?'

Edward said he was stuck in Le Havre. 'I need to get back to Doullens. But the trains aren't easy.'

'I'll come and get you. I've still got the Studebaker. Now that you're back I might as well tag along with you to Doullens. You can renew my local labour status can't you?'

Edward told him there would be another passenger – an English lady. Maurice at once assumed it must be Louise until Edward put him right. 'She isn't free to come over yet – it's a long story. I'll tell you over a bottle of the Mailly-Maillet Chateau's finest.'

'So are we going back there, then? To Auchonvillers?'

'Unless Banks has other orders for me when we get to Doullens. Mrs Turner's son is at Auchonvillers. I'd like at least to get her there.'

'I *see*, old man. I see!'

'No you don't see anything of the kind, Maurice. When can you be here? We're at the *Hotel du Port*.'

Burnell said all being well with the Studebaker which had been behaving itself all week he would be with them by lunch time the following day. 'I don't want to drive at night. Almost bound to be stopped by the *gendarmes*.' He rang off.

Edward replaced the receiver, this last remark still hanging in the air. Maurice's hoped-for friends on the coast had clearly not materialised. So presumably he hadn't been able to arrange for some appropriate documents regularising his status. Not for the first time Edward wondered what that status was. French deserter? English deserter? Wanted by the Americans? How much money, Edward wondered, had there really been in the trunk of that Studebaker? Did he actually care if it was all hooey? He knew if he put these questions to Maurice, he would be given another version of his past, leaving him none the wiser. Maurice Burnell was a man for the present, the here and now: the solver of all problems, Edward's genie of the lamp.

Maurice's timing proved to be overly optimistic. He did not arrive in Le Havre until well into the afternoon the following day.

As soon as he came into the hotel sitting room where Edward and Mrs Turner had taken themselves after lunch to await his belated arrival it was apparent that in the fortnight since they had parted, Maurice had finally shed the last vestiges of his French aviator's uniform. He was now kitted out in civilian clothes he had obtained during his short stay on the coast. It was evident that the small resort town of Wimereux had been unable to offer anything up-to-date and the result was a beach promenader's summer outfit dating back to before the war.

He saw the surprised look on Edward's face. 'Don't say a word. It's the best I could do under the circumstances and the military are hardly likely to be looking for a pre-war seaside *flâneur*. I'll be happier in my fatigues when we get back to Doullens.'

'Me too,' said Edward. 'I'll be glad to get out of this uniform again. This is Mrs Turner, I told you about. She's coming with us as far as Albert.' He only had a vague idea of where Albert was in relation to Le Havre but hoped it was not too much out of the way. He ought to be checking in with Lieutenant Banks before very much longer, otherwise Longuenesse would be reporting him missing. Edward had made a half-hearted attempt before lunch to put a call through to Banks, but Le Havre to Doullens on the very edge of no-man's land proved beyond the ingenuity of the operator.

Maurice pursed his lips at the idea of depositing Mrs Turner on her own in Albert. 'It's still a mess and the roads in and out are not good. Amiens might be better now. That's on our way.'

As it turned out the Studebaker barely made Amiens by nightfall, so all three of them had to put up there. The state of the town was still bad – much the same as Doullens, Edward thought, but it was larger and seemed to have been attracting more departmental resources. Several hotels were open for business, which was brisk. Nevertheless, Maurice managed to secure two rooms, one for Mrs Turner and the other he and Edward would have to share. Edward did manage to put a telephone call through to Lieutenant Banks in Doullens this time, only to find that the inestimable Miss Hibberd had already tipped him off that Edward was heading back in his direction.

Over a tolerable dinner at the hotel, which again Maurice had managed to organise without recourse to the bill of fare that the other guests had been given, and accompanied by a bottle of vintage cognac rather than the dubious bottle of open wine deposited on each table, he set about his usual practice of extracting more information from Mrs Turner than she might glean from him. It was obvious that she was equal to the contest. She had taken a shine to Maurice during the drive from Le Havre and they were already on first-name terms. At one point she had asked him how old he was and when he told her he had just had his thirty-second birthday on Armistice Day – which was news to Edward – she said, 'My son would have been a little younger than you, if he had lived.' Again there was the conundrum that Edward had avoided on the boat over – was her husband of barely a few weeks when he went down with the *Lusitania*, the father of her son Reuben. Edward had been too polite to ask anything which might have caused her embarrassment then, but the fact that she had now deliberately referred to his age, it was as if she wanted to be questioned about it.

Maurice had already heard about her marriage sadly cut short, but he had no compunction about solving the mystery. 'So you must have been married before…before Mr Turner?'

'Well, I was Mrs Westwood for a while when I was very young, but he died too – an accident haymaking. But I never married Rueben's true father. To tell the truth I don't think he was church-marrying kind. He wasn't what you would call a Christian, although he used to say we were all one under an equal sky, which I always thought amounted to the same thing. There – have I shocked you? I hope not. But these things seem to matter less and less to me now. It's probably all this war and death. Who cares if I was married to my dead son's father? There's no such thing as a respectable grieving mother is there? Just another grieving mother.'

Edward was not shocked. He had already seen enough of the aftermath of death and destruction, even if he had missed the process itself, to know that survivors like Annie Turner could never be judged by mere convention. It all needed rewriting now; what things of worth should remain, and what trash should be discarded. But there again it made him compare her with Louise, the only other woman in his life; she, like Annie Turner, mourned a fatherless son. But unlike her, she was still trapped in an iron net of convention wound round about her by, of all people, Herbert Grace. She would probably never be his wife and would never be his widow. Her son would never be acknowledged by him even now he was dead. Cornelius's true father, was he alive or dead himself, in America? He had almost become a fiction. But she deserved to say all those things that Annie Turner had just said.

She announced she was going up to her room as soon as dinner was finished, despite Maurice pressing her to stay on with Edward and him to share a nightcap. He, too, had clearly taken her statement of emancipation to heart and wasn't going to allow her to withdraw simply to observe female etiquette. 'C'mon Mrs Turner – Annie – you can't expect Edward and me to see off the rest of this excellent bottle of cognac all by ourselves, now can you?'

However she was determined to get some sleep after several days of uncomfortable journeying and urged the two men to do the same. As she rose from the table they stood up to let her go. Maurice, who was becoming slightly the worse for wear, put his hand on her arm. 'If he wasn't a Christian, what was he – a foreigner?'

Edward remonstrated with him. 'Come on Maurice, that's enough. Let the lady go to bed.'

She looked levelly at Maurice. 'He was an American too.'

'Like your husband? Your second husband, I mean. Were they friends.'

Edward was feeling distinctly uncomfortable. But Annie Turner seemed to be acquiring a serenity from Maurice's interrogation. It was as if he had strayed into a private garden of hers where few, if any, ever went, and she was glad to let him wander there, keeping her company at a little distance.

'Yes they were friends – more than friends. They were like adopted brothers. I suppose I married Henry when I couldn't have the other one. They were so close it was as if they were one and the same. I had waited for them both but only Henry came back.' She wasn't really talking to Maurice or Edward: she was talking out loud to herself, voicing thoughts that must constantly go unshared. Even the fuddled Maurice had the good sense to see that he had asked enough and, gallantly kissing her hand, bade her goodnight. Edward accompanied her out of the dining room and saw her to the foot of the stairs. Pausing for a moment at the half-landing she asked: 'So is he English or French, young Maurice?'

'Some of both, I guess.'

'It was the French half that kissed my hand, I suppose. Good night.'

Back at the table Maurice had already downed another brandy. 'We can't leave her here. She's not safe – woman like that.'

'I should have thought a woman like that was particularly safe,' said Edward. 'Bags of confidence even if she has no French. Better here than Doullens anyhow.'

'I don't mean that. It's the way she thinks and talks make her unsafe. She's positively dangerous. Like an unexploded shell waiting to be defused. Who knows what kind of trouble she could be, just sitting there.'

Edward assumed it was partly the cognac talking, but even so he vaguely understood what Maurice meant. He too was having misgivings about seeming to abandon Annie Turner at the edge of no-man's land. She was becoming more than a passing stranger needing directions. They had inevitably bonded: she was the kind of person, when you met, you wished you had known them all your life. Plus, he had talked of getting her transport to Auchonvillers, although that was when he had been assuming going by train as far as Albert. Well, they had their own transport now, didn't they? The protesting Studebaker.

'All right, Maurice. Let's take her to Doullens. If Banks agrees we can go straight on to Auchonvillers but you'll have to take her somewhere reasonably civilised to put up if I have to continue elsewhere. Depends what Longuenesse have planned.'

When they all met for breakfast the next morning, Mrs Turner seemed unsurprised by the change of plan. It was as if she regarded herself as part of a joint enterprise. She even offered to take a turn at driving the motor car. 'Henry bought one – a Riley – before he left and I had a few goes on it, much to the village's horror.'

Maurice, who regarded himself as the current owner of the Studebaker, declined, explaining rather ungallantly that it was already bad enough sharing the driving with Edward. To pay him out, as the two of them were putting their bags in the trunk at the back, Edward asked him innocently what they should do if they were stopped by the military police? Maurice said that they were unlikely to encounter any this far south, least of all Americans. 'Those that are operating are still around the barracks and hospitals along the coast. Most of those are closing as fast as the numbers of patients remaining dwindles. Anyway you've got your uniform haven't you? And I've still got the chitty you gave me showing the car belongs to the GRD.'

The fact that Maurice had taken his question seriously was making Edward rather apprehensive. 'So what's happened to the payroll or whatever it was you liberated with the car? I suppose it's too much to suppose you have left it anonymously on the steps of a gendarmerie?'

Maurice laughed. 'No such thing, Edward. Much too much to trust to them. They'd take at least three-quarters of it and still do me for the other twenty-five per cent. It's safe enough and I intend eventually to reinvest it in the French economy.'

Edward sighed. 'I never know whether to take you seriously or not, Maurice.'

It took several hours to make it through to Doullens from Amiens. The road was still pitted with old shell holes in many places, and the verges were deeply rutted where vehicles had veered off to the left and right to avoid the worst of them. Every so often they encountered gangs of Chinese labourers working on repairs and had to wait patiently until they could continue on their way.

Maurice knew the road from Amiens to Doullens from the air. It had been a main transport route immediately to the rear of the front lines as they moved slowly back and forth. 'We used to use it as guide back when we had been out taking photographs over the Boche lines. When you had been shot at and flying through smoke and cloud it was easy to lose your bearings. It was a great relief to see this road again and know that you'd been flying back in the right direction. At least this road is more or less passable. When we go down to Auchonvillers and Mailly it becomes much more difficult.'

'Where my son is?'

'I'm afraid so. But as we are coming at it from the Doullens side the roads were not completely destroyed. Doullens was a clearing station for wounded during most of 1916 and after. It was never really fought over.'

'That's why it's still reasonably habitable for us,' said Edward. 'Graves Registration,' he explained and then realised that made the town sound a little macabre.

When they eventually drew up at the Southern Area headquarters, Lieutenant Banks was in the motor pool looking rather agitated. The only vehicle there was jacked up and had important-looking pieces of its engine laid out on a tarpaulin. His agitation increased when he saw Maurice Burnell in the driving seat of the Studebaker. He signalled to Edward to get out and took him to one side. 'I didn't know he was coming back, Dereham. We had a couple of French MPs here or gendarmes, I can't tell all their uniforms, just after you left — when was it? Week before last? They were asking about what's-his-name, Burnell. They said his name was Simon, you know, the French way of pronouncing it. Said he was a French deserter and might have stolen rather a lot of money. From the Americans, they said.'

'What made you think it might be Maurice?'

'Well, they mentioned an American car.'

'The Studebaker?'

'Not as such — no. But I couldn't help thinking. And he used to wear French aviator's uniform didn't he? Bits of one, anyway.'

'What did you tell them?'

'Well, nothing much. I didn't want to suggest to the French authorities that we might be employing undesirables. Give the new Commission a bad name. Anyway we don't have a 'Simon' on our books. Things can be a bit tricky with the French at the best of times. They think we are being too slow finding our dead in this sector. More and more people are beginning to return to what was their land. They want to start farming again and at the moment the French authorities are keeping them back in our sector because there's so much still to do. But the French Urgent Work Service, I think it's called, want to get on with clearing the old ordnance out there so some kind of cultivation can begin. You can't blame them.'

'Why did the gendarmes come looking for this man here?'

'No idea. They might have said, but my French isn't up to it.'

'Well,' Edward fibbed, 'Graves Registration bought the Studebaker fair and square in Hesdin. I did the deal myself. Scarsbrook issued a chitty.'

'That's what I thought,' said Banks, momentarily relieved. Then he spotted Annie Turner descending from the back of the car and his look of agitation returned. 'That's a lady!'

Edward explained her presence. 'She's been told by the Enquiries Department in London that her son was killed in action near Mailly and had a battlefield burial. Probably brought in to Auchonvillers, although we know they can't always be sure of that.'

Banks's agitation increased. 'I suppose we are going to have to put up with more and more of this. We've got more than we can cope with already with what little manpower we have here, without having to provide Cook's Tours for grieving relatives. I don't know what London is playing at sometimes. They ought to come and have a look for themselves.'

'There was a Cook's Tour on the boat we came on. They were going to Passchendaele though.'

'Yes well, the northern sector is further ahead than us, by all accounts. That'll be because the King and the Prime Minister get to see what's going on there. I doubt they'll find their way down here.' Lieutenant Banks evidently had an enormous black dog on his shoulders at the moment.

'You should put in for some leave,' Edward offered. It was not the most diplomatic of suggestions.

'Don't think I haven't. But the colonel said that as the senior Lieutenant I couldn't be spared – as you were away gallivanting in London.'

'Well, I'm back now. You should try again.'

But Banks was not to be mollified. 'You might be moving on. On promotion to Longuenesse.'

'Says who?'

'Miss Hibberd.'

'Well, it's news to me.'

'More to the point there's some bad news down at Auchonvillers,' said Banks, brightening up at this recollection. 'I've had to let Private Pilgrim and his gardeners deal with it unsupervised. As you can see our only transport is *hors de combat*. Still as you're back and obviously itching to get down there, you can take the Studebaker and Burnell and sort it out. Gets you out of Doullens if the gendarmes come snooping around again. Oh – and this lady too.'

Mrs Turner had been politely standing a little way off, but she must have been able to hear their exchange. She smiled at Lieutenant Banks. 'I realise people like me must be an enormous problem for you, Sir.'

Banks, however, was not inclined to be softened by blandishment. 'Actually no. You're the first.'

Edward stepped in. 'What's happened at Auchonvillers?'

'They were clearing ground at the back for more graves – away from the church, thank God. They hit an unexploded mortar shell. German, Pilgrim said it was. A really big bugger.'

'So what – did it go off? Was anybody hurt?'

'No, they followed the clearance drill, sandbagged it and sent for the disposal team. Then it went off. Took best part of two rows with it.'

Edward's heart skipped a beat. 'New rows or earlier?'

Banks couldn't say.

'What's happened?' Annie Turner had detected the sudden change of mood.

Edward told her that an unexploded shell had disturbed some of the graves at Auchonvillers. She asked him what that would mean.

'The army will be reinterring the bodies. It is, unfortunately, something we have to get used to – all this unexploded ordnance. This is one we must have missed when the gardeners were marking out the cemetery. Who knows how long it's been there. Auchonvillers has been in place as a battlefield cemetery at least since 1916. Perhaps it was there all the time. It's a blessing no-one was hurt or killed. The gardeners I mean. It does happen sadly.'

'Actually no,' Banks interrupted. 'The army burial party has moved out of that part of the sector. They're not due to revisit that area for a while. I haven't been able to get any sense out of the Adjutant-General's office, they're absolutely deluged because of the pace of demobilisation. I was told we might get some German prisoners to help out, but they couldn't say when. And there's no local labour to be had. We'll have to see to it ourselves with the gardeners. Nothing else for it. We're going to be taking it over from the army soon, anyway, as soon as the Commission sends us some recruits.'

Maurice had been listening. 'One last piece of action for the dead. Dead men and a dead shell. You'd think they could be left alone, wouldn't you?'

There was a silence, then Lieutenant Banks said. 'Yes, well. First thing then, Dereham. Perhaps we could all have a drink and a bite to eat in the mess tonight. Does the lady sing? There's a piano. Oh Lord! We've no facilities for ladies, Dereham.'

Edward raised a questioning eyebrow at Maurice.

'No I'm afraid I let my billet in town here go. Didn't think I'd be needing it.'

After a little discussion Edward agreed with Banks that Mrs Turner could have the cot bed in the first-aid hut.

As they unloaded what they needed for the night, Edward said, 'So have we lost our *estaminet* in Auchonvillers too, Maurice?'

'Nothing a bit of wedge can't handle,' was the reply.

Much to everyone's delight, Annie Turner was more than up for a few songs after mess supper. Eventually falling under her quiet spell, Lieutenant Banks accompanied her on the out-of-tune piano with some old folk ballads she knew, London music hall favourites not having really penetrated to her part of Cambridgeshire. However she did finish with *I dreamt I dwelt in marble halls* which brought a lump to the throats of the men there, especially when she said it had been a favourite of her husband's. 'I should have sung it at his funeral if he had had one. But this seems a very suitable place for it, doesn't it?'

## *18*

WHEN the Studebaker set down its passengers at the entrance to the cemetery at Auchonvillers, beside the still heavily sandbagged church, they were met by the first lines of graves with their wooden crosses in good order, unmoved by the blast from the shell. The flowers at the ends of each row gave them an air of peaceful repose. But on the far side, where the previously cleared area gave way to a dilapidated communications trench with its rusting corrugated iron reinforcement snaking off into the unrecovered farmland still scarred and rank from years of fighting, it was a different scene. Here the crosses and the plots they marked had been rudely uprooted, their human contents too, heaped into unseemly mounds.

Private Pilgrim and his small team of gardeners had been busy since first light. Their first task had been gently to unearth as many of the bodies that were obvious and more or less intact and lay them to one side. 'The others are going to be a bit trickier, Sir,' Pilgrim said.

This was very clear to Edward, whose heart sank at the sight. He asked how many burials Pilgrim thought had been uprooted or damaged.

'Can't be certain Sir. We couldn't find the register. Do you have it?'

Edward remembered he had left it in the church for safe keeping, before being moved up to Cabaret Rouge. He was pretty certain he had mentioned this to the Padre who had been supervising the army burial party operating in the area. But as

Banks had said, they had now moved on. Edward prayed the lists were up-to-date as some of the disturbed graves would have been amongst the most recent to come in. Pilgrim confirmed this: about half a row had been brought in within the last fortnight. 'Some of these were re-burials from Mailly. We had a problem there too. Not a whizz bang like this. Some kind of subsidence and they were being flooded in the rain we had a while back. So Lieutenant Banks agreed with the padre they could come here to Ocean Villas as there was only one gardener minding Mailly at the time and we'd left these sites prepared before we all went to Cabaret Rouge.'

Edward went back to the church where Annie Turner was sitting on some sandbags beside the door. 'I need the register. It should be in here. I'm sorry I brought you here in the middle of all this. It's no place for a lady at all. I'll get Maurice to take you back to Doullens and find you somewhere to stay.'

But Mrs Turner was not to be put off so easily. She had come too far and, besides, her son was somewhere in the cemetery. 'There must be something I could be doing here to help. That soldier you were talking to doesn't seem to have very many pairs of hands.'

Edward looked at her helplessly. 'Mrs Turner...'

'Annie.'

'Annie, then. Look – some of them are just going to be, well, not complete. It wouldn't be right for a lady.'

She took hold of his hand. 'I'm not a lady, Edward. I'm a strong farming lass. I'm not squeamish. And I'm a mother. At the moment I could be the mother of any one of those poor boys lying there. And I should think each and every one of them called out for his mother at the end. They all do. So don't put me back in that motor car just yet. Come on – let's go and look for this register. I need to see where Reuben is.'

Meekly, Edward let her lead him into the church. He could not bear to break it to her that despite what she had been told by the Enquiries Unit, her son could be in any one of half a dozen cemeteries within five miles around.

The register was in the font under the wooden cover where he had in fact left it for safe-keeping, having calculated that this was unlikely to be needed for christenings in the foreseeable future. To his relief the Padre had kept it up-to-date and had listed the most recent reburials. Annie Turner peered eagerly over Edward's shoulder as he scanned the lists. The names were in alphabetical order with the row and plot numbers shown by them.

'I'll need to go through all of them and mark off those men in the two rows which have been turned over. I didn't do a list simply by row as well – perhaps I should now. This sort of thing is bound to happen again.'

Annie Turner was anxious to help. Edward gave her half the register and he went through the other half. There were already several hundred entries in it and he was anxious not to miss any from the two or three affected rows: they would need to comb through several times to be sure. It was Annie herself who discovered her son's name after they had swapped over each other's half of the register to go through a second time: Edward had missed him on the first trawl.

She was very quiet and matter-of-fact. 'Here he is. Reuben Turner, ninth battalion Suffolk Regiment. He's in one of those rows – look. But the date is August 1916. How can that be, Edward?'

Edward told her some graves had had to be relocated from another cemetery nearby. 'Your son's must be one of those.' And he explained that when she had asked the Enquiries Unit in London they could not have been certain of his location.

'Well,' she said, 'he's here now, which is a gift of providence for me, isn't it? Having met you and all. Reuben's father always used to say that some things were meant, even if they were extraordinary coincidences. Still, no rush. We need to go through these names one more time at least. We missed Reuben first time, didn't we?'

After several more sifts through the register Edward was satisfied that they had all the names from the damaged rows, so he put the register back in the font and the two of them went back out to the cemetery. Private Pilgrim's little team had been busy laying out the relatively intact bodies under several tarpaulins. A number – fortunately not too many judging by the evidence they presented – had been placed uncovered on another three or four tarpaulins a little way off.

'Trouble is,' said Pilgrim, 'some of these lads weren't, you know, Sir, weren't all there when they were put in the first time. Having to move them from Mailly didn't help matters either.'

Dereham asked whether they'd all had identification tags, to which Pilgrim replied that some had and some hadn't. As far as he could recall two had been 'unknown soldiers'.

'Known unto God,' said Edward half under his breath.

'That's one way of putting it,' said Pilgrim thoughtfully.

'Rudyard Kipling said that the other day – in a meeting I was at.'

'So what do you think, Sir? Put them all in together?'

Edward consulted his list. There were three 'unknowns' in the affected rows according to their search of the register. Ideally he would have wished to talk to the Padre before taking a decision to create new graves for bodies that could no longer be identified. It should really still be an army decision; but for how much longer? The army was handing it all over to the Commission very soon; and besides the burial parties for this part of the sector had moved on. Banks hadn't thought they would be returning now.

There was nothing for it. He deliberately straightened his cap. Private Pilgrim instinctively came to attention. Slightly embarrassed, Edward said hastily, 'Stand easy Pilgrim. We'll have to do the arithmetic and then see what we've got left. Have your men finished here do you think? If so perhaps they can make a start in the morning preparing this area for new graves. Mr Burnell, you, and I will go through the lists to establish the known identities. Then I'll take a decision on those we cannot put a name to.'

'Mount a guard Sir – tonight? Would be wise Sir. It don't look like rain but we don't want vermin coming in. I have the shotgun here. See?'

'Good idea. I'll take a turn although I may have to just wave the gun about if anything bigger than a rat appears – I'm not much of a shot.'

'I'll take a turn too.' Annie Turner had been standing quietly to one side, listening. 'I'm a farmer's daughter. I've been shooting crows and rabbits since I was weaned.'

Pilgrim looked enquiringly at Edward who sighed. 'It's useless to argue,' he said.

Maurice Burnell appeared. He had been tinkering with the Studebaker in anticipation of returning Annie Turner to Amiens in the morning rather than taking her back to Doullens. 'It's one side of the triangle instead of two,' he said. 'If we'd known we'd be coming back to Ocean Villas we needn't have called in to Doullens in the first place. By the by, I've reacquainted the patron of the *estaminet* with our return, much to his delight and he has found a space for Mrs Turner too. He offered rabbit for dinner tonight, but I'm not so sure – in these parts.' He pulled a face. 'But I made a point of stocking up with a few supplies in Doullens. The patron's wine is still very good, I have to say.'

'Maybe not tonight, Maurice,' Edward said. 'Work to be done. You're taking your turn on guard duty – we all are.' He explained the situation with the reburials.

'So we've got to keep the rabbits off, is that it?' Maurice looked at Pilgrim's shotgun. 'I'd rather have my Maxim. But beggars can't be choosers.'

It had been a sensible precaution to mount sentry duty during the night. The line of rats and a solitary fox laid out in the dawn light bore witness to that. Annie Turner had herself despatched the fox and six rats all by the light of a bull's-eye just before midnight. As the self-confessed worst shot, Edward had taken a late turn as the first streaks of dawn were appearing and most of the invaders had already been seen off. As soon as the light permitted, Pilgrim's gardeners, stripped to the waist and working as if possessed, started levelling the disturbed ground and digging new plots for the reburials, while Edward's little team began the solemn task of identifying the bodies, now for a second or third time since their deaths. They first turned their attention to those who, though disturbed by the explosion, had remained more or less in place. Despite her protests, Edward made Annie Turner sit a little way off on upturned handcart and gave her charge of the list they had compiled from the register. The three men set about matching names and regimental details, stamped on the tin crosses fastened on the larger wooden crosses that had been the grave markers, with the compressed fibre identification tags worn by the bodies. This was grim and, in some cases, stomach-turning work and they said nothing, other than to call out to Annie Turner when the names matched. They marked the bodies successfully identified by laying the correct crosses on them, or just the tin labels where the wooden crosses had been made unusable by the blast: Annie made a note of these, too, on her list.

When it was done Edward counted up the tally of known graves and their occupants. 'How many does that leave, Annie?'

'Eight.'

'Does that include any of those who were not identified before?'

She ran her finger down the list once more. 'Well possibly, because you had two without tags but with named crosses very close, but you had another two without tags and one cross with no name. I'm a little confused.'

'Could have been two in one grave, Sir,' said Pilgrim. 'You'd need to get hold of the Padre to check that.'

Brothers-in-arms, thought Edward. 'Were any on the list two in one plot, Annie? They shouldn't have been, because these are all…' He was going to say 'all in one piece' but he left his thought unfinished. It wasn't easy for him having a woman there when there was this work to be done. It wasn't a situation he could have anticipated when he had impulsively become her knight errant and brought her here. But now his normal misgivings were reasserting themselves. However, he applied himself once more to the sad arithmetic of the job in hand. He should assume that those marked with their crosses were correct. So that meant there was one unnamed cross, and two unnamed whole bodies, leaving six bodies waiting to be accounted for from the other remains they had not yet examined.

'There must be more crosses, Pilgrim. D'you think the gardeners have found them all?'

Pilgrim said he thought so but he would see whether any more had been turned up in the ground-clearing they were doing.

'I'll go, Pilgrim,' said Maurice. 'I really need a smoke!'

'There *must* be more, Edward,' said Annie. 'We haven't found Reuben yet and he was on the named list. He must have had a cross.'

Dereham's heart sank. No, they hadn't found her son yet, which would mean his remains were under the other tarpaulin – unless by some miracle he was one of these two untagged bodies. It was not impossible: the Graves Registration Directorate had often painstakingly pieced together an identity from other scraps and clues even when name tags were missing, or he might have been buried on the battlefield by his pals who knew who he was. It would mean calling her over to look at these two bodies – but if Reuben were neither of these, she would insist on examining the others over there. He looked down again at the two in front of him. Only one had a face that might be recognisable. 'Can you make anything of these two, Pilgrim? Do you think there's anything that would have identified them in the absence of name tags?'

Pilgrim stooped down and brushed away the cold clay sticking to what was left of the uniforms of the young men lying on the tarpaulin. First he inspected the one whose face was still recognisable. 'Suffolk Regiment tunic markings, this one.' He turned his attention to the one next to him and then straightened up. 'This one too – Suffolks.'

'Annie, how many Suffolk Regiment were on our list?' Edward prayed that the answer would be two.

Again Annie ran her finger down the list. 'Two,' she said quietly. 'My son and one other. Both August 1916. Have you found him? She stood up from her perch on the handcart.

'Just wait there, please Annie. Just wait there.' Edward covered both the bodies with tarpaulin leaving the one with the recognisable face showing but completely covering the second. 'All right now. Have a look at this one. Is this your son, Reuben?'

Annie Turner gazed down at the dead face for what seemed like a long, long time. 'No,' she said. 'It is not.'

Maurice had come back from his smoke. The gardeners who had taken a fag break too, followed him across from where they had been working. All of them were silent. Something had come to pass.

Edward took hold of both Annie Turner's hands. 'This is not going to be very easy, Annie. He's not…his face is not…'

She snatched her hands from his grasp, bent down and carefully, almost reverently, pulled the tarpaulin back to reveal the entire figure lying there. As she looked down at him she started to catch her breath. 'It's him. That's my son Reuben. That's his father's jacket – his real father. Henry brought it back for him from America.' She broke down with deep, gasping pain and buried her face in Edward's shoulder. As he looked down over hers he could see what he took to be the remnants of a thin waistcoat showing under the soldier's tattered tunic. They often wore something like this sent from home when they were going into the front line. But this had a strange kind of what looked like embroidery on it. Birds perhaps?

It took the garden party another two whole days to re-bury all the bodies. By a simple process of deduction they were able to put a name to Reuben Turner's comrade from the Suffolks and accord him a named plot despite the fact that he had had no tag and his cross had not survived the blast. Sadly, the remaining fragments of men could not all be separated although a few compressed identity tags had survived, a testament to their efficacy. From the original register in the church font they were therefore able to create some 'believed to be graves' so that they had at least their own plot number and row. The remainder were accorded 'known to be buried nearby'. It had been a sad business indeed, but Edward had to be satisfied that the positive identifications were correct and that as much as could be done to register the existence and whereabouts of the remaining dead had been done. It was the first time he had taken charge of re-interments from the army and although he knew from what Lieutenant Banks had intimated, these would increasingly be taken over by the Commission, he had had to proceed only on what he had observed the army burial parties doing. He hoped fervently he had got it right. The extraordinary circumstance which had led to Private Reuben Turner's mother, Annie, perhaps uniquely, identifying her son in the flesh, amid the dereliction of the Western Front, seared into him the sacred responsibility he had, to be the eyes of all the other mothers whose sons were there.

Once again he found himself making a comparison between Louise Bolden and Annie Turner. Louise had had to take his word for the discovery of Cornelius. Missing or found she was never to see him again. Annie's boy had been literally thrown up by an enemy mortar shell nearly a year after the war had ended and three years since he had been killed. Compared with Louise she had had the dubious privilege of identifying him herself and she had seen him laid to rest. But was the grief of these two women who had never met, in any way different now, or was it still part of a huge single grief shared by them and all the others? Edward wondered if he had been the dowser hired by fate to divine the whereabouts of both their sons. He dismissed the idea. It was more the case that he had simply been present when both had been revealed, by events entirely beyond his control. He had just been a witness to random happenings, no more a cause of them than the man next in line when death had come to one and not the other. Things happened all the time without being remarkable; paths nearly crossed, trains were caught or missed, people met and they parted. All had consequences: it was futile to suppose that some were more unlikely than others. That only happened when you accorded yourself a special place in time and space. All life was an accident, however deliberately caused.

## 19

THERE was as yet no such thing as a telephone line to Auchonvillers, although Doullens had provided a field telephone which sometimes worked, enabling the mobile gardening parties in no-man's land to communicate with the gardener left in charge at one or other of the nearest cemeteries if it happened to be in range. Its reach did not extend to Doullens. In the absence of any specific instructions about their next priorities after the reburials, Edward set Pilgrim and his party a rota of clearing and levelling at six of the cemetery sites in the sector where new-found bodies were still being brought in on a daily basis.

Nevertheless he was getting anxious about his continued isolation at Auchonvillers and he told Pilgrim a little anxiously, 'If you run across the Padre, Pilgrim, tell him what we've been up to here. I don't think we should be cutting the army out entirely just yet.' There was also the question of Annie Turner to be considered. Ideally she needed to be taken to Amiens and seen onto a train. He had a word with Maurice who, in the absence of anything other than manual labour to do, had been busying himself taking photographs. He was in another of his improvised dark rooms in a blanketed part of the *estaminet's* cellar.

'I can take her to Amiens if you want. You're the guv'nor. It'll be good for me to get to a proper telephone, anyway. I thought I might sell some of these pictures to the Daily Sketch.' He thought for a moment and said, 'Better not ask for a credit though. Which is a pity.'

Edward had forgotten about Maurice's small difficulties with the French authorities. 'I shouldn't think the gendarmes read the Sketch, Maurice. Or the American MPs either – surely they've all gone home by now?'

Maurice shrugged in that way which made it difficult to tell whether he was all French or all English. 'Have you spoken to her about leaving?'

'Not yet – why?'

'I think she'll want to stay, that's all.'

Annie Turner was on her knees, busy dividing up some of the more established flowers in the oldest part of the cemetery prior to replanting the thinnings around the new graves, as well as carefully saving the seed from the flowers that had finished. Edward told her that it would soon be time to go. 'Maurice will drop me off at Doullens so I can pick up my new instructions from Longuenesse and take you on to Amiens. I'm sorry it's the long way round but he can wait to make sure you get a train to Paris all right.'

Not looking up from her trowelling she said in her most matter-of-fact voice, and punctuating her words with small silences of concentration, 'I'm nowhere near ready to go yet… I need to be with my boy… and these other… young men… for a while longer. I've only just arrived and they've been here so long already.' She stood up and picked up the trug of rooted flower plants she had so carefully gathered. 'Look what I found. This trowel and the trug. There are other things in the shed too. All for the gardeners. But it's obvious Private Pilgrim and the others have precious little time for gardening just yet, no matter what your Commission chooses to call them.'

'How much longer did you have in mind?

'A few weeks. Maybe more. I don't know yet.'

Edward felt his own resolve fading as it always seemed to when faced with Annie Turner's. But he made an effort. 'There's more gardeners promised. And proper horticulturalists too, who can make proper designs…and architects…All these wooden crosses aren't staying forever, you know. There will be white headstones, all in proper straight rows…as if they're at church parade. Officers and men side-by-side…' His voice trailed off.

Annie brushed down her skirts and the calico apron she had evidently appropriated from the *estaminet*. She gazed over towards the ruined communications trench and beyond. 'Well good. I was worried about the crosses. But it won't happen tomorrow or next week or next month. It's August now. Autumn and the rains are coming. Soon we'll be into winter and then another spring and nothing done, unless it's done now. This time next year it will all be docks and weeds again.

Edward protested feebly. 'We'll leave a gardener here. There's one covering the surrounding cemeteries. Some have their own to themselves.'

'Good. Well that can include me. You can take me on as a local recruit.'

'I'm not sure I can.'

'You took Maurice on – he told me.'

'Yes but you're a wom…'

'A woman, yes. The army has women – so why not your Commission?'

Edward didn't know the answer to that. It just didn't feel right to him. After all, it was still dangerous out here. What had just happened with the mortar shell proved that, and there were still thousands more being unearthed by the French recovery teams. You could see all the dud ordnance piled up at the side of the old plank roads, waiting for disposal. He tried another tack. 'You cannot possibly exist out here with what little luggage you have with you. You can only have packed for a couple of weeks – I know, I've carried your suitcase.'

Annie turned and gave him an old-fashioned look. 'Are you questioning *my* ability to wash out my smalls, Lieutenant Dereham?'

Edward wilted with embarrassment. He was aware of his own shortcomings in the clean underwear department out here where there were no local laundresses to call on and he generally had to make do with difficulty until it was time for a visit to Doullens. None of the mobile gardeners were any too fragrant either, but in this god-forsaken wilderness, it hadn't been noticeable until Mrs Turner alluded to the subject.

She pressed home her advantage. 'You can send a telegram for me when you get to Doullens. I'm sure it's not beyond the wit of man to get a trunk sent over. And I don't expect paying or anything. I do have money enough. Henry Turner left me well provided for, God bless him.'

Edward gave up. When it came to it, he didn't suppose he had the right to stop her. The French might be able to, but their Emergency Works teams were hardly likely to bother about a woman working in a British cemetery, or if they did would assume she was a Women's Auxiliary or some such. In any case, hadn't he told himself to stop thinking about women like Annie Turner, who had rolled up their sleeves and worked through this war, as if they had not left the drawing rooms of 1904?

Maurice still had his head under a hood in his darkroom. Edward told him he had been right. 'So I'll need to take the motor back to Doullens tomorrow, Maurice. You'll have to make do with the Albion if you need transport. I may have to move on – depends what news Banks has for me.'

Maurice came out from under the hood with a jerk. 'Don't like the idea of being left here without a car, old man. Don't like the idea of being Mrs Turner's chaperone either. She doesn't need one. If she's choosing to stay, that's got to be her lookout, old man. I'm sure you tried to talk her out of it, but I'll have a go if you like.' And he went off to find her. In a while he was back. 'No good, Edward. Gave me a real flea in my ear. Said one or two other things about me that I didn't know showed.'

'So will you stay?'

'No, Edward. No, I don't think I shall. You know – I think it's time I moved on altogether. Those boys and that mortar shell. It's made me think, really made me think.' He took a cigarette from his breast pocket and lit it. 'I didn't come here for all this.' He gestured with the glowing cigarette at the cemetery and beyond, across the churned ground where patches of tufted grasses had begun to reclaim their summer place and here and there poppies and cornflowers. 'None of us wants to be *here*. We've found ourselves here for reasons of our own. I'm hiding here – you're hiding here. Mostly from ourselves I might say. And then this place finds you out. Annie, too. She came here for a perfectly understandable reason. Understandable that is in the village halls of Cambridgeshire or wherever it is she's from. Understandable to all the young women spilling out of the Tivoli cinemas without any men on their arms after they've watched the newsreel. But now she's actually here, this place has found her out. This is a place that relates to nothing on earth. Only the dead are here. Dead men in a dead land. I'm just thankful I'm not one of them, Edward – although I don't know about you sometimes. Annie Turner has to stay here now, like some Vestal tending an eternal flame. But, you know, Edward, this place has found me out and told me I need to go and get on with my life. If you take my advice, you'll think about what this place has found out about you and do something before it's too late.'

Suddenly Edward knew that was right. For him, for now, the cemeteries were harsh, fierce places, barely wrested from the battlefields, their graves thrusting up all along the front like dragons' teeth so recently seeded in the anger of war, still harbouring its stench. But these unquiet sidings for the dead would all be transmuted soon enough: the living were seeing to that in their committees and their drawing offices. They were to become places of peace and quiet, gardens where Cooks would bring Annie Turner's successors for calm comfort and reflection. Not to feel the rage of the dead. And whatever had been his tenuous reason for coming here, if he remembered it at all, would no longer have any meaning here and neither would he. His own act of contrition was over.

He drew a long breath. 'Perhaps you're right, Maurice. Perhaps it's time for me to go too. Hand my papers in at Longuenesse or whatever it is one does. They were going to promote me anyway, probably to sit on more committees. Whatever it is, I'm done here. I've seen what lies only a few feet under all this and I'm not sure I need to be part of what's coming instead. I know it has to be, and it's for the best, but I'd feel a fraud.'

'So what will you do, Edward?'

'I suppose I'd better find something useful to do with all that money. Some way of giving it back.'

'Will you go back to that place you gave to the Medical Corps?'

'I don't like it much, but I can hardly go back to my mother's pokey cottage in Lower Sunbury as if nothing's changed. Anyway, I may not get out of this as easily as all that. I am technically a serving officer, after all, and I suppose there are procedures. It may take time. What about you?'

Maurice took a final drag on his cigarette and stubbed it out, careful to put the dog end back in the tin. He didn't acknowledge Edward's question. 'Mustn't leave fag ends littering the cemetery. Disrespectful. If I drop you at Doullens, d'you think I can keep the Studebaker?'

Edward hadn't thought about the transport. 'I don't see how. It belongs to the Commission now. Anyway,' he added mischievously, 'it might still be recognised. I'll tell you what. We'll go to Amiens together and I'll buy you another car. There's bound to be surplus knocking around. Then I'll take the Studebaker on to Doullens. I can manage that.'

Maurice tried to look offended. 'I don't need your ill-gotten money. I've enough of my own. But otherwise it sounds like a good enough plan.'

Edward was already beginning to suffer pangs of guilt. 'Look, Maurice, I know you can just disappear if you want to. You're only down as local labour. I can tell Banks in Doullens that you're off the books. I shouldn't think there's much owing to you...' Maurice made a dismissive gesture... 'But will you come back for Mrs Turner if I don't get the chance? We can't just leave her here indefinitely. Although, she wants a trunk sent…'

Maurice indicated, rather half-heartedly that he would. 'Or we can get Pilgrim to get her back to Doullens and she can become Banks's problem. He'd like that. She can sing in his concert parties.'

The next morning Maurice was up first. He brought the Studebaker round to the *estaminet* and parped the horn. Annie Turner appeared at the door, ready to see the two men off. The night before they had made a further, fruitless attempt to let them take her to Amiens, but to no avail. Short of putting a blanket over her head and manhandling her into the Studebaker there was no way they were going to get her to leave Auchonvillers. When Edward came out with his valise he was wearing his best cap and uniform, the one he had had made for the meeting in London. Private Pilgrim, who had also come to see them off too, stood smartly to attention and gave a salute which Edward returned elegantly.

Annie Turner took him all in and his bulging valise. 'You look as though you won't be coming back,' she said, and holding his arm, she kissed him on the cheek. Take care.'

Edward thought about having one last attempt to persuade her but he could see it would be no good. 'Private Pilgrim will look after you – won't you Pilgrim? He'll fetch your trunk from Doullens when it arrives.' He climbed up beside Maurice and with a final toot they lurched their way slowly down the remnant of the main street.

There had been no rain for some time, which in many ways was a blessing. However, it meant that their journey was made in a cloud of fine dust rather than being bogged down in mud. By the time several miles had passed, Edward in the front passenger seat was seized with a paroxysm of coughing. Both he and Maurice had motor goggles of course and scarves pulled up over their mouths but nevertheless the dust found its way through.

'Here, we'd better pull up for a bit and let the dust settle,' Maurice said. He stopped the Studebaker to one side of the road although there was no other traffic in either direction.

Edward took the scarf off his face to shake the dust out of it. The inside of it was red with blood. Not just a spot – a lot of blood. He glanced sideways at Maurice to see if he had seen it too, but he was busy searching for his cigarettes.

'Bugger! They must be in my bag.' He got down and went round to rear of the motor and opened the luggage trunk. 'Sorry Edward, my bag's under all my tripods and camera boxes. I put them in last.' While he was rummaging around, he called out conversationally, 'So have you given any more thought to going back to that place – Hillcote is it? You could pop the question to your lady from Hove and live happily ever after. Put all this behind you – all this so-called concentration of graves, all these so-called garden parties. Concentrate on a real garden party at your mansion instead. Who knows? I could be your best man – if I can lay my hands on a passport, that is.'

'She'll probably get married. Not to me though – to Herbert Grace.' Edward tried to laugh but the effort set him coughing again into the grubby handkerchief he had fetched from his pocket. It was stained with more blood and dirty mucous when he was able to examine it. 'I'd like to see the garden parties reinstated at Hillcote, though. My Aunt Rose used to have them every year. Mr Kirby would like that. If any of his boys made it home. I did think I might get him to grow roses for the war cemeteries. Set him up with a lot of ladies like Annie Turner to help him. Be a good thing to do with some of the money, don't you think?'

This little speech set him to coughing again and there was more blood. More than he could ever remember before. Suddenly he felt very weary. The blood on his scarf was like a red flag, arresting whatever life he might have wished for now. He desperately needed some space, time to think, away from the dust of the road. He especially didn't want his friend to see the blood – not after all this time free of it. 'Look Maurice, finish your fag round there at the back. I need to relieve myself over there,' he lied.

'Can't you go up against the wheel?' But Edward was already walking away from the road on the other side of the motor.

'Won't be a moment,'

Out of sight behind the car Maurice shouted, 'Well watch your step. Keep to that plank road. You may find an old dugout if you're that shy.'

## 20

THE taxi from Hindhead station scrunched up the gravel drive and came to a halt outside the front entrance of Hillcote Grange. Its single passenger alighted and handed over the fare indicated on the meter. 'It's some time since I was in this part of the world,' he said conversationally to the young man at the wheel, 'but I have a recollection that Hindhead had a horse-drawn cab.'

'That was my grandfather's. He's packed it in now and I got this when I came out of the army. Second-hand mind. But there was loads of commercials goin' for a song then. Drivers never made it back, see?'

'You were lucky then.'

'You could say. D'you want me to wait?'

'Thank you, no. I shall be a while.'

'Well, we have a telephone now. Here's the number.' As he handed over a card, the door opened. 'There, look you're expected,' he said and putting the cab in gear turned a wide circle on the gravel and headed back to the gates.

The door had been opened by a young woman of about eighteen or so. The visitor didn't think she looked like the parlour maid, so he was a little at a loss. 'Good afternoon,' he said hesitantly, 'I'm James Bellingham. I don't know whether I'm expected. I wrote to a Mrs Bolden here, Mrs Louise Bolden, but I wasn't sure if she would be at this address or not. You're not she, I take it?'

'No. That's my mother. I don't know whether she's expecting you, but please come in and we can find out.'

James Bellingham followed her into the hall, removing his hat. 'I also had an address for her in Hove. Caroline Crescent. I wrote to her there as well and said I would try here first but I didn't hear anything so I thought I'd better come on the day I'd suggested. I do hope it's not inconvenient...' He followed her through to a large sitting room at the rear of the house with French windows. These were open in the sunshine, looking out onto a large walled garden.

Bellingham was impressed at the sight of the beds of roses there. 'I say! What a splendid display. Quite puts my meagre efforts at Sunbury to shame. But you must have help, surely? Not easily come by these days for a garden this size. So many gardeners haven't come back. But yours did?'

A dark-haired, pale-looking woman dressed in grey silk had come in from the garden through the French windows. She came towards him with an outstretched hand. Bellingham found his gaze fixed on her almost violet coloured eyes which, with the grey silk and her pale skin, seemed to emphasise a feeling of deep sadness in spite of her welcoming smile.

'It's Mr Bellingham, isn't it? I hoped you would come and I'm so sorry I didn't reply to your letter. But I only remembered it yesterday by which time I supposed it was too late. Gee and I were so busy with the funeral last week it clean went out of my mind. You can thank the army for the roses. My solicitor, Mr Dereham – your partner, I saw from your letterhead – let them have the house for convalescing officers.'

'Funeral? Have you suffered a loss, then?'

'Yes. A dear friend who was living here. He was an invalid and I'm afraid he succumbed to this terrible Spanish flu that's everywhere now. He went very quickly because he was so low anyway. In a matter of days. It doesn't seem right does it? So many dead in the war and now so many more with this flu. Do you have news of Mr Dereham? I've almost given up hope of hearing from him again, but I know he's a terrible correspondent.'

A slight look of panic showed in James Bellingham's face. He glanced across at the daughter, Gee and then back at her mother, as if he had things to say but wasn't sure if they should be said. Mrs Bolden detected there was some difficulty. Tactfully she said, 'Mr Bellingham, I know you are a solicitor and your letter said you had important matters to discuss, which you would prefer to do in person. I assume they are to do with Edward's business with me, as he is not here. But you should know that Gee – Grace – is over eighteen now and not so far off being twenty-one. I have no secrets from her. Anything you want to tell me you can say in front of her.'

'Anything at all?' She nodded. 'Well if you're sure,' he said. 'Perhaps we should all sit down…I wonder, Mrs Bolden, if I might have a sandwich and something to drink. I left Sunbury quite early this morning and I haven't been able to…'

Grace disappeared out of the room and reappeared shortly with a decanter of whisky and some glasses on a tray. 'Mrs Kirby is making some sandwiches,' she said, 'and tea. But I brought this from the library. I thought Mr Bellingham looked as though he might prefer it.'

Mrs Bolden remonstrated with her daughter's forthrightness but Bellingham thanked her all the same and said he would take a glass while they waited for the sandwiches.

Suitably fortified, he opened his attaché case and spread the papers in it out on the low table in front of them. He took out a pair of horn-rimmed spectacles and put them on the end of his nose and peered down at the documents for a moment and then sat back and looked over them at the two women. 'Where to begin? Perhaps first I should ask you, Mrs Bolden how close you are to Edward Dereham?'

She looked anxiously at him. 'He's a dear friend but no more than that. He looks after my finances for me and did Grace's school fees until she left. All the payments are being made. Has something happened to Edward? Is that why you have come?'

'Amongst other things. I'm still not sure how I should break this to you – if you were, well – if he was more than a friend and a business adviser.'

'We weren't lovers, if that's what you mean. Oh don't look like that. I'm not afraid of the word, Mr Bellingham. I've been a kept woman for many years. Tell me – us – you keep trying not to say "was". He's dead isn't he?'

'I'm very much afraid so. The army say he's missing, but presumed dead.'

Louise reached out and took hold of her daughter's hand. *'Presumed dead,'* she said softly. 'Well that's an improvement on Cornelius. He was just missing all that time till Edward found him.'

'I didn't know that. Where shall I begin then?'

'At the beginning's as good a place as any,' said Louise. 'I do need to know it all.'

Just before Christmas the previous year, 1919, Mrs Bale, Edward Dereham's daily, had presented herself at James Bellingham's front door, saying that she had been to the office but there was no-one there. When he asked what the problem was, she told him that as she hadn't been paid for some time now and, as it looked as if Mr Dereham wasn't coming back, she was handing in her notice and the key to the cottage. 'There's nearly a year owing, but as I ain't done nothing but a bit of dusting, I'm not too fussed.' Bellingham was rather taken aback. He had been going into their office regularly to keep an eye on what little long-term business there was, which wasn't much, but it hadn't occurred to him to visit the cottage, assuming that Edward had a continuing arrangement with Mrs Bale.

He took fifteen pounds out of his wallet, which was all it contained at that time in the week and asked her if that would settle the matter. She took the money somewhat grudgingly and handed over the key and a bundle of post she had collected on her last visit. When he took this back to his study and examined it he had discovered a letter with army service franking addressed to Edward's mother. He had hesitated to open it for a moment, but then remembered he had been her joint executor with Edward even though he had left all the detail to him. So he opened the letter, in case it was something Edward needed to know about – not that he had any real idea how to get in touch with him.

The letter was from the Adjutant General's office in Aldershot and had an October 1919 date. James read the contents with shocked dismay. It said in rather a matter-of-fact way that it was 'with deep regret that we have to inform you that your son Second Lieutenant Edward Albert Dereham, General Service Corps, suffered an accident while on permanent secondment to the Directorate of Graves Registration and Enquiries of the Imperial War Graves Commission in France and was posted missing, presumed dead. Please accept our sincere condolences.' It went on to say that Edward's mother should address any further enquiries to the Commission in St James's Square, London, who would also forward to her any pay owing to Lieutenant Dereham.

Bellingham concluded that Edward must have given his mother's name and address as his next of kin, but he could not think why, unless it had been much earlier when he had been applying unsuccessfully to join up.

'Just that?' Louise asked. Her face had grown even paler and her knuckles were white where her fingers were clutching Grace's. 'Nothing about what kind of an accident? Cornelius's commanding officer wrote to me, you know, telling me something of what happened to him. I thought it would make matters worse when I first opened it, but the more I read it over afterwards, the more it helped. D'you see?'

Bellingham said that it had become evident, when he himself began making enquiries, that the circumstances of Edward's accident were unknown to anyone in authority, either at the Commission in London or, indeed, at Longuenesse where the War Graves people were based in France.

'So why do they presume he's dead, if they haven't found him?' asked Grace.

Apparently that information had eventually been reported to a Lieutenant Banks at a place called Doullens, Bellingham said. The people at Longuenesse had been as helpful as they could be and had promised to follow it up with their southern sector HQ in Doullens, which was where Edward had been working from. This had taken some while. When eventually he had received another letter from Longuenesse, reading between the lines it looked as though everyone in some kind of authority had lost track of Edward's whereabouts. However, this Lieutenant Banks had made exhaustive inquiries and, officially, the evidence all pointed to Edward having died.

'Even though they didn't find him?' Grace persisted.

'Hush, dear,' said Louise. 'Let Mr Bellingham tell it.'

'I know, I know,' he said. 'It's not at all satisfactory for those of us who…well…were his friends. But speaking as his executor and wearing my legal hat, a letter from the appropriate authorities declaring him dead is sufficient to allow me to proceed with tidying up his affairs.'

Grace sighed impatiently.

Bellingham gestured pacifyingly to her. 'There is more, Grace. Hold on a minute.'

Bellingham had, as Edward's executor, set about putting his affairs in order. He had gone through his office in Lower Sunbury as well as the bureau at the cottage. He had not come up with anything extraordinary; the usual local bank accounts with not much money in them, an insurance policy or two and Edward's will, of which James was the sole executor.

'But surely he had a bit of money from his aunt when she left it to his mother?'

'I'm coming to that. Let me just finish telling you about Edward, if you can bear it.'

Sometime in March this year there had been a knock at the door. Polly said there was 'a Mr Burnell' asking for him. He had obtained Bellingham's name from the brass plate outside the office and had asked about the village for his house. It turned out that he had been working with Edward in France. 'Interesting chap. Half French. He'd served with the French Air Service in the war and met up with Edward after his demobilisation. Taught Edward to drive, he said. I, of course, asked if he could shed any light on Edward's death.'

Burnell had clearly been taken aback that he knew about it and was anxious to know how that had come about. He particularly wanted to know if his own name had come up in any of Bellingham's dealings with the authorities, but it had not. Obviously relieved to hear this, Burnell told him about the journey from Auchonvillers. 'Edward had stepped out of the motor to attend to a call of nature, of all things and disappeared from sight a short distance off the road. There had been an explosion. Not a particularly big one. Burnell had heard it but hadn't seen it precisely as he was round the other side of the motor having a cigarette. He'd ducked down of course. That was his first instinct, I suppose. When he had emerged the dust was already settling and precisely where it had occurred was difficult to tell. Burnell called out to Edward but there was no reply. He went a little way down a kind of wooden pathway which was where Edward had gone, still calling his name but there was no sign of him. It was difficult, he said, to judge where a single explosion might have happened. The ground was very churned up and littered with shell holes. It's difficult to imagine, isn't it?'

'So he didn't find Edward's body either?' said Grace.

'No. But it was clear he was gone – and buried by the explosion. So he went back to this place Auchonvillers and spoke to a man there who was tending the cemetery. I remember his name, it made me think of Bunyan. It was Pilgrim. This man said he would take some gardeners – I'm sure Burnell said gardeners – to the spot and have another search. It must have been this man, Pilgrim, who eventually reported it. Burnell wasn't going back to Doullens. He said he had had to take the car up to the coast.'

'So why had he come to see you? Mr Burnell? If not to tell you about Edward? He must have had a reason,' Louise asked.

Bellingham said that was an interesting question and one which he had asked himself several times afterwards. 'He had quite a lot of banker's drafts in Edward's name. They were in Edward's luggage in the car. He said he wanted to turn them over to me, which had to be a lie if he thought I didn't know about Edward's death. Personally I think he had come sniffing around to see if he could find some way of getting them endorsed in his favour. Perhaps he was going to tell me Edward had sent him. I don't know. I asked him if that was all. Had Edward had any cash? He got a bit sniffy at that and said there were a few sovereigns in gold but they had agreed to share the cost of the petrol to Boulogne at black market prices. Anyway it was a good thing he did hand them over to me.'

'I should say it was,' said Grace.

'Yes indeed, young lady. Because the drafts were drawn on a private bank account in the City of London, about which I knew nothing. It turns out that Edward was extremely wealthy, thanks to the legacy from his Aunt to his late mother. I mean extremely wealthy. I don't know how his aunt came by it. This I assume was her house. The deeds were amongst the papers in a safety deposit box in Lombard Street, and much else besides.'

Louise looked thoughtfully at him. 'This house belonged to my friend who has just died. He was married to Edward's aunt Rose. All the money and so on must have been his really and he must have given it to his wife in her name.'

'And who was he – your friend?'

'I suppose it doesn't matter now. He was Herbert Grace. I expect you've heard of him.'

Bellingham drew a deep breath. 'So that explains it. Oh dear!'

'Why "oh dear"?'

'Because Edward's will, of which I am the executor, left everything to his lawful children should he have any, which I am not aware he did, or to his mother should he predecease her, which he did not. I'm afraid he didn't update it before he met his death.'

'So where does it all go?'

'To the Chancellor, unless I can conjure up some progeny.'

'Including this house?' Grace asked.

'I'm afraid so. There is a considerable fortune, I should say, which I have discovered in Herbert Grace's name. But I couldn't for the life of me fathom out the connection. There were details in Edward's Lombard Street box of a private bank in Antwerp, which I have pursued. Edward's papers at the office showed that he had power of attorney for Herbert Grace, which, of course, I knew nothing about, nor who Herbert Grace might be. So as Edward's surviving partner I was able to take it on for the practice. It turns out that Herbert Grace had considerable holdings in diamonds in Antwerp which seem to have survived German occupation. But of course, now that he has died, they will go to his next of kin. Unless of course, Mrs Bolden, he, ah, made a will in your favour?'

'Not that I know of. There was nothing in his papers here or at Caroline Crescent. He owned most of that too, you know. Edward told me. But Grace is his daughter. So it will come to her when she's twenty-one won't it? But it's a shame about this house having to go to the old Chancellor. Well, I don't mean that exactly. But I quite like it here.'

'Can you prove Grace is his daughter? You said I could speak freely Mrs Bolden.'

'Well his name is on her birth certificate. He insisted. He wasn't all bad, you know.'

'Good enough. Good enough. We haven't gone for probate yet so we could probably put this house on the market and Grace could put in a bid for it which I could accept. The diamonds are worth something over half a million pounds. Also I found several jewellery boxes in Edward's safe at Lower Sunbury. As they were in a small valise with Herbert Grace's initials on them I must assume they were his property being held in safe-keeping by Edward. The jewellery is worth a very considerable sum, I should say, and should come to you Grace in due course.'

After that they walked out into the garden. The early evening scent of the roses was almost overpowering.

Bellingham breathed it in deeply. 'That reminds me,' he said. 'I asked Burnell if Edward had said anything to him just before he took that last short walk into no-man's land. He said Edward had said he would like to come back here and restart the garden parties his aunt used to hold before the war. I can see why.'

'We'll do that, won't we mummy,' said Grace. 'We'll do it for Edward and Cornelius.'

'And your father,' said Louise and a tear trickled down her cheek. 'A garden party for the dead.'

# Epilogue

ONE November morning in 1923 Jacques Bucamp, who had just turned sixteen and was grudgingly considered by his grandfather able to be trusted with the horses, had begun ploughing one of last pieces of their land to have been declared safe by the Office of Agricultural Reconstitution. Despite the declaration Jacques knew full well the dangers of unexploded ordnance lurking beneath the earth. But he and his grandfather were as anxious as the Department of Agriculture was to get as much of their land as possible producing again. Even so, he stood the horses to at the beginning of each new furrow and slowly walked the next ground to be turned, by himself, before risking his precious animals.

While doing this for the fourth time that morning he saw something glinting dully in the pale sunshine in the furrow he had just completed, beside him. He stooped down to examine it more closely before touching it and found it to be an army cap badge. He knew it was not a French because, when he had rubbed it clean on the seat of his trousers it had a lion, a unicorn and a crown on it. Putting it in his pocket he continued his reconnoitre to the far side of field. As sure as he could be that it was safe he returned to the two horses, set the ploughshare and moved them off, keeping half an eye on the spot where he had found the badge. As he came alongside it, turning the new furrow he felt the share shiver slightly, as if hesitating, and then moving on. It had encountered something harder than the earth, but not by the feel, stone or metal. But Jacques was taking no chances. He lifted the ploughshare clear and when the horses had walked on a few more yards, he looked back at the ground they had just tilled. What the plough had sheared were human remains.

What was left of the body was removed the next day by Jacques and his grandfather to the shelter of their rebuilt barn. Although they knew that strictly speaking such remains should be left for a British army burial party to deal with, they were in no mood to wait and further delay the ploughing. When the small exhumation team arrived some days later, having been contacted by the War Graves caretaker at the nearest cemetery, they found very little to identify what was left of the body. The scraps of uniform, suggested an officer, but an identity tag had not survived. The General Service Corps cap badge remained in Jacques Bucamp's trouser pocket as a souvenir. It probably would not have added very much to establishing the identity of the officer or how, or indeed, when he had met his death: the War Graves records, recently taken over from the Directorate of Graves Registration, could shed no light on this isolated discovery. There was no record of a battlefield interment at the spot, although the Bucamps had been somewhat vague as to where precisely that had been, not wishing the authorities to institute more searches of their field.

The nearest cemetery had already been declared closed to new interments, so the remains were taken further on to the cemetery at a place called Auchonvillers which was still open. They were allocated a plot by the permanent caretaker there, a Mr Pilgrim, and the following spring an English lady, one Mrs Turner, who had decided to take up residence in the village, came in as she was accustomed to do, to plant out some of the marigolds and cornflowers from her little nursery, which seemed to do well there. Eventually, too, the grave received one of the new headstones, with the simple epitaph, 'A soldier of the Great War. Known Unto God.'

# An Afterword

*A Garden Party for the Dead* is not intended to be a precise history of the early days of the Imperial War Graves Commission. It is very much a work of fiction, with fictional characters. But they are playing out their lives and interacting with one another in an extraordinary time and space historically. In that respect the fictional characters occasionally come into contact with people who really existed too, perhaps, above all, the millions of the dead of the Great War, whom I have represented in a handful of imagined soldiers.

More specifically, Fabian Ware was the head of the Directorate of Graves Registration, and the driving force for the Imperial War Graves Commission which developed out of it. As such he would have been part of meetings like the one that Edward Dereham was summoned to attend, even though I have imagined it. Similarly, the Prince of Wales, later to become Edward the Eighth, took a close and active interest in the many sensitive issues and controversies surrounding the burial and lasting commemoration of the Great War dead. I do not know whether he attended any meetings at which Rudyard Kipling was present, but it is by no means impossible.

All the other named characters and events are imagined. Nor have I tried to squeeze them into otherwise detailed, historically accurate events. Rather, I have attempted to create an artist's impression of what it must have felt like to them, still toiling in the desolation of the western front in those early months after the guns fell silent on Armistice Day 1918. As with an impression on canvas, *A Garden Party for the Dead* fixes changing and fleeting moments into one small space. Much is left out; I have indulged in sleight of hand for the sake of the story. When Edward Dereham arrives in France, the role I have created for him in the Directorate of Graves Registration is imprecise and frayed at the edges. It brings together functions which, properly, might have been those of more than one person and more than one rank. I hope that does not matter: in the end: I hope you have been left with an accurate impression of what must have been their collective experience.

A word too about Maurice Burnell. Maurice first found me in *The Middle Room*. A persistent survivor, he made a reappearance in *Madame Lamartine's Journey*. It remains to be seen whether he will demand to be accounted for in the future.

Annie Turner, *née* Lilley, came into being in my first book, *The Equal Sky*. Her fictional son, Reuben Turner, is named after my second cousin of the ninth battalion, the Suffolk Regiment, who is buried at Auchonvillers, but there all resemblance to him ends.

For those who do seek a purer historical account of the early days of the Imperial – now Commonwealth – War Graves Commission, I would refer them to *The Unending Vigil. A history of the Commonwealth War Graves Commission, 1917 – 1967*, by Philip Longworth. Published by Constable 1967. I have referred constantly to this work. But, as I say, I was writing a work of fiction.

Stephen Reardon

# Acknowledgements

∞∞

The author would like to thank his small group of editorial advisers who have generously given their time to make *A Garden Party for the Dead* a better book: they are, Roger Birchall, Simon Dugdale, Ian Herbert, David Hughes, Dr Sarah Maxwell, and Jane Reardon. Grateful thanks, too, to Michael Greet, the Archive Assistant at the Commonwealth War Graves Commission, for suggesting and providing access to helpful records and correspondence, and to David Cook, for help with some of the legal issues in the plot.

Principal published references consulted were: *The Unending Vigil. A History of the Commonwealth War Graves Commission 1917 – 1967,* by Philip Longworth. Published by Constable 1967. © The Commonwealth War Graves Commission; *After the Ruins. Restoring the Countryside of Northern France after the Great War,* by Hugh Clout. University of Exeter Press 1996; *Battlefield Tourism: pilgrimage and the commemoration of the Great War in Britain, Australia and Canada 1919 – 1939,* by David W. Lloyd. Published by Oxford: Berg 1998; *The Battle of the Somme. A Topographical History,* by Gerald Gliddon, published by Sutton Publishing 1994.

*About the author*

Stephen Reardon was born in High Barnet, England in 1947. After graduating in 1968 his career spanned thirty years working as a civil servant in press relations, publishing and advertising in various government departments in London. He worked in several administrations with ministers and Secretaries of State, latterly as a Director of Communications and press secretary. Parting company with Whitehall following the 1997 general election, he joined the management board at the Institute of Directors as Head of Communications. Leaving to write in 2004, he published his first novel, *The Equal Sky*, in 2007. His subsequent novels have been *The Middle Room*, published in 2009, *Madame Lamartine's Journey*, in 2015, and now *A Garden Party for the Dead*, in 2018.

He lives in Twickenham, England, with his wife, Jane. They have a son, Ben, a daughter, Iona, and three grandchildren, Ronnie, Stanley, and Romy.

*Also by Stephen Reardon*

***The Equal Sky***

Unprecedented winter flooding in Cambridgeshire in the winter of 1886 causes a river to give up the skull of an ancient British warrior, and farm bailiff's son, Henry Turner, feels drawn to the discovery. When he is forced to leave his country calling, he takes the post of groom in the London house of a former army officer, who also has an estate in turbulent Ireland – and a sinister past.

In a street brawl, Henry saves the life of a Sioux Indian, an interpreter with Buffalo Bill Cody's Wild West Show, which is in London for Queen Victoria's jubilee celebrations. Together the two men set out to determine the ancient warrior's will, and to resolve their shared love for one woman.

*"An excellent first novel…this is a very well researched book, the tale gathering pace as you become more involved with the characters and the plot. It is extremely readable and one of those books you continue to think about for days after you have finished it."*

*Reader review on-line*

## *The Middle Room*

Recently-married Florence Draper listens to the nightly air raids on London in the blitz. She re-lives the stories of the bombardment in the siege of Paris seventy years before, told to her by her grandmother, a French cook who had lived through it, and had experienced the starvation and improvised food in a *grand hotel*.

Florence's new husband, who speaks French, has been seconded by the army to be a clerk with the Free French in General De Gaulle's London headquarters. He is approached by a French officer whose family had knowledge of the part Florence's grandmother played all those years earlier in smuggling a valuable work of art across the Prussian lines.

*"It is very rare these days that I pick up a novel that I can't put down but this one did it for me. Stephen Reardon has an unerring ear for conversation and for period details… food, intrigue and history. What more can anyone want?"*

Reader review on-line.

## *Madame Lamartine's Journey*

Ex-newspaperman turned government press chief, John Colebrook, is told his face no longer fits in Whitehall with the new administration after the 1974 British election. Sent home to cool his heels while his future is decided, he is secretly approached by Sally Hegarty, a rising young civil servant. She enlists him to investigate discreetly the wartime activities of a prominent industrialist. It is then Colebrook finds himself under surveillance, as he learns of Claudette Lamartine and the real reason for her perilous journey through occupied France to Lisbon in 1940, and as he begins to uncover a murky wartime conspiracy whose instigators may still be active in public life.

*"…a damn good read! It gripped me from the start and held my attention right to the end. It's a powerful narrative, with excellent characterisation, sharp and pacey, knowing writing…clever and humorous in the right places."*

*"…I couldn't put it down…you are in the author's good hands as you move through the labyrinths and intrigues of Whitehall's corridors, the drinking holes of Fleet Street, ex-pat life in Lisbon, and war-torn France. Superbly drawn characters take you through a rich journey you should not miss."*

*Readers' reviews on-line*

*To purchase any of Stephen Reardon's books and to read articles and further background to the author and his novels please visit [www.stephenreardon.co.uk](www.stephenreardon.co.uk) and follow the links, or go directly to lulu.com or amazon.com*

Printed in Great Britain
by Amazon